The Silence that Remains

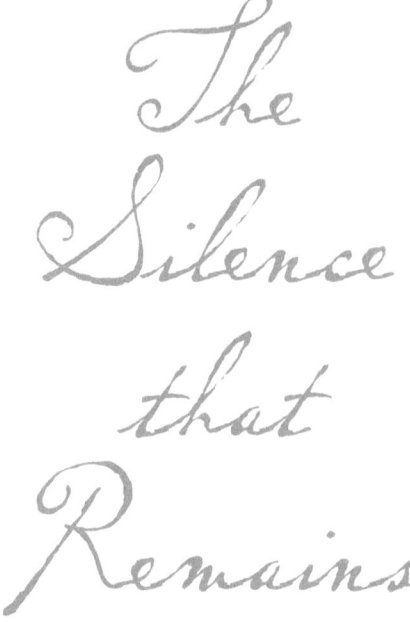

A NOVEL

MEG WINGERTER

M·P·P
www.MissionPointPress.com

Copyright © 2026 Meg Wingerter
All world rights reserved.

This is a work of fiction. All names, places, and incidents are the products of the author's imagination or are used fictitiously. Any resemblance to actual events or locales or persons, living or dead, is entirely coincidental.

No part of this book may be reproduced, stored in a retrieval system, or transmitted in any form or by any means electronic, mechanical, photocopy, recording, or otherwise, without the prior consent of the publisher.

Mission Point Press

Published by Mission Point Press
www.MissionPointPress.com

Cover and book design: Deirdre Wait
Cover photographs: Adobe Stock

Hardcover ISBN 13: 978-1-968761-09-7
Paperback ISBN 13: 978-1-968761-10-3

LCCN: available upon request.

Printed in the United States of America

To Justin,
who never stopped believing
in this book,
or in me.

1955

Annushka

I told a series of half-truths to get here.

When the woman stamping travel papers asked, I said I was looking for my late father-in-law's sister, to give her a few of his things. I would have had to bribe her if I were trying to go to Moscow or Leningrad, or any of the cities where you need a residency permit. But no one was trying to illegally set up in a backwater like Tambov Province. I packed up a few worn-down things in case they decided to search my bag. No one did, though. I've been told I have an innocent face.

The railroad took me as far as the city of Tambov, but from there the only way was to hire a ride from a peasant with a cart. I brought cigarettes for that sort of thing. I can't stand the smell of tobacco, but they're as good as currency, sometimes better. A hunched old man demanded two packs to take me back to his village, and I could hardly argue, since winter had closed the markets and I might not have gotten another chance for days.

We rode in silence for maybe the first hour, bouncing over the ruts and bumps locked in place when the autumn mud froze. The brown grass, roughly the same color as the mud, was unchanging as far as I could see, so I played a game of guessing what happened on these roads. For a while, I followed tracks left by a truck, which suddenly cut off—it must have bogged down and been abandoned.

"When did they tow it out?" I asked.

"What?"

"The truck that left those tracks." He looked at me suspiciously. "In my village, the mud could almost swallow a wagon whole. Though our mud was darker." It probably hasn't changed color, but I can't help thinking of my home in the past tense. If there are people there, talking about my mud as theirs, I can't imagine them. I don't want to.

But it's a safe topic. Russians are always happy to talk about their mud, like they do their parents and children, with a strange mix of complaints and love. From there, we went on to agriculture, then to who did and didn't do their share at the kolkhoz, the communal farm. I don't like to think about kolkhozes, but I let him say his piece before asking if he knew my father-in-law's family.

"Chekhov," he murmured, stroking his silver-stubbled chin. "No, can't say I've heard of them."

"His sister's name is Olga Aleksandrovna," I said as casually as I could.

"Oh, Olga Aleksandrovna? She's been dead for years."

"Did she have any children? My father-in-law passed not too long ago. I wanted to tell them myself, not just send them a letter."

"Good girl," he said. "Most young folks don't bother about the people they left at home." I let him go on about the ingratitude of the young for a bit before gently steering him back to Olga Aleksandrovna. She had three children who survived to adulthood—two good ones and one wastrel who was drunk more than he was sober. The old man, who told me to call him Volodya, promised to introduce me to the daughter, and I couldn't let him see just how grateful I was. I didn't want to answer questions about why it was quite so important to me.

The village Vitya grew up in was much like any other: little heaps of wood and thatch that only look worse when the steppes turned green around them because their faded gray-brown stands out. It's the sort of place where men beat women, and women beat children, and everyone is exhausted before they're old. I don't think my village was like that, but maybe I'm fooling myself.

Olga Aleksandrovna's daughter was just another worn-out, middle-aged peasant who looked older than her years, but she was pretty once. I could see the remains. No peasant woman is pretty after her early twenties. The sun bakes and wrinkles their skin, and their bodies don't go back to their previous shape after pregnancy, like some city women's do. It doesn't matter if a woman is pretty when her purpose is to raise children and sling hay bales.

I'm not beautiful, but I could see that she thought I was and hated me just a little bit for it. "You think you're one of us," her eyes said, "but you have no idea what we've suffered." She didn't know what I'd suffered either, but the worst parts of my life happened when I was a child, so they don't show on my face. I gave her my green headscarf when I noticed she was eyeing it. I guess she saw it as a trade, because she finally spoke.

"You didn't have to come here," she said. "My uncle dying has nothing to do with me."

"I didn't exactly come for your benefit," I said, and her eyebrows rose. She didn't expect me to confirm her suspicions. "I have a son. His father's dead, and now his grandfather. And there are some things I need to know, for his sake. Anything you can tell me about the family's history would help."

She settled heavily into a chair near the stove. I could tell from the way she moved that she was wearing a band across her lower belly to hold her organs in, as so many women like her have to. "There's nothing to tell. Nothing different from everyone else."

I hesitated. "Did your mother ever say anything about her brother? That he was—different?"

"You want to know if the crazy runs in the family." I lowered my eyes, but I nodded. "Mama told me her brother lost his mind in the war—not this last war, the tsar's war. Burned down a house after he got back. That's all I know."

I believed her. No one around town knew much more. There were fragments of old gossip about a farmer named Chekhov marrying a woman from a traveling tribe, fragments generally told with a wad of spit directed at the ground.

The man who ran the village clubhouse in what used to be the church tried to help me, but there was nothing beyond records of births, baptisms, and deaths. I thanked him anyway and went to wander between the rows of graves before returning to spend the night at the one guest house run by the kolkhoz.

I found Vitya's mother, Elizaveta Chekhova, marked with a neat headstone. Something that looked like it might have been a hastily erected cross leaned against the stone, though it had mostly been reclaimed by the earth. I didn't look around before I crossed myself. If the clubhouse man saw me, he'd just shake his head at a superstitious country woman. And he might have been right. Because I wasn't praying to God at that moment. I was begging these people who are part of the past to give me some shred of information that absolved me, that said it wasn't my fault three lives were wrecked. But all I heard was the wind blowing snow.

I gave Volodya another pack of cigarettes to take me back to the train station. Once I arrived, I found a public phone and went through the ordeal of dialing Moscow, knowing that I'd have to immediately hang up if the wrong person answered.

"Alo?" the voice on the other end said with Diana's French lilt. I sighed with relief.

"Nothing," I said. "There's nothing here beyond what he already told you."

"I expected as much," she responded. "Can you describe it, though? To set the scene."

I told her everything I observed, down to the color of the mud, and I heard her pen scratching in the background.

"Thank you," she said when I'd finished. "I'll send you something for your time."

"There's no need," I answered.

"Oh, don't be foolish. I know how little they pay you. And I've put you to so much trouble, going out there." We both knew the real trouble hadn't yet begun, but we couldn't say that on a line that anyone could be listening to. "I'm going to send some textbooks for your son. He should start learning French soon."

I said I understood and hung up. I didn't doubt she would send me textbooks, but I could never let my son read what she wrote in the margins. This was dangerous. If I were caught, which I would be if I ever shared any of it, I'd spend the rest of my son's youth in a prison camp. But I agreed to accept it anyway, because I owed it to her. Hers is one of the three lives I have to atone for.

1905-1922

Diana

I was five when my father first told me he had plotted to assassinate the tsar.

I had walked into the sitting room in our apartment. His head was bowed in sorrow over the newspaper. I stood on my tiptoes to peer at the paper on his desk, which was larger than our sofa. I could already read, though I have no idea who taught me. Men and women of letters were always coming and going from our apartment on a fashionably shabby street on the left bank of the Seine. It would be a few years before I discovered that not every home in Paris functioned as a stage for a rotating cast of intellectuals dressed in workers' clothes, laboring over their speeches and newspaper articles.

Some of them would hide sweets in their jacket pockets and faux-scold me when I filched some, then pat my little blonde head and tell me how pretty I was. My parents never did that. They were old Bolsheviks par excellence, and they took the responsibility of raising the next generation of revolutionaries too seriously to allow for that sort of thing. You young people probably don't know what that means, since the old Bolsheviks who didn't have the good sense to die early have all been killed. You join the Party for the perks and promotions. They did it knowing there was every possibility they'd end up on the gallows.

I knew I was to stay quiet and out of sight when they were writing, until I was old enough to contribute something of value. My father wasn't writing then, though, so I bumped him in a way that might have passed for accidental. He startled and looked at me as if I'd materialized out of thin air.

"What happened, father?"

"The tsar and the emperor of Japan have concluded a peace treaty." I didn't really know what this meant. He sighed heavily. "They stopped the war."

I had known Russia and Japan had been fighting for as long as I could remember, and that everyone was excited about it. I didn't yet understand imperialism, that both countries were trying to grab bits of Manchuria and Korea. "Maybe they'll start another war soon," I said.

"No, Diana, they won't. Even the tsar wouldn't be that stupid. The people were starting to rise, and it frightened him enough to give just a little. Just enough to quiet them."

"Did they win?" I'd heard all my life that we were waiting for the people to rise.

"No. All they got was a little more pay and a few more holidays, but they don't know to demand anything else." I didn't say anything. He sighed again, probably at my underdeveloped sense of class consciousness. "Happy, comfortable people will never be desperate enough to overthrow their oppressors. Revolution comes from pain. Do you think I was happy when I worked with The People's Will to try to kill the tsar's father?"

"Non, papa." That seemed to be the correct answer, though the question was perhaps asking a bit much of a child that age.

"Of course I wasn't. Foolish people will spend their whole lives trying to scrape together the little happiness their rulers leave them. Our job is to see that they know they are miserable and what to do about it. Bolsheviks don't try to make people happy. We try to make them into what they can become. Do you understand?" I didn't, but I said I did.

I knew we were Bolsheviks before I knew what the term meant, but I only learned we were Jews by accident. My father's name was Sergey Muskin—Sergey the Muscovite, as Russian as could be desired. Even after he died, I never knew his real name. It was practical. If you were caught plotting the tsar's death, there was no guarantee your loved ones wouldn't pay the price, so it was best to break from them as thoroughly as you could. But I was still young, and it hadn't occurred to me that you could leave a name or a life behind.

My mother had brought me to hear a speech he was giving near a factory. A few workers had gathered to listen, and we stood near the back. I thought it was a good speech, and a few of the grease-stained workers seemed to like it, but the foreman didn't. He got up next to my father and started yelling about foul, conniving Jews, out to exploit them, plus plenty of words I didn't yet understand. And the men decided they liked that better than anything my father said. My mother hustled me home and forbade me to ever talk about it.

After that, my father wrote the speeches and gave them to Comrade Slutsky, who had almost blond hair and the kind of nose people seemed to like, to read publicly. Sometimes we'd go watch him speak, and I'd notice my father leaning forward slightly, mouthing the words, frowning when he thought Comrade Slutsky paused at the wrong moment.

I kept my promise and never told him I'd witnessed his humiliation. I did say I thought it wasn't fair that Comrade Slutsky got to give the speeches now.

"It's not a question of fairness, Diana," my father said. "What matters is that they hear the message. And they won't hear it from someone like me."

I didn't really know what "someone like me" meant. I was vaguely aware that Judaism was a religion, but my parents had made clear that all religions were poison, so how could that have anything to do with him? I didn't know anything about the concept of Jewish culture, literature, or thought. I can only assume now that my parents believed it would get in the way of the new proletarian culture—a culture that belonged to everyone, and therefore, no one. I couldn't ask what "someone like me" was at home, so I asked Comrade Slutsky's wife.

I felt comfortable with Citizen Slutskaya, probably because she always smelled like soap. You can't be intimidated by someone who's always elbow-deep in laundry. Women who joined the Party were comrades, too, but the ones who were just wives were called citizens. Even though we weren't in Russia, most of them kept up the custom of adding an 'a' to women's last names.

"What's a Jew?" I asked.

"Someone whose ancestors came from ancient Israel," she said without looking up.

"Why does everyone hate them?"

Citizen Slutskaya wiped her hands on her apron—I never saw her without an apron—and thought a moment. "That's how the capitalists stay in power. Focus the workers on fighting each other, not fighting their oppressors. And the Jews are always an easy target."

"Am I a Jew too?" I asked.

Citizen Slutskaya hemmed a bit. "I suppose so. In a way. Not that anyone can tell with that blonde hair. But we're building a world where it won't matter."

She must have told on me, because I got a long lecture at home about how I was not to get any ideas about going to a synagogue or swearing off quiche Lorraine. (Where I would have gotten those ideas, I don't know, since I'd never met a religious person in my young life.) I was a French citizen and would someday be a good Party member, and that was all I needed to be.

I didn't really understand any of it, but I did feel that I now had a stake in the new world my parents were building. If we were going to create a future where it didn't matter if a person was a Jew, I wouldn't need to worry about whether I was one. The promises that rebuilding the whole world would be difficult, painful, and bloody made no impression. I'd scraped my knee and bled a few times, so I felt quite prepared for whatever the revolution might bring.

I was shipped off when I started to have opinions and the temerity to voice them.

A few of the wives and female Party members came to our apartment to discuss how they were going to educate the next generation, squeezing together on the couches and trying not knock over each other's coffee. I don't know where the other children were, and I was under strict instructions to entertain myself quietly.

In the future, children would be raised in communal nurseries after they'd been weaned (or perhaps there would be professional nurses, they never quite sorted that out), but that was a long way off, and they had to make do until then. My mother was of the opinion that the French public schools were hopelessly bourgeois. Why just that day, I had come home asking for a pretty blue hair ribbon like the one Jeanne-Louise had been wearing and argued I should have one because Jeanne-Louise had a different ribbon for every day of the week! Clearly, this would not do.

They batted around the idea of starting a school, but good Bolshevik poverty has its disadvantages. It was Citizen Slutskaya who brought up the ballet school at the Opera Garnier. Of course the opera was a bourgeois hotspot, she'd said, but the school taught discipline above all else. And while she hadn't said it, it would keep the children out from under their boots six days a week, leaving them free to work and organize.

My father wouldn't hear of it initially—art was a frill that would disappear with the ruling class. But my mother was determined to have her way. A proletarian culture would need artists to guide it, she said. My father didn't argue the point.

"Remember, you're not there for the rich men to look at," he told me when they dropped me off for the first time. He seemed so out of place in plain workers clothes under enough gold leaf to make Midas think they'd overdone it. "You're to take the training and use it to become harder. Like iron. Do you understand?"

I was eight when I entered the school, so I didn't, but I said I did.

I also didn't understand why I had to go stay with someone else. I cried while I packed up my things. My mother told me it was for my own good. In the future, all children would be raised together, without anyone spoiling them. This would help me become a new woman, ahead of my time.

I lived with Citizen Slutskaya, Comrade Slutsky, and their daughter, Nadya. A few of the wives had volunteered to take charge of the political education of one or two other children so the female Party members could use their talents to further the cause. I liked Citizen Slutskaya. But I gradually realized that wives would never lead the people, never be remembered in the history books. They would do laundry for the heroes manning the barricades. (I read Victor Hugo at a young age, so for the rest of my youth, I was sure that barricading the streets would be a vital part of any respectable revolution.) I imagined my mother doing great things while Citizen Slutskaya explained to me why my shape was starting to change. Sometimes, I'd think about when my mother would decide I was old enough to take my place beside her in the great struggle. But she never did, and I tried not to dwell on it.

Student ballerinas were paid a small fee for each performance, so most of the girls were the children of workers. I tried to tell them about the coming workers' state where everyone would be equal, but most didn't listen. I had expected them to receive the message with joy. The world called them "petits rats" and condemned them as whores but condoned the rich old men who bought them. They were just the sort of people we were trying to help, but all they wanted to talk about was getting one of the rich men to marry them so they wouldn't have to keep dancing. And the few that would listen tended to lose interest when I told them we'd all still work, but it would somehow be better.

I started to think maybe some of the male Bolsheviks were correct, that women were too frivolous to involve in politics, but Citizen Slutskaya had an answer for that. Capitalists valued women for their reproductive capacities rather than their productive ones, so women were merely being rational when they put so much energy into being pretty and flirting. It made me less ashamed of my own sex but no less frustrated that I couldn't start my own Party cell.

We had a few lessons in reading and mathematics and were forced to attend Sunday services, but the rest of our time was spent learning the positions. People who imagine dancers as carefree butterflies floating after the opera patrons clearly have never broken a toe from overuse and kept dancing through the pain. But pain just fueled my stubborn streak. I would not be defeated. Maybe this was what it meant to become iron. And, truth be told, I quite enjoyed the feeling when I finally mastered a move.

I progressed through my classes and was taken into the corps de ballet by the time the war came. Already I could see a future as a soloist, maybe even the coveted name on the poster, a drawing of my increasingly willowy self en pointe below. I hadn't yet realized that you can't be both a prima ballerina and a full-time revolutionary.

I considered myself reasonably well-informed for a fourteen-year-old, but I never entirely understood why an Austrian duke being shot in Serbia suddenly meant French boys and German boys had to go kill each other.

The war seemed very romantic to many of the chorus girls, and to quite a few adults who should have known better. In a rare break of routine at the opera house, we were allowed to bring flowers to give to the soldiers departing on trains for the front. I viewed it as a performance of sorts. I didn't care if France or Germany won, and I had no desire to fall in love with a boy who might be dead in weeks. But I smiled in the way that was expected and handed out flowers with tri-color ribbons. Once I kissed a flower before handing it to a boy, just to see if he would blush. He did. Nadya liked that little touch and used it herself, though I think it lost its magic when used on every boy within reach.

There were still people alive who could remember the war with Prussia, but memory seemed to fail them. It was as if they had never considered that young men would be blown to pieces. Some of the artists and thinkers who floated at the edge of the Bolsheviks knew what would come, and they despaired. But my father was pleased. Russia was fighting too. This was the second war, the one he thought the tsar wouldn't be stupid enough to start. Our time was coming.

Notebook of
Lt. Viktor Aleksandrovich Chekhov

20 August, 1914
Somewhere in Masurian Lakes region

Second Army moving quickly today. Too quick. Supply lines left behind. Not sure where First Army is. Hope headquarters knows.

Men in good spirits. Sergeant (Konstantin Fyodorovich Orlov) talking about museums to see in Berlin. Maybe students not trained enough? Conscripts doing better handling their guns. Want to train them more, but no time. Orders to keep marching.

Why don't Germans push back? Want us here? Not good.

30 August? 1914
Somewhere in Masurian Lakes region

Germans want us here. Pincer trapped us. Don't want to think about how many dead. Second Army gone.

My men broke out of encirclement. No orders now. Not sure where First Army is. East seems like right direction to start.

Found relatively dry area with trees and bushes to hide. Hope no German snipers near. No way to check. And men need to rest.

2 September? 1914
Some goddamn swamp

Lost two to snipers. First one was hit in the leg. Medic put on tourniquet. Another carried him. Slowed that man down. He was shot through first man's body. First one died right then. Second not so lucky. Couldn't order another to carry a dying man. Couldn't stay with snipers around. No choice but to leave. Should have killed him to finish it? Can't kill own man in front of others. Maybe couldn't do it if we were alone.

May all be dead soon anyway.

4 September? 1914
More swamp

Keeping men low and quiet. Another unit captured near us. Can't help them.

11 September, 1914
Near Insterburg

Found First Army. Confirmed Second Army gone. Gen. Samsonov shot himself. Probably best thing to do.

Men finally resting and eating. Not fit to fight for weeks. May not get weeks to rest.

Had a drink with other officers. Tried to talk about lost men. They said no good to talk about it. Probably right. Not their first battle.

12 September, 1914 (think after midnight)
Near Insterburg

Briefly lost mind and thought could go back for men. Too tired to think. Orlov stopped before could wander off and get shot for deserting. Stupid, stupid. Men already dead.

Need to write to wife. Send it now, in case they have to leave me. Then try to sleep. Maybe another vodka for that.

Diana

The parade ground quickly became an open-air slaughterhouse, but for us, life went on much as it always had. People went to the ballet. The only difference was that the performances were more patriotic in their subject matter than before. Until someone had the brilliant idea to send pretty children to cheer up the wounded soldiers.

There were men without arms, without legs, with rags over their sightless eyes. Nadya fainted and some of the girls turned back. I went down the rows of beds, smiling and parroting the phrases we had been told. "Thank you for your bravery." "We welcome you back." "God bless you." Well, I refused to say that last one. You can get away with not doing all sorts of things, if you don't call attention to it. I suppose my parents would have been disappointed if they'd known that I didn't make a speech about why there is no God, though.

Then I came to the man at the end of the row. The bottom of his jaw had been blown off. He might have been only a few years older than me, but he had eyes like the statues on the cathedrals—blank from watching centuries' worth of human hatefulness. I stared. I couldn't help myself. Then he seemed to see me. And his eyes burned. I blurted out one of those three platitudes and moved on as quickly as I could without running.

I didn't cry, or faint, or vomit. I pretended nothing was amiss until I was in the room I shared with Nadya and the lights were off. I wanted to cause pain. To the Germans, or the French government who sent men to that fate for nothing. Was this my conversion? I'd supported the revolution intellectually all my life, but there's a difference between thinking something would be a good idea and being willing to kill and die for it. I wasn't even willing to make a speech that would earn me extra chores, for heaven's sake, and my attempts to start a ballet soviet had gone nowhere. Every good Bolshevik had a conversion story, and I felt, at the mature age of sixteen, I was lagging behind. I tried to tell myself the man's suffering wasn't pointless, that without knowing it, he was helping to bring about the end of those who'd destroyed him. I told myself that, over and over, until I almost convinced myself I believed it. But as good as I was at tricking others, I could never quite fool myself.

Notebook of
Maj. Viktor Aleksandrovich Chekhov

---

11 August, 1916
Volyn Province

Promoted again. When did I become a captain? Near Warsaw, maybe, in '15.

Army stopped short of Kovel. Won't be retaking Lana's village this time. At least 50 km from the northern part of the line to Brest. But we're taking back land instead of giving it up. First time since '14.

Enough shells, guns, everything now. Except maybe men. How many officers lost, if I'm a major? Don't want to think about it.

14 August, 1916
Volyn province

No movement for a few days. That's good. Men are exhausted. Autumn rain will soon turn all the roads to mud. At least a few months of rest to come. Maybe more, if the winter is too cold for guns.

15 August, 1916
Volyn province

Hope other men didn't get unkind letters like Lana's. Bad for morale if their wives act that way.

She asked me to come home. Said the war is lost anyway. Right after this victory! Maybe the news hasn't gotten there.

And if I couldn't come, to send her every cent I could for little Masha. I do! God knows I don't drink much or visit the brothels. She says it's hard. War is hard. How many men died just this month? She'll have to work with what I can send. And she hasn't done what I asked, getting another picture of Masha. She's four now, and I only know a baby just starting to walk.

Diana

I found out the tsar's government had fallen the way everyone else in Paris did: from the newspapers. We read about how the cost of bread had risen past levels the female factory workers could afford, even when their men sent home war wages, and how their demonstration became a riot, and their riot became a revolution.

We had always had some hope that the workers of the world would overthrow their oppressors to end the war, but I don't think anyone expected it to start in Russia, which we all considered the most politically and culturally backward of the European nations. Then again, it was an unfinished revolution. The new "provisional government"—a placeholder until they could hold elections—wasn't going to give them land, peace, or bread. They'd just exchanged the tsar for a puppet of the bourgeoisie.

Still, it excited everyone in a way that nothing had since 1905. I remember coming home and hearing Comrade Slutsky and my father arguing about whether they had to let this bourgeois revolution run its course, or if Russia could almost skip over one of Marx's developmental phases. Being seventeen, I was inclined to think anything was possible if we just worked hard enough, but no one cared what I thought.

Notebook of
Col. Viktor Aleksandrovich Chekhov

3 March, 1917
Volyn province

There's no tsar anymore.

Messenger came to tell me someone else died, and now I'm a colonel. Then he said there's no tsar. A riot in ~~Petersburg~~ Petrograd pushed him out. And the tsarevich, the prince Alexei, gave up the throne, too, and then the tsar's brother, the Grand Duke. And then I guess they ran out of Romanovs.

Will have to listen to what the men say. The tsar was a bad commander, I can say now. And the men thought his wife and the mad monk she was fucking (maybe not?) were traitors. This might be better. But who do we report to? The messenger said there will be elections for a new government. But what until then? An army needs stability.

Wonder if all nobility will go away. Colonels are nobility. Do I have a title now? Don't know. Seems wrong to ask. If someone gives me a title, fine. If not, won't mention it to Lana. No loss.

15 April, 1917
Volyn province

Caught a man dressed like a factory worker telling the men to lay down their arms. Said the Germans would do the same. (When have the Germans refused to fight? They have discipline, if nothing else.) Or that they should turn their guns on their real oppressors, the politicians. Konstantin Fyodorovich said we should let him go. Because it's a delicate time, and killing him would only inflame the men. Don't get that choice, though. Treason is treason.

Maybe see if command will let me just flog him instead. Wouldn't count on it, if I were him.

28 April, 1917
Volyn province

There's more of them. Where are they coming from? Don't they understand that men can't just choose not to fight? What's an army then? Who's going to stop the Germans if they decide to run us over?

Hearing that now they say to kill your officers, too, not just the politicians. Will have to time my latrine visits carefully. Stand in a mixed group, so no one takes a shot.

7 May, 1917
Volyn province

The men formed their own soviet (council). What the hell do privates need a council for? Their representative told me they're working on demands for improved conditions. I'd like better rations myself, but demanding them won't get me anywhere.

Konstantin Fyodorovich went to one of their meetings, even though he's an officer too. Said they've decided to vote on my orders and are discussing an eight-hour workday. The Germans don't fight on the clock!

So many deserting. I couldn't shoot them all, even if we caught them all. And I'm not allowed to anymore anyway.

Konstantin Fyodorovich says I have to persuade them. Persuade my own damn men. And how? What can I offer them, when the so-called factory workers say they can just go home and divide up their landlords' fields? My god, the world is mad.

18 June, 1917
Volyn province

Kerensky (new Minister of War) came to speak to the men. He speaks well. Patriotism, honor, sacrifice. The men love it. Not sure about him, though. Had his arm in a sling, but didn't move like he was in pain. May not matter.

There's another push coming. High risk. If it works, maybe we have an army again. If not, might as well give up and hand the Germans whatever towns they want. Will do everything I can to make it succeed. But that's not much.

September? 1917
Red Cross house

One of the nurses told me what day it is, but now I can't remember. Don't want to ask her again.

Here convilessing for at least a month. That doesn't look right. I could spell that word before. Doesn't matter. Don't need spelling to use a plow and sickle.

The war's lost. Kerensky's pretty words didn't help when the shells started exploding. The men ran toward the fight, then ran home like boys beaten at a game.

Tried to keep my unit together for an orderly retreat. I was on my horse, then I was on the ground. Couldn't hear anything. Everything was blurry and too fast, like God wanted it all over with and sped up time. Don't remember much after that.

Will go home once they say I've convelessed enough. (Still not right?) They say the peasants are dividing up the estates. I'll get my share and feed my family. We can sell our grain to the tsar or the kaiser, I don't care which. No, no tsar anymore. Can't get used to it. Doesn't matter. I'm going home.

Diana

It was a cold, dreary November night, and Nadya and I just wanted our beds after a long day of rehearsals. When we got back, though, we could tell we wouldn't be sleeping that night. Every Bolshevik in Paris must have been packed into that apartment. Most of them already had red noses and watery eyes.

Someone crushed us in an embrace. "We've done it, children!"

The provisional government in Petrograd had fallen. It had lived only about eight months. My father was good-naturedly yelling at Comrade Slutsky. "You see, I told you the bourgeois regime wouldn't last our whole lives!" I remember feeling that I was part of something great, that we had achieved something unheard-of in human history. Then someone thrust a glass of vodka into my hands, and I don't remember much after that.

And then we waited. I kept dancing, but only to fill the time. It was obvious I would never have a career as a ballerina. This was just a way of preparing myself for the physical rigors of the revolution. Any day, the German and French soldiers would see that the real enemy wasn't the other side, but the capitalists who made money by sending the workers to destroy each other.

But one month passed, then two, then three. Spring approached, and the workers showed no sign they understood the world was being remade. The adults redoubled their efforts to raise the consciousness of the French proletariat. But some of them began to frown and whisper. Did we need something more? A provocation? Something to destroy the public will to fight the capitalists' war? Or a bold first act to give the people something to rally around and fight for? After all, Russia was far from Paris, and perhaps people had dismissed the Bolsheviks as hopelessly backward, just like they had the tsar's government. I fantasized that they would choose me to set off a bomb in the opera house, burying the fat old men who bought little girls beneath their own marble and gold leaf.

I was thinking about that on a Friday afternoon in March as I strolled along. The opera house was closed so the Christians could celebrate a Jewish man dying in agony. I was imagining how I would help rid the world of that rubbish when the blast threw me off my feet.

There had been a church less than a block from me. And now there was none. A German shell had done what my father's speeches never could.

I picked myself up and ran in. People were moaning and screaming. I stepped over a child's arm, severed at the elbow. I didn't know what to do. A hand grabbed my ankle. A girl about my age was pinned under part of the ceiling. Her blue eyes locked onto mine.

"Help me," she gasped. I tried. I lifted and pushed, lifted and pushed, until I'd freed her chest, then her belly, then—*dear God.*

The blood gushed out where her pelvis and legs should have been. Her skin turned to ash. She was sweating. She was afraid. I took her hand and stroked her hair. I thought I heard her say "Pray." I didn't know how to pray, and it wasn't the time to tell her there was no God, so I just asked anyone who was listening to save her. She was gone before I had to come up with anything else. Others had rushed in to rescue the survivors by then.

I stumbled to my parents' apartment, even though it was farther than Citizen Slutskaya's. My father was writing something with the door open. I told my mother what happened, as best I could, which wasn't very well since I couldn't stop crying. She kept shushing me, and my father shut the door so he could concentrate.

"This is good," she said. I thought I had heard her incorrectly. "It's a blow to their will to fight this war and a reminder their god won't protect them. We need them to turn away from both before they're ready to embrace our message."

"That girl is dead," I said, like she hadn't understood what I'd told her.

"People die, Diana. Many more will die before the revolution's over." I turned away and sobbed. "Now, stop crying. If you can't rejoice, at least take it like a grown woman." Everything she said made perfect sense. What were the lives of however many dozen people in that church, compared to everything the capitalists had destroyed over the last three years? And it wasn't even our bomb. There was no moral balancing required, no need to justify the end, since there was no means. But I still wept. "I thought I'd raised you to be stronger than this."

I screamed at her that she hadn't raised me at all and that I hated her. Which I did, at least at that moment. But I also hated myself because I was weak and sentimental, and I was beginning to realize that wouldn't change, that I'd never really been converted. I was just like the artists and writers who floated at the edge of the Party and never did anything—the kind of person I'd always despised because my parents despised those people. I wasn't made of iron. I would pretend after that, and they would pretend to believe it. But it was a lie. We all knew it, and I hated her for demanding that I keep up the appearance so everyone could believe they'd raised a good Bolshevik. I should have seen it for the excellent preparation for my adult life that it was.

Notebook of
Col. Viktor Aleksandrovich Chekhov

1 April, 1918
Petrograd

Nothing to update for months. But now I have a command again, so I must record.

Red Cross released me in December. Went home to Tambov. Lana took Masha there to get away from the fighting. They stayed with my sister and her family. No, not at the end. They stayed in the next house until they died.

I don't remember what happened. I saw red paint on the door. My sister said they were dead. And next thing I knew, the house was on fire. I had two boards in my hand. I made a cross in the churchyard. I didn't have time to carve their names before the village pushed me on the next train.

I have a lock of Masha's hair in a handkerchief. Dark like mine, curly like Lana's. My sister must have given it to me. I just don't remember.

Stop. This is a colonel's notebook, not a girl's diary.

The train went to ~~Petersburg~~ Petrograd. I got off. Nowhere to go, so I ended up at Smolny. And I volunteered. The Bolsheviks (they call themselves that) didn't trust me until I told them I wanted to kill the tsar slowly. Why? For the men? Or because armies carry disease to wives and children? Don't know. They didn't ask. But they gave me a unit.

Thank God they didn't send us when the mob broke into the rich people's wine cellars. My men would have joined in. But they're getting better. No more soldiers' committees voting on orders.

My sergeant, Konstantin Fyodorovich, found me again. He's the commissar. Still not sure what they do. Make speeches, I guess. Which may not be entirely worthless. Still don't understand why we're about to fight another war. Don't think the men understand either. But I need the work. It's hard enough to exhaust me. Only way I'll ever sleep.

Maybe he'll ask for transfer. I didn't mean to hit him. But when he said my wife and baby must have driven me crazy fast to bring me back so soon, I lost my mind for a second. I didn't really hurt him, but I apologized.

17 May, 1918
Petrograd

Drills getting better. Men might not run away when we have to fight.

Still don't understand what we're doing. Reds (us) want to end the tsar's war and carve up the landlords' estates. Fine. What do Whites want? Konstantin Fyodorovich says they'll bring back tsar. Don't believe it. No one could want him back in charge. Probably not even his wife.

Konstantin Fyodorovich says we're fighting those who'd make us slaves again. Free men, fighting to free the rest of Russia, no matter the cost. Free it from what? Doesn't matter. There's going to be another war. Have to fight it until somebody wins.

Diana

Sometimes I wondered if my generation was cursed. The Spanish flu was cutting people down faster than the German bombs. At first, we still held rehearsals to maintain discipline, in the hope that some of us would live to perform for people again. For a while, the whole thing seemed distant, an inconvenient interruption. Then one little chorus girl started coughing during rehearsal. She turned blue that night and died the next day. I never even knew her name. Three others followed her. Then they closed the theater.

This was before antibiotics. People were accustomed to the idea that not every child would live to grow up, and that if you heard grandmother cough, you'd better prepare to say goodbye. But this disease was killing strong, healthy people. It's cruel, that men who survived the trenches coughed themselves to death.

Some of the girls stayed home every possible moment. I couldn't bear to do that. At Slutskaya's apartment, people were still trying to come up with the right slogan to convince the French proletariat the capitalists had sent them this plague on purpose. I knew it wasn't true, and I said so. They said literal truth—exactly where the flu had come from, and why—didn't matter so much as the truth that the workers were being exploited, and only they could provide a solution. Rigid adherence to the rules was what allowed the capitalists and bourgeoisie to stay in power, and to insist on it was to play into their hands. I imagined myself telling Lenin how corrupt his Paris comrades were, but I didn't know how to send a letter to the Kremlin, so I found seedy little cafes and bars whose owners were willing to defy all the orders and stay open. It was foolish, at best, but I'd never had entire days with nothing to do but think, with nothing pushing me to my physical limits.

I met an Italian artist who seemed to be there for much the same reason. He, too, was a Jew by birth but not conviction. He asked me, without any flattery or promises, if I would sleep with him. I found the directness rather refreshing. And I didn't want to be blown to bits or drown in my own lungs' fluids without knowing what it was to "be with" a man.

There were others after that. It wasn't about love, or even passion, exactly. I wanted a kind of oblivion, to stop thinking about how I couldn't bear what I knew I needed to, couldn't believe the only thing that gave all of this carnage meaning. I tried drinking, and cocaine powder, just once—I couldn't see what all the fuss was about in either case. Merging my flesh with someone else's was the only thing that let me sleep well afterward. After a thorough cleansing with vinegar, of course. I had no desire to be a mother, much less to raise a child with any of those lost men.

It wasn't rebellion. Every good Bolshevik knew marriage was a bourgeois trap—a glorified form of prostitution. Of course, my parents were married, and as far as I knew, neither had brought home any lovers, but they'd always taught me that my body was mine, to do with as I pleased—so long as it didn't interfere with Party work. Which meant no lovers from unacceptable classes and no pacifists. The men I played with were all radicals, or they thought they were. They read seditious literature and mocked bourgeois morality, and some made halfway decent art. Mostly anarchists, though I never got a coherent explanation of what they planned to do if there was no one to call if someone grabbed their paintings and ran. It didn't matter. The politics was just something to give the whole thing a patina of legitimacy. For Bolsheviks, sex exists to support politics. I thought I was rather clever, turning that on its head. We all think we're very clever when we're that young.

Notebook of
Col. Viktor Aleksandrovich Chekhov

28 August, 1918
Outside Kazan, Tatarstan

Whites have Kazan. Trotsky (war ~~minister~~ commissar) says they plan to march from there to Moscow. Good luck getting there before the roads turn to mud. This will be my unit's first real action. Are they ready? At least we have enough boots and rifles.

Heard when a unit retreated in another battle, Trotsky had commander shot, then random men. Not sure if it was one in ten, like the Romans. Need discipline, yes. But must be something between this and letting them vote on their orders. Sometimes retreat makes sense. Keep men alive to fight another day. Won't have that option, God help me. Hard to sleep, knowing that. Does Trotsky sleep well? Only saw him at a distance, but he looked alright. Tired from work but not tormented. How?

7 September, 1918
Outside Kazan

Shelling started today. Not enough units to surround the city. Will Whites try to hold onto it, or escape on Volga River? Depends how many boats they have.

8 September, 1918
Outside Kazan

No change today. Whites either didn't have artillery to fight back, we destroyed it, or they plan to flee.

10 September, 1918
Inside Kazan

It's ours. The Whites left by the river. We're securing the city. Superiors are worried they left saboteurs or ambushes. I doubt it. Most people don't want to live in the middle of a war.

Will go to the religious houses in my part of the city. Set an example for the men, not to loot the altars. Start with the Orthodox church. If anyone supported Whites, it's them.

3 p.m.

Visited churches. All quiet. Just old priests and monks. "You're polite, for a Red follower of Satan," one said to me. Maybe he wanted to see what I'd do. I laughed.

On to the synagogue. No trouble there. People say the Jews like us Reds, since the tsar kept burning their villages. Maybe some of them do, I don't know. Most probably just want to be left alone.

5 p.m.

Ordered hotels and boarding houses to take in survivors and feed them. Gave out my sleeping pills, one each, until I ran out. They need them more than I do.

Should start this entry over, it's all out of order. God, never thought I'd write something like this.

When I went to the synagogue, there was blood seeping under the door. Don't know if I was supposed to go in, just me and my aide, but there's no protocol for that. For battles, yes. For prisoners, yes. If you find a massacre? No.

There must have been a hundred of them, strewn everywhere, like they'd tried to run or fight back. Didn't count the bullets, but they were imbedded in the walls, chairs, everything. They'd done something worse to an old man, strung him up and cut off pieces. The rabbi? Don't know. Couldn't make sense of it. Bodies make sense on a battlefield. Not like that.

My aide asked if I wanted him to go bring some men to dispose of the bodies. Must have said yes. He went, and I started turning over corpses, looking for anybody with a spark of life. Dozens dead before I found one alive. Little girl with dark curls, covered in blood. Thought she was dead, too, until I felt she was warm. She screamed when I picked her up.

"We're here to help," I said. Help. How could we help? Took her outside and had someone get her a blanket and some soup. No one could get her name. She was old enough to talk, but she probably couldn't remember how. Called her Masha for now.

We found five others. Two had small wounds and would have died if we hadn't come then. One woman was able to speak and said the Whites had done it before they left. Why? She just looked at me. "When has anyone ever needed a reason?" she said. She wasn't wrong. God. They have to pay for this.

There's no one to punish now, not since they fled. They'll pay in the next battle. The men will remember this. Forget commissars, they'll know why they're fighting.

Midnight?

Don't know if this requires an update. Couldn't sleep. Heard shooting. Very close. In my section. Should have woken someone, but didn't think of it. Went looking.

Ran into Konstantin Fyodorovich. Why was he up? Must not have been able to sleep either. He said he didn't hear anything. Was I sure? I was. I heard it. Didn't I? But it was quiet then. He said it must have been something else, or the battle ringing in my ears. That if anything was happening, I was the first one he'd want responding. But nothing was happening. I don't understand. I know I heard it. Didn't I?

I'd take a sleeping pill, but I gave my last away. Maybe there are some in one of the pharmacies the Whites didn't completely loot. Vodka will have to do. Just for one night.

11 September, 1918

There was shooting. But it wasn't a White uprising. It was another massacre. This one in the church.

It was much the same, except smaller. Just the priests and monks.

At least I think so. They were in their night clothes. Herded into the sanctuary and shot there. Konstantin Fyodorovich said the locals must have taken revenge on their oppressors. Naïve. Doesn't want to believe we could be involved. I know it was us. I know the sound of an officer's pistol.

Must arrange a lecture for the men about not taking 'exterminating our class enemies' so literally. Not that I blame them, wanting revenge. But we can't be like the Whites. God help poor Russia if either way she's ruled by murderers.

Diana

Eventually it all ended, the war and the flu. The world went on, and the capitalists divided it up.

The theater reopened. That was a relief in at least two ways. First, it gave me something to do. Second, it put bread on the table, since the Bolsheviks in Russia were a bit preoccupied with a civil war and no longer sent funds to support their brethren in exile. Neither of my parents had ever been anything but a professional revolutionary—a notoriously underpaid vocation. So I danced for the capitalists to support the Bolsheviks. It was better than waiting to drop dead from flu or shrapnel.

All the conversations at my parents' apartment centered on one question: When will we go? Everyone's mind was in Russia, but reports suggested their bodies might face considerable trouble there. Mother told Father he could go if he wished, but she and her daughter were not going to set up a home in a country that still was on fire. "A war is no place for a ballerina," she said. Was the note of condescension there, or did I read it in? It doesn't matter. I heard it, and I hated them for despising my work that stocked the larder.

I went to the Italian artist. Not for comfort, exactly. He couldn't offer that. More to know that someone else was more lost than I was. He was poor company for anyone who intended to find her way, but I can't be the first person who dealt with her problems by going to someone who could only make them worse. And I thought, when he said that nothing mattered and we were all on the way to the grave anyway, that he was at least doing me the favor of being honest. I know now that it was all an excuse for him to do whatever he wanted, and to hell with everyone else. But who among us hasn't made that mistake when we were young and stupid?

It would have taken longer for me to come to my senses if I hadn't found his handkerchief stained with blood. He didn't deny he had tuberculosis—we were all dying anyway—and he didn't apologize. I went and sat on the steps in front of his building and wondered if he'd condemned me to a slow, agonizing death. If so, I'd helped him do me in, and so had all our friends who sat around drinking all day and never tried to do anything other than slap a little paint on a canvas. I cried because I was afraid, and then I seethed. I went up to confront him, but he was already passed out drunk, so I took one of his paintings to a stable and planted it squarely in a pile of manure. It hardly changed the work's quality. And then I went home.

For months afterward, I was sure any tickle in my throat was the beginning of my death. I pleaded in my head, though there was no one to bargain with. "If I don't die, I will do something. I won't be a waste like them. I will serve the people. I'll help create something new under the sun."

Notebook of
Col. Viktor Aleksandrovich Chekhov

---

27 February, 1921
On a train

En route to Tambov to put down peasant rebellion. Hope my brother-in-law isn't in it. Wouldn't mind shooting some of the others, after they abandoned Masha and Lana. Might not even mind shooting him.

6 March, 1921
Tambov Province

Trip took longer than it should have. Railway's in terrible shape.

Not sure what my men are here for. The "Greens" (why does every group of fighting men need a color?) have a strategy of popping up, raiding grain stores, and melting away. Suppose we'll just guard the grain and fight them if they come. What else is there to do?

10 March, 1921
Tambov Province

Ordered to accompany two Chekists to villages to get grain. Thought Cheka just listened for the wrong kind of talk. Apparently, they do much more.

So we're bodyguards now. Should be easy. Bandits look for unguarded targets, not ones with a whole unit around them. Wonder why the people are sheltering them (they must be). Seems easier to just turn over the grain.

11 March, 1921
Tambov Province

Bad start with the Chekists. They ask lots of questions I don't know how to answer. They thought that was suspicious. Said I'm not a politician, just doing a job. That was wrong. The man said he could have me shot. I believe him. Thank God Konstantin Fyodorovich talked him down. He said I'm useful, despite needing to work on class consciousness. 'Useful' is the best I can hope for.

12 March, 1921
Tambov Province

Arrived in target village. Chekists' plan is to bring village together and demand they turn over grain and any bandits. Do they need a whole unit for that? Doesn't matter, we're here.

There is no grain.

Nothing in this village but people with dead eyes. Those children won't survive until harvest. If there is a harvest. The ground is dry. Winter wheat needs snow.

Told the Chekists it was a mistake. Someone wrote down the wrong village, or someone didn't understand what's happening. The man threatened to shoot me again. Said it wouldn't get him any grain.

When the peasants didn't turn over anyone, they grabbed a man. Why him? No reason. And they shot him. In front of everyone. No warning. Just shot him. And then they grabbed another. There was a little girl on his leg. Screaming. And I had my pistol out. Pointed at the one who kept saying he'd shoot me. Don't remember deciding to draw it. And then Konstantin Fyodorovich stood between me and him. How did he get there? "You can't change this," he said. I think that's what he said. Wasn't hearing right. Then I was surrounded. My men took me back to my tent. Not sure if anyone's guarding me. Haven't looked. Someone must have my pistol. Was going to shoot myself and save them the time. But I don't have it.

If my superior reads this log, only one thing left to say. We'll all burn in hell for this.

1 June, 1921
Moscow

No one shot me. That's all I know.

In a hospital. Another head injury. How? Think I remember a fire. If I'm alive, the Chekists must be dead. The others must not have said what I did. Should probably burn this. Maybe not. If they kill me, don't I deserve it?

7 July, 1921
Moscow

Released. Doctor said I'm not fit for combat duty anymore. But not so disabled they'll discharge me. Told to expect an office assignment. Would rather never wear a uniform again. But no real choice.

20 July, 1921
Moscow

Heard the new commander, Tukhachevsky, used poison gas to kill all the peasants hiding in the ravines in Tambov. Would be tempted to run in with them.

Tried to write to my sister. She's probably already dead. If she isn't, probably will never know.

Assigned to the military academy. Comes with a room and Red Army rations, though I'm not working hard. I give some away. Every corner has a starving woman or child. Or both. They see a uniform and ask to trade for bread. Even the children. Sickening. Can't trade. I give it to them. One girl said someone will knife me if they know I have bread in my pocket. Fine. Seems right.

31 December, 1921
Moscow

Nothing to write for months. Teach, sleep, teach, sleep, teach, sleep. Expect more of the same next year. (This is new New Year's. They changed the calendar. Don't know why. Don't care.)

My job is to teach the lessons of the tsar's war. Don't know why they trust me to do that. Someone must have lied shamelessly. Konstantin Fyodorovich must have. Who else?

They're good boys. Makes me sick to think in a few years they'll be shooting their neighbors. But at least being here gets them good rations for now. Don't know what would happen to them if they weren't here. Probably would be shooting their neighbors already.

31 October, 1922
Moscow

Vladivostok fell. No major cities left in the Whites' or the rebels' hands. Now it's going to be just mopping up the little uprisings. Hope they just give up. Why should more die?

They may have found a way to keep it going, though, seizing the churches' property to pay for food. Don't care myself (God isn't taking good care of his faithful people), but some of them will. People will fight for God when they've given up on everything else.

31 December, 1922
Moscow

We're now the Union of Soviet Socialist Republics. New name, new year, new hope? The war is ending. Then what? Everyone who lost a wife and child finds a widow? There are so many. No, no. How long has it been since I slept without pills or vodka? I have no business thinking about loving anyone.

1923-1931

Diana

From that point forward, I dedicated myself fully to preparing for revolutionary struggle. In my work, I attempted to raise the class consciousness of my fellow ballerinas. In my spare time, I abandoned sensual frivolity and devoted myself to the study of Marx, Engels, and our great leader, Lenin. Since my return—and how can it be anything but a return, to a person of Russian heritage?—I have taken advantage of the warm, comradely help offered to improve myself. My only ambition is to serve the Party, and to help the proletariat to prepare for its rise.

That's all a lie.

Vanya, the man who did makeup at the Bolshoi Theater, told me I needed a convincing conversion story if I wanted to join the Party and helped me cook one up for the committee that would decide whether to admit me.

Vanya was the first person in Russia who I genuinely liked. Most of the ballerinas thought he rejoiced too much when the Party lifted the ban on sodomy, but I didn't object. Good God, after some of the things I'd seen the artists do, why would I? He liked me and tried to help me to win over the ballet master, who didn't appreciate a foreigner being thrown into his ranks. There was so much I didn't understand—so many little cues that the others knew how to read and interpret, and that had somehow gotten lost when the exiles were raising their children. Not to mention that I couldn't follow how they mashed up words in any way that pleased them. I'd learned passable Russian from Citizen Slutskaya, but it never flowed for me like it did for them. My parents and many of the other Party members spoke German at home, since they assumed the "most advanced" proletariat would be the first to rise up. I was completely unprepared for Russian life.

Not that it was all my fault. The other dancers all thought the French were weak, decadent, and lazy, and while I didn't entirely disagree, they might have given me a chance to prove myself. I'd hear them whispering about Muskvina the diva, Muskvina the Jew, and all my supposed sexual exploits. I was tempted to tell them they didn't know the half of it, just to see if any of them would faint from sheer prudishness.

But I didn't mind that so much. Every theater has a few mangy alley cats in the chorus. And I didn't yearn for their approval, with their petty intrigues to move even half a rung up the ladder, and their shameless flattery of people they mocked once their backs were turned. No, what kept me up at night was what I'd seen on the way.

We'd arrived in Odessa not long after the Whites had fled. An old associate of my father's met us at the dock and bundled us into a train car. It was guarded. I didn't understand why until I saw the people riding on the roofs and fighting in the other cars. Wouldn't the comradely thing be to invite some of them in?

"They'd eat you alive, miss," the guard said. As we passed through the country on the way to Moscow, I caught glimpses of people with skinny limbs and swollen bellies, and I wondered how literally he meant it.

My parents didn't talk about them when we got to Moscow, and I actually wondered if I could have imagined it. But how could I have? I'd seen people with their limbs blown off or their skin burned by mustard gas, but never any who were starving. So I told myself it was the cruelty of the Whites, destroying fields as they ran away. I wasn't sure why we hadn't yet fixed it. I yearned for Comrade Lenin to show up at the ballet and explain it. I couldn't get rid of my doubts, so I simply folded them up like someone's grandmother's quilt and tucked them away until a superior mind could open my eyes. I was ready to rebel against my parents and their lies, but I wanted to believe that what we were building would work. After watching the capitalists put men in the meat grinder for years, how could I bear to believe anything else?

That yearning for illumination only grew as I worked my way up and the ballerinas became more vicious, as their wives of the Nepmen somehow found furs and diamonds, and as an unofficial flesh market opened after our performances. We called them Nepmen because they'd done so well under the New Economic Policy, which allowed a little bit of trade while the country recovered from the civil war. I'd expected them to behave like swine, but seeing our comrades line up to ply girls with champagne and use their positions to talk them into bed was a surprise. Hadn't we all agreed it was time for that to end? But no one said a word.

Increasingly, I dreamed I would enlighten Lenin. He would be unaware of how these so-called Bolsheviks were behaving as badly as the Nepmen, and I would be the only one with the courage to tell him. And he would be so grateful he would praise this brave French girl: a loyal Communist, a true servant of the people, practically the daughter he never had. I saw it, and it sustained me.

Notebook of
Col. Viktor Aleksandrovich Chekhov

---

2 September, 1923

No longer need a campaign notebook, but the commissar has assigned us to write. To track the development of our political consciousnesses. Apparently, this is something Bolsheviks do.

My political consciousness must not be developing well, or he wouldn't have given me the assignment. True, I was grading exams during the lecture. But I wasn't asleep. That should count for something.

I wonder if the boys told him I'm unreliable. Some of them think so. But so did last year's. And they liked me by the winter break.

The commissar says we'll take a field trip at the end of the week to help develop our consciousnesses. Hope it's not a battlefield. Can't stand the idea of listening to him talk about what it all meant, to those of us who were there. Guess I'll have to stand it.

5 September, 1923

Not just my political consciousness that's slow. I've forgotten how to talk to women. Made a damn fool of myself.

The field trip was to the ballet. I don't mind ballet. I'd be lying if I said I understood all of it. How can I, when they don't talk? But anyway, it was clear it was about the Revolution. Though if I'm honest, I spent the whole time watching the lead dancer.

She played a countess. So I guess she wasn't the lead dancer. We were supposed to be looking at the one who was leading the worker-dancers. But who could look at anyone but the countess? Golden hair, white calves, the kind of body … I'm probably not supposed to write about that.

I tried to talk to her after. I did talk to her, but I sounded like an idiot. Should I send flowers to apologize? Can't hurt. But yes, it can. I can humiliate myself again. Probably will. You don't learn, Chekhov, you don't learn. No wonder the commissar's making you do extra homework.

Diana

It was a clear, starry night, but I was in a foul mood. Nothing in particular had happened—nothing that didn't happen any other night. But for whatever reason, I couldn't abide the thought of pretending to listen to pompous windbags pump up their war records while the alley cats purred and simpered. So, after the performance, I slipped outside for a moment of quiet.

No such luck.

An average-sized man followed me out. I tracked him out of the corner of my eye. He didn't walk like a drunk, but even a sober man may decide to grab a woman on her own. He waited; I don't know for what. Finally, he spoke:

"Excuse me, comrade, but I wanted to congratulate you on your performance."

"Thank you, comrade." *Go away, go away, go away.*

"Do you smoke?"

"No." I did, on occasion, though I tried not to make a habit of it.

"Mind if I do?"

"Please yourself."

"I was very moved by your performance."

"I'm sure you were." It was rude, I knew, but he didn't seem to be taking the hint that I wanted nothing less than to talk to another supposed admirer.

"I like your accent." I didn't respond. "Where are you from?"

"Paris."

"Then what are you doing here?"

"My part, to build socialism."

"You'd better be careful. When you dance like that, you'll make hearts break for the poor countess." That finally annoyed me enough that I turned around and locked eyes with him. I might have laughed it off, but I wasn't going to be played with by a man too stupid to understand the moral of the show.

"If you think I care a centime for those parasites, I will bid you good night, sir."

"I didn't mean—" He tried to grab my hand, to get me to stay, and I told him he'd better warm up those cold fingers, because they were the only thing that would touch his dick. Vanya thought that was clever when I told him about it the next day.

I thought that was the end of it, until a bouquet arrived in my dressing room. The urchin who delivered it said a man was waiting outside to find out if I took it. I was tempted to dismiss it out of hand, but I decided to read the card. It was an apology, though I suspected he still had no idea what he'd done wrong. Men are like that. I told the urchin to tell this Viktor Aleksandrovich Chekhov that he could wait if he wished, because I wasn't about to run out in my leotard.

He was still waiting when I had changed and sauntered out, a little slower than I usually walked. I stopped a few steps above him and looked down. He was pacing and stubbing out a cigarette. He had dark hair with just a few grays threaded in, which stood out in the streetlamp light.

"I came to apologize," he said.

"For what?"

"For insulting you when I was trying to compliment you. And touching you with my cold hand." I scoffed. "I've never been good with words, but I wanted to say you're talented. And beautiful. That's all."

"I accept your apology."

He hesitated. "Do you want me to leave you alone?" I would have said yes the night before, but I didn't answer that night. "If you aren't busy tonight, come have a cup of tea with me."

"I won't sleep with you."

"I didn't expect you to." I gave him my most withering look. "There are women who would make this easier, if that was all I wanted."

I did smile at that. I might have turned him down and gone back to my dormitory just to make a point, but I had nothing to do and I wasn't sleepy. "Have me back in an hour."

We went to a little tea house with sticky tables and a seemingly permanent cloud of cigarette smoke over everything. He wanted to hear about Paris. I told him it was something like Moscow, which wasn't true. Moscow, with its rings of wooden buildings around the central fortress, felt like it had never fully left the Middle Ages behind. But it seemed insulting to say so.

"Where were you when you heard the tsar had been deposed?" I asked, because everyone who was at least my age had a story about that. I guessed he was about thirty, maybe a decade older than myself.

"At the front, writing a letter. I'd just gotten word someone had promoted to the heavenly choir and I'd been given his rank of colonel. The messenger asked if I'd heard what had happened in Petrograd. We called it Petrograd then, because St. Petersburg was too German. I thought it was something about the monk Rasputin. He'd been killed just a few months before."

"What did you feel when he told you?"

"I thought he was joking. Though that would have been a bold joke. No tsar for the first time in centuries. I didn't know what to think. I tore up the letter I was writing. Can't send a letter written under a tsar into a tsar-less world."

"You didn't rejoice?"

"It was all the same at the front. We took an oath of loyalty to the new government and kept fighting—well, for a while. By the time I was wounded, no one even bothered to see if I was fit to go back. So many had deserted."

"What kind of wound?"

"You are direct, aren't you? Head. A shell burst too close to me, and I blacked out. Maybe that's why I don't understand what historical materialism is. Too brain-damaged."

I tried to explain Marx's theory of historical development, and he managed to ask questions that were good enough to show he was paying attention, but not good enough to suggest he understood much of it. I might have felt somewhat superior if I hadn't been humbled as soon as the samovar arrived. Apparently, every Russian learns to work a tea urn by age eight. Why didn't my parents teach me that? Making tea would have been a useful skill. He offered to do it, but I said I needed to learn so I could fit in. Then he made a joke about stars not being made to blend in instead of mocking me, so I decided to give him what he wanted. Why not? He couldn't be any worse than some of the men I'd been with, and a little physical stimulation might do wonders for my mood if he happened to be any good.

I took him down into the orchestra pit and perched on the bars at the edge, where I could look up into the dark theater. He was out of practice, but I said yes when he kept asking me if it felt good. The asking felt better than anything he did with his penis, to be honest.

I was surprised when he showed up the next night. I'd assumed he'd gotten what he wanted. But I wasn't averse to seeing him again, and I didn't string him along before agreeing to have tea.

"So why did you join, if it was all the same to you whether there was a tsar or not?" I asked, to see if he'd answer honestly.

He hesitated. "We all lost so much in that war we never needed to fight. When I came back, there was nothing for me. And I wanted him to pay for that. Not that he meant for it all to happen. But he didn't stop it."

"So it was personal."

"Yes. I ended up in Petrograd and found their recruiting office. They needed officers. And when I said I wanted to rip the tsar's guts out, they decided I'd do."

"And did you do it?"

"No. Somebody must have killed him. But not me. I spent the first half of '18 just getting my unit to follow orders."

"And once they would follow orders?"

"We were part of the push to retake Kazan. That's in the Tatar's part of western Siberia. On the Volga River." I was glad he hadn't made me ask. "We got it back. It was ugly, though. Even as war goes."

"What do you mean?"

He hesitated. "People die in wars. No getting around that. But people died who didn't need to. Women, children, old men."

"The Whites killed them?"

"Some of them."

"You make it sound less than glorious."

"War's never glorious. Until we talk about it years later. Then it gets better."

"I wanted to be here, doing my part. Not dancing for the capitalists," I said.

"You would have died when the rations ran out." He looked like he wanted to cut out his own tongue. "I mean, you don't have any fat to draw on. Everyone went hungry."

"Even soldiers?"

"Sometimes."

"Even children?"

"Almost always."

"What did people do?"

"Some died. Some got lucky. Those who could went back to their villages. The ones stuck here tore down houses for firewood and traded everything they owned for potatoes." He shook his head. "Sometimes traded themselves, if you know what I mean. Even kids."

I knew the truth, of course, but I'd never known anyone in Russia who would tell it. I decided this man was worth spending some time with. He might not know anything about Marxism, but that could be taught. Honesty and a solid grasp of reality couldn't, and both seemed shamefully lacking in this country.

We'd go on long walks around Moscow and he'd tell me stories, mixing his cadet days with tall tales of the tsars Ivan the Dyspeptic and Vladimir the Rotund. I'd tell him all the things I was reading, and he'd listen like a man who wanted to learn. That, as much as anything, drew me in. Respect for female intellect is so rare. And when it came to other things, let's just say he improved with practice and was eager to learn there, too.

"How would you feel if you were bedding a Jew?" I asked him as we lazed in the sheets one afternoon when rehearsals were canceled.

He thought a moment. "I'd feel that I shouldn't have eaten sausage before using my tongue that way." I punched him lightly on the shoulder. "I wouldn't mind, if she didn't mind bedding 'half-gypsy scum'."

"You grew up in a traveling circus?"

"No, but my mother did. My father was a peasant working a few strips of land in Tambov. You've probably never heard of it. There's no reason you should have."

"Peasants married traveling girls often in Tambov?"

He snorted. "No. People like my mother didn't have any rights. When my father died, the others in the village said it was God's punishment. I was five. Too young to work his strips. And they would have been perfectly content to let us starve."

"So what did you do?"

"My mother went to see the landlord. They made some sort of arrangement. She said he was kind to us." He paused. "Mostly she did laundry. Though the landlord's wife liked to assign her to scrub chamber pots. I thought it was because of what we were. Then I found out she didn't have any other choice."

"No, of course not. How could she refuse the man who owned you all?"

"His parents had owned my grandparents, but not anymore. The tsar had emancipated us by then. Not that it did us much good. He still owned the land we had to rent, which was the same thing as owning us."

"My parents would have told your neighbors they should have turned their pitchforks on him, not you."

"They would have called you trouble-making Jews and run you off." He shrugged. "I don't mean to offend. It's what they would have done. We weren't revolutionaries in Tambov. Bandits, occasionally. Not revolutionaries. Though I did almost hit the landlord with a candlestick."

"Good class instincts," I said.

"It wasn't about class. Once I saw him …" He shuddered. "I'm sure you can guess. I've always wished I'd hit him. But my mother talked me down. She said she didn't mind. That she loved him. I never believed it. But he did send me off to study in Petersburg instead of having me arrested for threatening him."

"That's how you became a soldier."

"Yes. I think everyone assumed I was the landlord's bastard son. That's why they put up with a boy who was darker than all the rest of them and didn't know which fork to use. But I learned." He shrugged. "Well, I learned a little bit. I don't know if I'd remember which fork to use if I got invited to an officers' ball. But it doesn't matter, since they don't have those anymore."

"So you would have been there when the workers rose up the first time."

"If you want to put it that way."

"Did you see it start? Bloody Sunday?"

"No. I was in chapel when the worst of it happened. It was only later that we heard the crowd wasn't armed, that they just wanted to bring the tsar a petition about ending the war with Japan."

"Did you fight?"

"No. They called us out later to support the Petersburg garrison in case they couldn't contain the crowd. All we did was stand in the cold for hours."

"What do you think about at a time like that?"

"I decided I'd aim high, over the heads of women and children. If I hit a man, well, his life wasn't worth more than mine. But I wouldn't harm a woman or a child. And I wouldn't order men under my command do it, if I ever got a command."

"Didn't you think of joining the workers?" I asked. "Turning your gun on the people who would have ordered you to shoot at children?"

"Never once. We just didn't think that way then. Well," he hesitated, "I guess some people did. People decided who they were that year: monarchists, reformers, revolutionaries, everything else. I decided I was a good soldier." He looked away quickly, and I wondered for the first time if he was lying to me. I couldn't imagine what he could be lying about, though, so I let it drop.

It was a strange feeling, wanting to see him every day. I didn't call it love. I'd assumed it would take the bravest genius the revolution could produce to sweep me off my feet. He wasn't a genius, but he was good. Undeniably good. Good enough that I wanted my parents to meet him, unlike my past lovers, who I took great pains to ensure they never knew about.

My father kept quizzing him about his opinions on obscure points of Marxism, even though I'd told him what sort of person Vitya was.

"He's a soldier, father, not a politician," I reminded him as we passed around the salad.

"How can soldiers fight if they don't understand their cause?" I didn't have an answer for that.

Vitya paused. "With due respect, soldiers follow orders. It's not for us to decide the rightness of those orders."

"So you'd have killed women and children if the tsar had ordered you to?"

"No."

"But you said you followed orders."

"Father, stop." I really wanted them both to stop talking. I shot looks at my mother, trying to ask her to call him off, but she didn't.

"I was ordered to murder innocent people, and I refused."

"You expect me to believe the tsar let you live?" My father pointed his fork accusingly, like he was going to stab Vitya with it.

"It wasn't the tsar. And I believe the Chekists would have killed me if the peasants hadn't killed them first." I gasped. This was not a story I had heard. "Forgive me, I didn't mean to shock."

"The only shocking thing is your ignorance," my father said. Vitya didn't argue that point. "Our war was not against innocent people, but against social parasites. Your duty was to exterminate them. You should have been shot for that."

"Father!"

"Sergey!" That was finally too much for my mother.

"I knew I'd rather die than live knowing I'd done that."

My father shook his head. "You understand so little. What is necessary for the future of the proletariat cannot corrupt you."

"Killing always corrupts you. If you had ever fought, you'd know that." That hit a tender spot. My father ordered him out of the apartment.

Why had I thought I should introduce them? This wasn't the old world, where my father could give me away or withhold me. But I let Vitya leave. One day passed, and then another, and I didn't reach out. I knew I shouldn't, even if every fiber of my body wanted to. Our kind of people didn't love people who didn't love the revolution. Yes, I'd started calling it love at some point, and why shouldn't I? I had as much right to it as anyone else.

I knew I could defy my parents and love whomever I wanted. There was no law preventing it, I was twenty-four years old, and I made enough of my own money dancing to live independently from them. But if I chose Vitya over them, I was also implicitly making a political choice. Not that he cared enough about politics to demand that I agree with him. And I was comfortable enough holding two thoughts in my mind: that our cause was worthwhile, and that many horrible things, avoidable or not, had happened on the way to achieving it. We all knew that was true. Vitya was just the one who had the courage to say it, or lacked the political instincts not to say it. I didn't understand why others couldn't see it that way, and why my father thought men like him would be the death of the revolution. My mother said that was because I'd let feelings turn my head backwards.

I ran the problem by everyone I knew, and the results were utterly predictable: Party members told me to master myself, and ballerinas told me to follow my heart. It made me wonder: how could I be sure I wasn't acting like a silly chorus girl, the kind I'd always despised? I couldn't know with certainty. I hoped for the deus ex machina to be lowered to the stage and solve my problem for me—Lenin, or some wise senior Party member, telling me I was absolutely right. It's never a good thing to wish for someone to do your deciding for you, but that's what I did. What can I say? I was young and inexperienced, and not ready to deal with the harsher truths of life. At least I grew out of it, unlike so many people.

Notebook of
Col. Viktor Aleksandrovich Chekhov

---

3 January, 1924

Commissar hinted my consciousness is not rising as fast as it should. Well, it's been three months since I last saw my tutor. Not so motivated to study without her. Missing her.

For God's sake, man, stop pitying yourself. You're alive. You're fed, sheltered, and clothed, even though you're not working very hard. All you have to do is keep your eyes open in the lectures. And you had no business thinking you could be a husband anyway.

21 January, 1924

Landed on the floor when they shot off a cannon. Office mate was just startled awake, so no one saw. Why can't they send great men off with church bells?

It's Lenin. Will have to comfort the boys. They love him in a way I never loved the tsar. Don't understand it, but doesn't mean it's not real.

What will happen? Can they pick someone else to lead? Or will it be another war? Half of my students killing the other half? Don't think about that now. Boys will need someone to keep a level head.

22 January, 1924

My tutor is here. She's still sleeping. Didn't think two could fit in that bed. Didn't sleep well, but did sleep a little bit without pills. How long since that happened?

Probably won't see her again after this. Better to have something and lose it again, or not have it? Doesn't matter. I wasn't going to turn her away, not when she was crying. Probably not anyway at all. You don't learn, Chekhov. Nothing to do about it now. Maybe I can get a few more kisses before she leaves again.

Diana

They gave us the night off to mourn with our families when Lenin died. I went to the military academy instead. I couldn't endure sitting through speeches about how we were going to carry on our leader's vision, and how we'd have no time for womanly tears.

A boy stopped me and thought that made him very important. But he went and got the tactics professor. We stood facing each other in a large entryway, where everything echoed off the stone. The boys were asleep, and probably most of their professors were too.

"They told us to go home," I said. He nodded. "I couldn't go there. They'd tell me to stop crying and resolve to fight on." Still nothing. "Do you want me to leave?"

"No."

"Is there somewhere we could talk?"

"I have a room to myself."

He went in and slammed some drawers before letting me in. The room was small, just a bed with scratchy gray blankets, a chest of drawers, a desk, and a chair. I sat on the bed and patted the rock-hard mattress next to me. I wasn't in the mood for a gentleman to offer me the chair.

"Why are you here?" he asked, then winced at the harshness of it. "Why did you come to me?"

I tried to explain. All my reasons for coming back to an ex-lover sounded childish, and my reasons for letting him go in the first place sounded worse. "I needed to see you."

"But why?"

Words were useless, so I leaned on his shoulder and wept until I was finished. Then I unbuttoned my dress and climbed on top of him and made us both feel better. He didn't object.

He was gone when I woke up. I got dressed and waited. It was his room, so he had to come back. I sat down on the bed and kicked my heels against the edge of the mattress. Then I noticed a half-shut drawer.

There was a bottle of vodka, one of headache pills, and one of sleeping pills. None of them shocked me. Then there was a photo, in a plain wooden frame, of a woman and a baby with a mop of dark curls. I put the photo back in the drawer and slammed it shut. I paced and wanted to scream, but I laughed instead. How utterly perfect, that I had agonized over my feelings for an adulterous pig. I repeated what my mother had said—"Monogamy is a bourgeois trap"—but I still wanted to kick him in the knees, and maybe higher.

"You might have mentioned a wife and child," I said when he came in with rolls and steaming cups. I pulled out the photo to confront him with the evidence.

He looked very tired as he set our breakfast on the desk. "Dead. Six years now."

"I'm so sorry." And I was. Both that it had happened and that I'd been ready to scratch his eyes out.

"You didn't know."

"Your daughter was beautiful."

"She was."

"What was her name?"

"Maria Viktorovna. Masha."

"What happened to them?" I wasn't sure if I should ask it, but it was the next logical question.

"Cholera. Armies carry diseases."

"During the tsar's war?"

"Yes. I wasn't the only one who lost a child that way. In either war."

No wonder he'd wanted to disembowel the tsar. "Why didn't you tell me about them?"

"I didn't want you to think I was asking for your pity." I did pity him, though, because he looked so tired, like we'd been sparring for hours instead of talking for minutes.

We cried together. That was the first time a man ever cried in front of me. I stroked his hair and made low, comforting sounds because there was nothing else I could do. And I thought about how angry I'd been, and why, and what that meant. And since Lenin was dead and could no longer be insulted, I'd tell all the others to go to hell. What was all this emancipation for, otherwise?

He didn't know what I was thinking, though, and kissed my forehead like it was goodbye when we both had to go to our work. I stood on my toes to kiss his lips. Maybe it wasn't appropriate after what we'd talked about, but I wasn't going to waste any more time.

"I want to see you again," I said.

"I thought—"

"I don't care."

Neither of us was eager to formalize it. He was convinced he was always one mistake away from being thrown out of the Party—which might have been true—and I knew the married ballerinas ended up leaving the stage, even though we officially had all the rights of men. So we met after classes and performances, wandering the city and stealing moments in flophouses here and there.

"Did you ever meet women like this when you were a young soldier?" I asked as we split a bottle of wine after a performance.

"I had a few romances before my mother died," he said. "After that,

I had to look after my sister. And I was married by the time I was twenty-one."

"And you behaved after marriage?"

"I did."

"You must have loved her a great deal." I winced as soon as I'd said it. We'd never talked about the woman in the photograph, not after that morning. I'd never known how to ask about her without reopening old wounds or sounding jealous of a woman who'd died of a horrible disease.

"I don't know," he answered. "I thought it might be love, at the time." He looked at me. "You want to know about her?"

"Yes," I said. I didn't see the point in pretending otherwise.

"Lana and my sister became friends. Svetlana Alekseyevna. She wasn't especially pretty, but she was a good worker. 'You'll never have to worry about your home if you marry a woman with calloused hands.' That's what one of the captains told me. He said it's good for an army man to have a dependable woman managing while he's fighting."

"No ballerinas then."

"I don't think we had any in Brest-Litovsk."

"And did she manage it all?"

He looked away. "As well as anyone could have."

"I'm sorry—"

"You didn't do anything. I just didn't understand how hard times were toward the end of the war. She wrote, begging me to send more money when I'd already sent everything I had. I didn't have any patience. Not when we were losing a thousand men for a few kilometers of ground. I don't think I could have changed anything. But I could have been kinder in my letters. Not just told her to find a way. But they didn't tell us anything about that at the front."

"I'm sure she understood."

"I don't know if she did. We didn't know each other very well when we got married. Her parents had six daughters and needed to marry them off. She wasn't a beauty, and I wasn't rich. But we weren't a bad match. And once we had Masha, I didn't care about anything else. As long as she kept the home running and didn't sleep around when I was on duty, that was enough. All she asked was that I not beat her and not drink up all my pay."

"Was that asking much?"

"It was more than most of the women in my village got. But no, it wasn't all that hard. I never wanted to go out drinking then. Not when I could be with my daughter." He laughed. "All the other lieutenants said I'd lost my mind, that I thought Masha was the first human to crawl or walk or talk. But it's different when it's your child."

I shrugged. I could hardly imagine my father, or even my mother, doting on my every word and movement. He was better able to read women than most men and quickly moved on.

"Now explain to me again how we'll know when we've reached communism?"

Maybe it's for the best that he never seemed to understand it. He read the papers, just enough to see how loudly they called for rooting out the "bourgeois specialists" and "careerists" who had to be tolerated for a time, until there was a new Red generation to replace their expertise. Every time I saw my father, he went on about how these leftovers would gum up the works with their half-hearted communism—with a pointed look that said he could think of someone I knew who fell into that category.

But it wasn't men like Vitya they came for. My father, who'd been a respected professor of Marxist theory, turned out to have been hopelessly wrong about everything.

The Party was changing. My father's views on the long-term impossibility of socialism in one country without a world revolution would have been perfectly acceptable a few years earlier. But in

1927, they were a dangerous deviation. Does anyone care about that anymore? At the time, it meant everything.

Because if socialism in one country was impossible, the Soviet Union was bound to collapse, and that was a bit of an awkward philosophical underpinning for a government. Not that the ordinary people knew or cared. I asked Vitya what he thought, and he said he supposed that if countries wanted to be socialist, or didn't want to, it was of no importance to him so long as nobody decided to go to war over it. But it was never really about giving the people a philosophical foundation to believe in. It was about which side you had chosen, the Trotskyites or the Stalinists, though they didn't call themselves that then.

Before the revolution, the exiled members would spend hours discussing even the finest point of Marxist theory. Usually it ended with some shouting, but they'd reconcile over drinks a few days later. When we first arrived, there were some consequences for an unorthodox view, but really, they weren't much more severe than having to wear a figurative dunce cap for a while. At least, not for Party members. The understanding was that you could debate policies within Marx and Lenin's framework safely and were only an enemy of the people if you wanted to replace the government.

Then the men at the top had banned factionalism—even the ones who would be shot as traitors a decade later signed on, thinking themselves safe, I suppose. How can you ban talking to like-minded people? But they did. What none of them seemed to realize was that whoever held the most power could decide that anyone who disagreed was a factionalist and a traitor. Or maybe they did and thought they could grab the top spot for themselves. My father agreed with them, never thinking he could somehow be part of a faction. But then he was labeled a Trotskyite shortly after Trotsky was exiled. It was somehow worse than being a tsar's officer at that moment.

My father renounced his views and denounced himself with increasingly colorful language as the Party line changed, but after a while, it changed so fast he couldn't keep up with what he was supposed to believe. It wasn't just whether we needed a world revolution. It was a hundred things.

I knew he'd fallen behind in the dance when the newspapers began running articles about him and the other professors who had agreed with Trotsky. What was the unforgivable sin? Was it about needing a world revolution, or that the peasants had to be forced onto communes? They eventually did create the communes. Then it became a deviation to believe the peasants should be allowed to work their own land. I should remember what the final mistake was, but I simply can't. It might as well have been about whether men should wear brown or black shoes.

The respect I had fought for in the ballet evaporated overnight. Whether I performed beautifully or missed a step, I was always Muskvina the foreign, Jewish diva, shamelessly trying to outshine the others or too self-satisfied and lazy to try at all. They demoted me to the chorus line. I still performed with every ounce of energy I had. I wasn't going to prove them right.

"You should probably stay away from me," I said to Vitya one night when he came to pick me up for dinner. I was trying to light a cigarette because this was the sort of day that demanded one, but I couldn't make the lighter work.

He took it and lit the cigarette with no trouble. "Why? You don't like me anymore?" I could tell he wasn't serious in the way he said it, which exasperated me even more.

"Have you read the paper?"

"Not closely enough, I guess."

"My father's on page four."

The headline said, "University professors apologize for factionalist deviation." And below it was my father's picture, along with five other men in disgrace.

"You think I'd make it worse for him?" he asked.

"I think we'd make it worse for you. A man who cares about his career doesn't see a woman from a suspicious family."

"Who said I cared about my career?"

"Don't you?" A Red Army officer in a family of deviationists? Unthinkable. But being my Vitya, he didn't care about his career—at least, not enough to stop seeing me. He kept coming to the ballet, right on schedule, until they dismissed me. It was the same day the university decided it no longer wanted my father's services.

I went back to my parents—I couldn't very well live in the military academy. The three of us sat around the table, staring at the fish, potatoes, borscht, and fresh bread the maid had laid out as a homecoming meal. We picked at it for a while in silence. Then I took a thick slice of bread, slathered it with butter, and ate it. Then another. Then another. I was buttering my fourth slice when my mother reprimanded me.

"Stop that, or you'll be too fat to be a ballerina when they take you back." I wasn't even hungry anymore, but I took another bite out of pure spite. "I didn't raise you to wallow like this."

"Oh, let her stuff herself," my father said. "She's finished. I'm finished." He pushed away from the table and went into his study. I helped the maid clean up. When I looked in to check on him, I saw him staring at the wall. He didn't seem to see me.

I got my coat and went to wander the city. I wanted Vitya, but I decided I would give him this chance to come to his senses, to leave me like a sensible man. So I just took streetcars in random directions until dawn. Then I went back to my parents' building.

I knew as soon as I entered the stairwell and saw my father's old shoes on the bottom step. They'd slid off. And there he was, blue and lifeless, hanging by a belt from the handrail.

I didn't scream. I went and woke the building manager and then climbed the stairs to my parents' apartment. My mother was still asleep. Good. I wanted them to cut him down before I had to tell her so she wouldn't run out and see him. She couldn't have borne it.

Why don't schools teach you what you're supposed to do when someone dies? It's something almost every student is going to have to face eventually. I broke the news to my mother after they cut him down—well, I broke it in a sense. I said there had been an accident. She wanted to run to him, but I stopped her. And we were there, weeping on the sofa, with no idea what to do next, when I heard Vitya pounding on the door and yelling for me.

I opened the door and he wrapped me in his arms. "I saw them taking … It looked too big, but … The ticket seller said you'd gone."

"I'm fine," I said after he let me go, even though I clearly wasn't. "I just found his shoes." And he crushed me in his arms again. I stood there, my head on his shoulder, letting myself feel protected. My mother gave no sign she noticed I wasn't beside her or even that there was now another person in the room. Then someone else knocked, more formally.

It was the superintendent, whose main job seemed to be liaisons with the woman watching the door. "The apartment will be reassigned," he said. "Please have your things out by the end of the day." He handed me some papers, which I didn't bother to read. I saw Vitya's hands curling into fists, but I shut the door before he could use them.

"Get your clothes, Mother," I said in French, because I didn't think she was in any state to remember Russian.

She still looked at me as if she didn't understand a word. "My clothes?"

"Yes. They're giving the apartment to someone else."

She pointed her finger at Vitya. "You son of bitch—"

"Not him. He's my lover." Maybe she just saw a uniform or was too overwhelmed to think of anyone but my father. "We have to go."

"Where?"

"I don't know."

There was nowhere to go, so Vitya took our books and my father's papers back to his room while I checked into a hotel. He didn't ask what they were, even though my father had been declared a subversive. "You can go through them when you're ready," he said.

I didn't give any thought to the papers, though. I had to find a job. Yes, my father had left us some money, but not enough to live on indefinitely, particularly at the rates that a clean, orderly hotel would charge. I wasn't qualified to do anything other than dance, so I begged to audition for increasingly obscure troupes. None of them wanted me.

"You could always marry me," Vitya said.

I half-laughed. "And the three of us would live in that little room?"

"Until they assigned us an apartment." He sounded serious. "Or you could get a job in a shop. I bet one of the fancy ones would take you."

"Why? What do I know about shops?"

"You're French. People will assume you know about clothes and things."

I went to the store catering to the Nepmen's wives and pretended to know about "clothes and things." Not the top store. But a relatively good one whose manager wanted it to seem better than it was.

"Do you share your father's views?" he asked me.

"No, of course not," I said, because that was what was expected. They couldn't have someone who believed in the wrong type of communism helping women pick out silks and furs.

Notebook of
Col. Viktor Aleksandrovich Chekhov

4 June, 1928

Last entry. I'm not a soldier anymore.

Comrade Muskvina came to check on her husband's books. What did she think I'd do to them? Anyway, they were all there, and we agreed I'd keep them until she and Diya find a permanent place.

Someone must have seen and known who she was. I got called into the office. I told them the truth, that it was nothing to do with politics, everything to do with a woman. They said they could ignore bad judgment about subversive families once, but never to see them again. I said no. None of their business. I don't think the paperwork is done, but they told me I'm no longer part of the Red Army. Fine. This could never last forever. Now it's just a question of finding a place to stay and getting someone to help me carry all these damn books.

Diana

The job didn't come with an apartment, but it did pay enough to keep us off the streets for a bit longer. I was in high spirits when I went back to the hotel—until I opened the door and saw Vitya leaning against the dresser while my mother sat on the bed. Books sat piled on the floor like icebergs.

"What happened?"

"They threw him out of the army," my mother said. She didn't say why, but I knew it was because of us.

I didn't want to cry in front of my mother, but I couldn't stop myself. Vitya put his arms around me. "Don't worry. It was going to happen eventually. I'll find a factory job tomorrow. Or construction. They always need men for that. And I'm not too old to work." He kissed me. "I don't regret anything."

I made him spend the night. He slept curled on the couch while my mother and I took the bed. "It was all there," she said in a voice just audible above his light snoring. "I was worried."

"Vitya is more reliable than you think," I said.

"Yes, a sturdy, reliable, stupid peasant. Not the type I thought you would defy us for."

"I won't listen to you call him stupid. He sacrificed everything for us."

"For you."

"It's the same thing."

"No, it isn't. He loves you, so he doesn't care what they say about your father. It doesn't matter to him whether it was just or not. Your father and I could be common bandits, for all he cares."

I barely heard the part beyond "he loves you." I knew he did. And I knew that I loved him back. I just didn't expect her to be able to see that.

"I didn't believe you when you said he didn't give a damn about anything," she said, which was not true. I had said he didn't give a damn about politics. "Probably just as well. No one tries to cut down a worm that's just crawling along."

"Don't call him a worm."

"Fine, fine. If we're going to be stuck in this frozen shithole, you could have chosen worse than him. Though if your father were alive, I don't know what he'd say."

"Well, if he'd cared enough to stay alive for us, then he could have spoken for himself," I said, then instantly regretted it. "I didn't mean …" But she just rolled over and pulled the blanket over her head.

Vitya did find work quickly, in a tool-making factory. "The job comes with a room," he told me as we ate sausages from a street vendor on my lunch break. "Nothing fancy, but it's four walls and a roof."

"So no one has to get married for a place to sleep," I said.

"No. But we could get married anyway," he said.

"Don't joke."

"I'm not joking." He pulled a plain gold chain necklace from his pocket. "I wanted to get a ring, but I guess they banned those. So I got this. A while ago. I was waiting for the right time. Then things kept happening. But it's still here, if you want it."

"Yes," I said, even though he hadn't exactly asked. I had never imagined that moment of saying yes, not even when I was a little girl.

If I had, I probably wouldn't have imagined setting down a sausage and joining our grease-slicked hands as gray people blurred past us, their little worlds going on as before when mine would never be the same again. "Yes."

The manager let me off, and we went to the registry office that afternoon. It was only after we got there that I thought I should have brought along my mother. But it was too late, so we made an arrangement with another couple to act as each other's witnesses. No vows, no wedding party, just signatures on a piece of paper. We kissed on the steps of the building, and Vitya fastened the chain around my neck. "My beautiful wife," he said.

There was no nonsense about becoming one flesh or that no man should divide what God had joined together. But when we laid together again for the first time after, it was obvious that something had happened—a deep, invisible something—and nothing would ever be the same again. I was a wife. Well, there were no barricades left to man anyway. And since I was twenty-eight, even my mother was willing to concede that it was time to surrender to monogamy.

There was no honeymoon, since we both had to work the next day and were sharing a room with my mother. Once, I snuck him into the back room where we unpacked newly arrived clothes, because it was the only place where we could have a moment of privacy. Later, we'd go to the courtyard behind the factory apartments, but it took time to be assigned a room there.

And so my only child was conceived on a pile of fur coats while we both tried not to alert the night watchman by moaning or giggling.

I didn't hate my father until we were going through his papers.

I wasn't too big yet, but five months had passed, so it seemed safe to assume our room would soon have to accommodate a fourth person, though a small and immobile one. I told my mother that some of the books would simply have to go to make room for a cradle, unless she wanted to move her mattress to the hallway or the communal kitchen.

We went through each one, looking for old letters or anything that she couldn't bear to sell. I was thumbing through his favorite copy of Lenin's collected works when the note slipped out and landed against my belly. Maybe it shouldn't have surprised me, that his last message was a letter explaining that the Party had been his life and to be without it was unbearable. The only mention that he'd had a wife and daughter was a sentence in the margins, asking us to send his note to *Pravda*, so everyone would know he had been an honest Communist to the end.

I threw the book at the wall because I didn't want to scream in an apartment where the walls seemed to be nothing more than compressed dust.

My mother forgave him. I never did.

Sometimes I would turn over in bed, pull Vitya's arm around me, and beg him to promise he would never be so selfish, never leave me, never care about anything more than our family. I did it more often when I felt our child starting to move inside me. And he always squeezed me and promised. I love him for that.

I hadn't exactly chosen a child, but I hadn't stopped it. I'd more or less fallen into motherhood. Abortions were legal in the first three months, and if I'd still been a ballerina, I might have done it. But Vitya wanted a child, and I wasn't sure if I wanted one or not, which seemed like not enough of a reason to get rid of it. Sometimes, when I was swollen and uncomfortable and other people's brats were running wild in the apartment, I wondered what I'd done, and if those communal nurseries would be ready any time soon.

But I loved him when he arrived. That surprised me. What does nature do to make us want to clean and cuddle a screaming, puking stranger who torments our nipples and ruins our sleep? Somehow, we overlook all that and believe we've created the finest creature ever to walk the earth, some perfect mix of the best parts of ourselves and the men we love, with none of our deep flaws. And then the thought of turning him over to the state to raise seemed like cutting out my own heart. Though if I could have given him to them once in a while, just long enough to take a nap …

It was exhausting, working and coming home to take him off my mother's hands. But Vitya tried to help. He learned to cook, though not well, and he changed diapers, though he always seemed to slip a pin in the baby's flesh. The other men teased him mercilessly for it, so I knew he loved me. He was best at bouncing little Aleksander Viktorovich—Sasha—up and down to quiet the crying. Which was a blessing. The man in the next room only screamed at his wife to shut up their baby.

Not that Vitya was perfect. He had a habit—no, not a habit, that implies control. And I know he wasn't in control of himself in those moments. No one would choose to blank out at the smell of spoiled meat, no matter how distasteful he found it. I took on the duty of monitoring the icebox closely for the whole communal apartment, because I was frightened by the look in his eye, wild and far-off at the same time. It seemed entirely possible he could do anything in that moment and have no idea what had happened in the next.

Occasionally, I'd wake up and find him out of bed, standing at the dresser, apparently stroking a handkerchief. I sneaked a look one day and found a dark, matted curl. I thought of the baby in the photo and put it back without any questions.

I never complained about his quirks, though, because he took care of us. I don't mean the job, though it allowed us to live well enough. Not well, exactly, not by French standards. But well enough. I had to wait in long lines to buy whatever they deigned to sell me at the food stores, but my son was pink and healthy, and my husband never complained.

No, when I say he took care of us, I'm thinking of times like the day he got some of the other men to work together to make a sled for the children from unusable parts at work because no one could find one in the store. Our son, dressed in so many layers that he was as wide as he was tall, would waddle out to the courtyard, and Vitya would pull him around on that little sled, round and round, until they both could barely keep their heads up. And then we'd put Sasha on his little mattress and sing lullabies until he was asleep, then crawl into our bed that wasn't really big enough for two adults. He would give me a quick squeeze, then roll on his left side because I'd told him he snored less when he slept that way.

I wish I could remember more of those years. We were happy, mostly, and when we weren't happy, we were together. But so much of that time seems like a sleep-deprived blur, with lucid moments of watching my husband play-wrestle our son on the floor or my mother telling the French fairy tales I had learned from other girls because there was no time for that nonsense in the Muskvin home. In a way, I was absurdly jealous of my own son.

"Would you really have given me to the state?" I asked one night when we were doing dishes. It was a stifling Moscow August, I was foul tempered from a long day on my feet, and I hated dipping my hands into the hot, soapy water while my dress stuck to my back.

"Why would you ask me that?"

"I want to know the answer."

She stopped. "I don't know. I suppose so."

"Why?"

"It would have prevented you from being spoiled."

"You think I'm spoiled?"

"No more than anyone else."

"That doesn't make sense, Mother."

"Spoiled for life as a social creature. Parents love their children. It's biological, but not social. If a child believes he's the center of his parents' world, he'll never be a true Communist. He'll never love everyone equally. He'll always expect someone to put him first—like you and your peasant do." She shook her head. "Your father was right. The Russians aren't hard enough inside. You've already spoiled at least the next generation. Sometimes, I think the orphans are the only hope we have."

"Says the woman building blanket forts with her grandson."

"I'm too old to fight anymore. That's for all of you." I looked at her and realized that she was. I'd never thought of my mother as particularly old—she still carried herself like some great lady reduced by circumstances to live in an apartment that always smelled like cabbage—but her hands shook a little as she dried the dishes and put them away. I'd been ready to have the argument about how she'd sent me away as easily as a dog she was tired of feeding, but suddenly she seemed too frail for that.

"Was it worth it?" I asked. I left the question open. Was it worth pushing away her only child, uprooting her family to move to a place whose language she never seemed interested in learning, watching her husband die because he couldn't throw away everything he believed fast enough? For me, it was, because I'd fallen in love, though it would have been so much nicer if Vitya had found himself in Paris instead of the other way around. But for her? I knew the answer, but I wanted to hear her say it. One moment of honesty in all this.

She looked me straight in the eye. "Yes," she said. "We're building something that all mankind will thank us for. Our great leaders ..." I stopped listening. And I silently promised myself that, while I might spoil my son, I'd never lie to him. I was finished lying to myself.

1932-1935

Annushka

I suppose I wouldn't exist if the world hadn't fallen apart.

My father's family lived near Odessa, and in 1914, he was taken into the tsar's army, like most of his village. My mother's side lived in Galicia, which is part of the Polish People's Republic now. But then, it was part of Austria-Hungary, and her brothers had to fight for the emperor, even though they understood maybe a half-dozen words in German.

They never talked about the war; I only knew this because eventually I was old enough to ask why my father had one leg he couldn't walk on and uncle Tolya only had one eye. I never noticed any enmity between them about it, but why should there have been? Both were Ukrainian, and neither of them had any choice in which empire had swallowed their villages up.

And those wounds might have saved their lives from everything that came after. Once the civil war started, the Reds and Whites were grabbing any man they could to fill out their ranks. The new Polish state was doing something similar. I could never sort out who had fought whom, or why, from the bits of adult conversation I managed to overhear. Now I wonder if that's because they never knew themselves.

My mother's family left Galicia to get away from the fighting in 1919. I don't know what would have happened to her if they'd stayed, but she wouldn't have met my father. It was either an accident or God's plan that brought her family, exhausted and carrying nothing but some bundled blankets, into my father's village. The better-off peasants needed workers, because so many men had been lost or injured too badly to go into the fields again. So they stayed.

Somehow, they got by, and my parents met. I wish I knew the details. All I remember is my father talking about seeing a wisp of a girl in a green headscarf, and my mother saying she could never see my father as crippled after she saw his dark eyes light up with his laugh. It's hard for a child to know what love is, but I've always believed it was something like that.

I know so little about their lives together. They left my father's village and went north to Kharkiv Province because of a drought and to get away from the grain thieves. The area around the city of Kharkiv always drew people in times of famine. When the harvest disappoints, the forest provides.

I don't know if their first little girl got sick after she came north, or if she was just too far gone by that point. She had a little cross in the churchyard that said "Anna Heorgiyevna Kolisnychenko, 1920-1923." It might still be there. My mother would go and pull any weeds sprouting around it every Sunday. It wasn't until I was much older that I wondered if they had started calling me Annushka by accident. Little Anna, instead of Nastya, as most little Anastasias are called. My father always cursed the Communists for destroying the patch of land his family had farmed for generations, but he never talked about tiny Anna in her grave.

When we would kneel to pray before bed, my mother always had one petition: "May Annushka never know hunger." I was too young to understand that she was answering all of my questions there. But I was sure I'd never go hungry, since my mother had prayed that. I believed it with all my little soul.

The Silence that Remains

I was born in 1924, between wars and disasters. My earliest memories are a blur of running through wheat that towered over me at harvest time, baking with my mother, watching my father turn blocks of wood into anything he wanted, and feeding the goats my aunts kept for cheese and wool.

I told you how the Russians love to talk about their mud. So do we, and I still believe we had the best mud the world can offer. It was as dark as used-up coffee grounds, so good that we barely had to fertilize it when it dried enough to plow. It probably still is. I can't imagine how even the worst farmers could have ruined it since my childhood. I suppose I could get on a train to go back and check. But I know it could never look the same, never be as rich and nurturing as it was when I was too little to understand how lucky we were to have it.

I've wished so many times that I could go back in time and savor all of those things I didn't know were changeable and precious. But I was just too young. I only know those must have been good years because I was surprised when the world went mad around me.

In some ways, it seems like the revolution had passed Kharkiv Province by.

By that point, everyone had accepted Soviet authority, the way they accepted sun or rain. There were a few men who'd tried to fight to create a nation for us Ukrainians, with our brothers and sisters who'd been divided up in Poland or elsewhere. It would have been dangerous if the authorities had ever found out who those men were. But the village had decided, without ever discussing it, that we'd all claim to know nothing about it if any city people came.

Some of our neighbors had joined the Party, but the rest of us looked at it as a harmless quirk, like collecting bottle caps tossed from the windows of passing trains. We went to church on Sunday; they went to meetings at their club. I remember some of the older children caroling, with two paper stars on a stick: a red five-pointed one and one that looked like the Star of Bethlehem. They flipped it as they went from house to house, to whichever side increased the odds of getting sweets. At the time it all seemed perfectly natural.

That all changed when the outsiders came. I was six. They were city people, there to try to convince us to join something called a kolkhoz, a collective farm. There had been city people who'd come a year before, looking for hidden grain. We had turned over everything we had rather than let them arrest my father or one of my uncles. We'd lived on vegetables from the garden and cheese from the goats' milk that winter, supplemented with pine nuts and whatever else we could forage. I was hungry for bread, but I had something to eat, and looking for nuts and mushrooms was still a kind of game. I didn't understand how many different shades of hunger there are yet.

But these outsiders were different. They didn't just want our grain. They wanted us to give up our animals, our tools, our vegetable garden, maybe even our house to this kolkhoz, where the whole village would work as one. My father laughed at them. So did most people. Who were these city people, coming to tell them how to run a farm? But then they stopped laughing.

At first, all I saw was other children walking by carrying clothes or even toys. I didn't understand. I thought the city people were just giving things away, and I wondered when I would get my turn to pick something. Then I saw another girl carrying a doll I knew had belonged to a girl a few years older than me named Raisa, whose family owned the nicest cottage in our village. It was the type with a porcelain face, not a rag doll like the rest of us played with, and I knew it was the same one because it was missing the thumb on its right hand after some rough handling by one of Raisa's brothers. She never would have parted with that doll willingly.

I was supposed to be running some errand for one of my aunts, but I went to Raisa's cottage instead. The people who lived in rundown huts were taking things out and carrying them away. I'd never seen anyone act that way before. Two grown women were even fighting over the curtains. And the city people weren't doing anything to stop them. Raisa and her family were sitting in the grass, watching it all, not saying anything. I could see Raisa's shoulders shaking, and I knew she wanted her doll back. I ran back to our cottage to get one of mine.

My dolls were nothing fancy, just bits of worn-out clothes tied together, but I felt rich to have more than one. It took me a long time to decide which one I could part with. I settled on Tanya, my newest doll, who wore the prettiest dress but had heard the fewest secrets. It still hurt to take her away from her sister dolls, but I knew Raisa would take good care of her.

Most of the villagers had left by the time I got back. The city people were arguing with Raisa's father about something I didn't understand. No one was paying much attention to the children, so I went over and told Raisa to stop crying.

"Doesn't she have a pretty dress?" I said as I handed her my doll, who seemed beautiful in an old red kerchief. Raisa looked at me like she didn't understand what I had said. "Rag dolls are better than city dolls. You don't have to worry about breaking them."

Then one of the city women saw what I was doing and grabbed Tanya out of my hand. "These people are kulaks," she said. "You don't bring presents to your oppressors."

I knew enough Russian to understand that the word meant "fist," but I couldn't make sense of why she was using it. They were fists? Everybody has fists, if they want to use them. But she didn't explain it. She just gave me the doll back and told me to go home.

"What's a kulak?" I asked my mother as she put me to bed.

She didn't say a fist. She sat quietly on my mattress before settling on: "A rich peasant."

"Is that bad?"

"The Communists think it is. And they'll make trouble for anyone who says otherwise."

I was at an age where trouble meant being sent to bed without supper, but I could tell from the sound of her voice that this was grown-up trouble, different from anything I had yet encountered. "Are we rich peasants, Mama?"

She looked around our cottage. We had curtains, but not lace ones. No one in our home wore rags, but no one had shiny shoes either. We had enough food, but we grew or raised almost all of it ourselves. "I hope not, Annushka."

I'll never know what happened to Raisa and her family. A few days later, they were loaded onto wagons, and that was all. I heard the adults say they were going to be taken to Siberia. That seems like it could be true. But what they were expected to do there, how they would live, if they would ever be allowed to return, no one knew.

After they were taken away, my father and uncles decided we would join the kolkhoz. I wasn't allowed to listen while they discussed it, but there are no real secrets in a cottage. I laid very still, with my eyes shut, and listened to them say the city people would come for us next. I tried to ask about it the next morning, but no one would explain what it all meant. "Hush, Annushka. Hush." As if not talking about it would make it go away.

We were allowed to stay in our own house because there were no barracks yet. I remember them coming for the goats. Some of our neighbors killed their cows and horses, rather than let the kolkhoz take them. You won't understand, if you're not a peasant, but that's like burning down your own house. My mother said that was wasteful, that it was better to get a small share of the goats' milk than nothing at all.

For a while, the city people kept letting me do my old chore of milking. They didn't know how to hold the teats, so the mother goats would butt them. It didn't occur to me to wonder why they didn't have one of the grown-ups do it. Now I know it's because children were the only ones who still wanted to be useful.

I didn't really understand what was happening. My uncles had always worked from sunup to sundown during the planting season, but I would see them around the house in the afternoon, having a drink or lying in the shade. Other children's fathers and older brothers did the same. I think they planted enough wheat and potatoes to feed the village, but nothing more.

"Why are we planting for them?" my uncle Tolya asked. "Let them grow their own bread."

The city people made everyone gather for a lecture on laziness, but I don't think it was that. It was like some kind of illness had come over the village and turned people into ghosts of themselves, just drifting along with no interest in anything. I tried to ask, but I didn't yet have the words for the question. "Hush, Annushka. Everything is fine."

The men had misunderstood them. Yes, it was a dry year, which reduced the harvest, but we would have all gotten by if the city people had let us eat what we'd grown. But of course they didn't, or I wouldn't be writing this so strangers like you would know the truth.

It wasn't just that they took everything that the fields produced that year. When that wasn't enough, they went door-to-door, looking for flour. The women would try to beat them off with their brooms, but it never did any good. They took anything edible they could get their greedy hands on.

Lara, my favorite aunt, would gather with some of the other women and talk about it in low voices, then switch to talking loudly about mending socks when anyone came near. I tried to worm my way in, but they always sent me off. "Go do your chores, Annushka."

One morning, I saw her take a sickle, even though it wasn't harvest time. I could hear people yelling, and she came back with a big sack of potatoes slung over her shoulder. We ate some, then she and my mother hid the rest in the forest, with precautions so they wouldn't spoil before winter.

The second time, Aunt Lara brought back a sack of wheat. The third time, she didn't come back at all. After she took the sickle and went out, men on horses thundered down our village's one street. My mother told me to come hide behind the thick iron stove in the middle of the room. She didn't tell me to hush. She kept her hand over my mouth until it was over. For weeks afterward, I asked when my aunt was coming back, but no one could ever answer. I don't know if she was sent to Siberia or shot.

After they'd arrested enough people to silence the rest, they came for the church. I don't know if that was always the plan or a way of punishing us. They took the priest's clothes and threw him out. Then they ordered the men to lower the bell from the tower. It would be melted down to make machines. My mother cried, so I cried, too, but I was secretly certain that God would destroy these Communists, like he drowned Pharaoh's army. I stood back because I didn't want to be swept away by accident when He came for them. But the Communists just took the bell to destroy and went on their way.

Eventually, people stopped trying to fight back. They were too tired. We'd think the Communists had taken everything, then they'd come back and find something else to take. But they never found that bag of potatoes hidden in the woods. I think the shadows from the trees and the birds' calls scared them.

I was never afraid in the woods, though. They weren't just a place to gather nuts and whatever else God might provide. They were a sanctuary, a place where there were no Communists and everything was right. Sometimes they reminded me of the church—branches stretching over me to meet each other, like the beams pointed toward Heaven, and the insects droning like cantors. I was too young to understand what I felt, though, or why it made me think of the church. I just knew I liked it in some vague, confused way.

Those woods saved my life, I know. I've heard whispers that people in the southern provinces only had grass.

My uncles ran away to try to find work in the coal mines in Donbas, even though we were forbidden to leave the kolkhoz. I don't know if they made it. We didn't go because my father couldn't walk so far on a shattered leg. Sometimes I would lie awake, hungry, and hear my parents talking about whether my mother should take me and run. That talk intensified every time the Communists and the poor people they brought with them came and tore our house apart looking for food. We were hungry, but not starving, so they knew we'd hidden something. The last time they came, they threw us out of our home. But it could have been worse. They didn't take our clothes.

We didn't dare sleep in barns. They were all state property. So I showed my mother and father a little clearing I'd found near a stream we could drink from and not too far from the few potatoes we had left. I remember my mother crying as I led her. "Don't worry, Mama, the woods aren't scary," I told her, and she tried to smile for me.

We tried to make the potatoes last, but nothing lasts forever. We planted the eyes in the clearing, but potatoes will only grow in their own time. We collected as many pine nuts as we could, but it wasn't enough. We had to walk further and further to find nuts, acorns, berries, mushrooms, anything.

I'd always been taught that stealing was wrong. But I was so hungry that I didn't question it when we went into the fields at night to cut grain. It was dangerous. It was theft of state property, which I now know would mean years in the camps. But it was that or starvation.

You may judge us. But if you do, you've never been truly hungry. People did things they never would have done before. Stole from their neighbors. Dug up old graves looking for jewelry they could trade for food. My parents never left me alone for a moment, even when they were cutting grain. A woman in our village had gone mad, cut up her youngest child, and eaten his heart and liver. She'd been arrested, of course, but what about the next one? If people could do that to their own children, what would they do to someone else's baby? I was almost nine, and felt much older, but I wouldn't be able to defend myself from an adult with a knife.

We had to work quickly when we took grain. My parents would each cut a few heads of wheat, and I would gather anything that had fallen to the ground. Then we would take it back to the woods, grind it as best we could, mix it with anything else we had to eat, and cook the whole mess over our campfire. It tasted terrible, but it was food. That was all that mattered.

There was a full moon on my last night in the village. We were almost finished collecting grain when one of the men they had guarding the fields found us. His name was Volodymyr Oleksandrovich. He had lived three houses away from us. My father pleaded with him to just let us slip away. But they rewarded the guards with a loaf of bread for every grain thief they found. He blew the whistle.

"Run, Annushka," my mother said. She had told me that if this happened, I was to get to the forest, no matter what. My father grabbed that man and punched him in the head so he couldn't follow us.

I ran, and after a while, no one was behind me. I went back to the little home we had made and waited for my parents. I was still waiting when it was light, and when it got dark again.

On the second day, I went to find my own food. I collected some berries, but they weren't enough, and I'd already eaten all the pine nuts

I could reach. Then I happened on a bird's nest. The parents had left their babies, and they were squawking for food.

I killed them and cooked them over our little campfire and ate them without a second thought.

When it was clear I wouldn't survive in the woods, I hopped in the back of a cart to the city of Kharkiv. It's a fine city, with gold-domed churches and factories of every kind. But that wasn't what I was looking for. The grown-ups had said there was food in the cities. But they were wrong, or if there was, it wasn't enough for all those starving men, women, and children. I saw so many swollen people, sitting and begging because they didn't have the strength to do anything else. Then they'd slump over, on steps or against a wall, and never move again. Some would be walking, pleading, trying to convince someone they could work, and die just like that. On their feet one minute, dead the next. Everyone saw them, no matter how much they denied it later.

I might have died, too, if it hadn't been for a round, pleasant woman named Mrs. Liebowitz. I was begging in front of the building where she lived. So many others had walked by without even a glance at me. But she went upstairs and came down with a little slice of bread. She told me I could come back tomorrow for another slice. I think she hoped enough people would do the same to keep me alive. It was a fine hope.

One day, she asked me to follow her. I was so tired I could barely walk and kept swaying and bumping against her. We stopped at an orphanage.

"I have three children, and I can't feed a fourth," she said. "If I could, I'd take you in. Now do as they tell you and live." She hugged me and walked away. I was too weak to chase after her.

The orphanage did feed me, though it was mostly watery porridge. I had to share a bed with a little girl I didn't know because there weren't enough mattresses to go around. I don't think the orphanage ladies were cruel. There were just too many starving children. I can understand that now, though at the time, I thought they were Satan's sisters.

I remember the first time I saw a child die there. He was so weak he couldn't even feed himself, with a skeleton's arms and a belly so swollen that fluid leaked out through the fragile skin. I was going to feed him a little bit of my porridge, but one of the orphanage ladies stopped me.

"It's kinder just to let him slip away," she said, gently. "His stomach can't take food anymore. There's no hope, child. None at all." And by the next morning, he was gone.

I hated all the Russians for a long time. How could they be so cruel as to sit comfortably in their cities while people starved all around them? Now I wonder how much they didn't know. Surely the men on top knew. But the ordinary people ... Did no one searching for food make it as far as Moscow and Petersburg? Were they cordoned off from all the suffering, like someone had shut the city gates against a plague? Or do they just remember it that way now, to feel better about looking away?

I think that maybe someday I will feel safe enough to ask a certain person, but I won't get an answer. He will want to know why I asked, and once he knows that, he won't be able to admit if it suited him to look away, because I would be within my rights to hate him, like all the others. And I'm beginning to suspect that what he wants most is for me to like him.

I quickly learned the value of allies in an orphanage.

Dima was a thief. I say that without judgment. Vitya was a soldier,

I'm a baker, and Dima is probably still a thief, if he hasn't gotten himself killed. He'd sneak out of the orphanage and steal food from stores or people's bags. My job was to come up with lies if someone wondered where he was. I'd been taught not to lie, but I persuaded myself that lying to these Communist devils didn't really count. I'd also been taught it was wrong to hurt other people, and the grown-ups had made it clear that rule didn't apply to everyone.

Dima would come back with food and give me a small portion. He'd call me his little sister. I wonder, now, if he'd lost a sister and decided to replace her with me. It was rare that anyone noticed he was gone, and he seemed like the sort of boy who could take a whipping and keep doing exactly what he pleased.

But I didn't think about it then. I was just happy to have someone looking out for me. I told him that when my parents came and found me, I would beg them to take him home too.

"Keep dreaming, little sister," he would say, then he'd mess up my hair. "You keep dreaming." I was young enough I didn't read in the obvious meaning and we didn't quarrel. If I'd understood, I would have at least poked him. They were coming back, and that was all.

I learned to start hiding my real thoughts when I was eleven. That was when the orphanage women decided they would no longer tolerate any talk of parents. Parents were gone; parents had never existed; there was no such thing as parents.

The famine had been over for a year. Kharkiv, as far as I could tell from the orphanage window, was trying to pretend nothing had happened. People still toppled over in the streets, but from weakened hearts, and no one dared suggest that months of starvation might have had something to do with it. Those people did not die because they starved; no one ever starved in the Soviet Union; starvation was confined to the deep, dark past, and we must not speak of it. I took quite a few hits on the wrist for trying to say what I had seen. Not that I was very good at saying it, as a child. But good enough that the orphanage women had to stop me.

I suppose they had their orders. Nothing had happened, and no one could believe otherwise. Maybe they thought, because we were children, they could make us forget everything we'd seen. I fought them hard on every point. I don't know how many times they hit me, sent me to bed hungry, or told me how I'd never amount to anything because I wouldn't get into the League of Young Communists and the Party when I was old enough. Sometimes I'd scream back that I didn't want to join their club, and they'd hit me harder.

It was the same at school, until the teacher kept me after class one day. Her name was Comrade Ivanova, and I hated her. Everyone said she was an old Bolshevik, going out with grain thieves during the civil war before she settled into teaching. I don't know if it's true.

"How old are you?" she asked.

"Eleven."

"The age of criminal responsibility is twelve. They just changed it recently." I wasn't sure what that meant. "You could be shot next year if you don't learn how to behave. Do you want to be shot, Anastasia Georgiyevna?" She always pronounced it the Russian way, with a G instead of an H.

I didn't answer. I'd never given any thought to being shot. I assumed I didn't want it, but it also didn't seem like a real possibility.

She undid the top buttons on her shirt and pulled it aside, so I could see a pink circle near her collarbone. "When you are shot, the only thing in your mind is how you'd give anything for more time. How unimportant your reasons were now that you'll never see another day." I looked away. "You're very young. So much life ahead of you. I hope you learn to govern yourself so you can experience it."

That night, I laid in bed wondering what it would feel like to be shot. A part of me wanted to defy them right up until death. But what if my parents came back and I'd already been shot? They'd have to put me in the cold ground next to little Anna.

Maybe Comrade Ivanova thought she'd make me a good Communist, but she didn't. All she taught me was to say yes when I meant no, to smile when I wanted to cry, and to agree to one thing and do the opposite when her back was turned. Sometimes I'd look around and wonder if everyone else was lying, too, or if they had somehow forgotten. But how could they? How could anyone?

A slightly older girl in the orphanage explained it to me. Her name was also Anastasiya, but she went by Nastya. "You'll never win," she said. "So beat them at their own game."

Nastya also believed in God and that her parents would return, and she intended to survive until they did. So she shouted whatever they asked her to shout, then mocked it all to me when we were lying in our beds. I couldn't fake enthusiasm the way she could, though, so I pretended to be stupid. It was less degrading to repeat their rubbish if I acted like I'd believe the Earth was flat. It was the only way I had of clapping back at them, of saying, "I see through all your lies." The orphanage women and Comrade Ivanova knew I wasn't stupid; I think they knew what I was doing. But they had too many tasks on their hands, so anything that wasn't open defiance was acceptable to them.

Sometimes I wonder what happened to Nastya. She left the orphanage a few years before I did, and I never heard from her again. Is she cackling at the stupidity of it all to her husband after a long day of drudgery? Did she fake it well enough to set herself up in a better position? And what happened if she did? That might be how they get you in the end.

1936-1939

Diana

I laughed when the men on top began to fall in '36. Cancer had already taken my mother, and there was no one to make me ashamed before the girl who'd wanted to man the barricades.

The first were Zinoviev and Kamenev, who were accused of conspiring with the exiled Trotsky to murder other members of the Politburo. My father had actually agreed with them on many policy points. But they hadn't intervened when others in the Party had hounded him to death because they were quite comfortable, certain that their triumvirate with Stalin was unshakeable. I didn't believe they were foreign spies or saboteurs or any of that nonsense. But I didn't care. They were all guilty of something, so why shouldn't they eat each other alive?

I never expected ordinary people in the factory where my husband worked would also have to pay the next year.

After we had finally gotten Sasha to sleep, on one of those endless June nights they have in Russia, Vitya told me how they'd all been called in during the middle of the workday.

"Higher quotas?" I asked.

"That's what I thought. But they told us Marshal Tukhachevsky had confessed to spying for the fascists. You remember him?"

"One of the heroes of the revolution. A good comrade."

"Depends on your definition of good. He used poison gas on rebelling peasants. But not a traitor."

"Did you say anything?"

"No."

"That's wise." I paused. "But what's that got to do with making metal bits?"

"I don't know."

The marshal was put on trial with a few others who'd supposedly plotted to turn the army over to the fascists. I might have followed the coverage, false and inflammatory as it was, if the manager of the shop where I worked hadn't been missing the next day.

I suppose he wasn't missing; someone knew where he was. We just weren't told. There was a new manager who told us the old boss had been arrested for selling poisoned perfume. Which was ridiculous. We all knew it. I think even the new manager knew it.

I didn't say a word, though. I was ready to keep my head down and do my work. Why couldn't the new manager have just accepted that? But we had to denounce the old manager. It was like a strange play, all made up of people shouting curses at someone offstage. But I shouted them, too, like all the others—no, louder. With my accent and my heritage, I couldn't afford to seem less than totally aflame with righteous rage. When the world loses its mind, you have to act crazy just to survive.

I hoped Sasha would be oblivious to it all, but children never are. When I got home after a long time in line to buy cheese, I overheard him talking to Vitya about it. A game of Reds and Whites had gotten out of hand again. Vitya generally left homework duty to me, unless he'd had to drag our son out of a pile that was beating whichever boy was out of favor.

"Papa?"

"Yes?"

"They found more enemies today."

"Yes, I heard. But you're stalling."

"No, I'm not."

"Well, math doesn't have any enemies."

That must have kept his head down for all of two minutes. "Papa?"

"Yes, my son."

"Did you see him? In the Revolution?"

"Who?"

"The enemy general."

"Only once or twice. He never spoke to me."

"Could you tell he was bad?"

I think Sasha was too young to understand why his father took so long to answer. Anyone who'd held a command in that war was bad, he'd told me, and I wasn't sure he exempted himself from that judgment. "You can't always tell if a man is bad, Sasha. Certainly not by looking at him. Some bad people pretend to be good. Sometimes people think a man's bad, but he's really good inside."

"The teacher says he's bad."

"I hope she's right. Now, math."

A few days later, a man in a uniform came to visit me at work. We sat in the back, where the merchandise waits to go on shelves and racks. All I could think of was that I'd seemed insufficiently enthusiastic in denouncing the manager.

But he wanted to talk about one of my customers. Somewhere in the early '30s, the Nepmen's wives had disappeared from our store, if not from the face of the earth. Now, we served Party wives. The days of women comrades wearing boxy dresses to show their Bolshevik austerity were over.

The one he wanted to talk about was a vain, snobby woman who drowned her existential conflicts in shoes, but that was no reason to arrest her. I didn't tell him that, though. I answered as best I could.

No, she never told political jokes. Yes, I had my suspicions about where her husband got the money for all those high heels. Yes, I suppose it was possible she was in on the poisoned perfume ring, though I'd never seen her tamper with a bottle. I didn't like it, but I also knew that refusing to go along with his line of questioning wouldn't save her. And even if it would have, I would have sacrificed a thousand of her kind to protect myself and my family.

Still, I couldn't sleep after I got Sasha to bed. Vitya hadn't come home. That wasn't unusual for some of the men, but he almost never went out drinking with them. I opened a pack of those awful Soviet cigarettes and started smoking them, one after the other, as I imagined increasingly terrible fates for him.

I was less than gracious when he walked through the door. "Where the hell were you?"

He looked taken aback. "Working. Is there any supper?"

"That's all you have to say?"

"I told you this morning. Comrade Smirnov—"

"Yes," I said, remembering the bargain he said he'd made with one of the better-connected workers. "Yes, that's right."

"Don't you want to know what he had?" I didn't care at all about what questionable goods Smirnov had gotten hold of. "It's for your birthday."

"That was two months ago."

"I know, but all Comrade Smirnov's connection had that week were skillets." He handed me a brown paper package. "Bonne birthday."

He made himself a sandwich while I tried on the stockings he'd traded for. One had a little hole, but it wouldn't be visible with shoes on. I would have been pleased any other day.

"Did you hear about Kaminsky's accident?" he asked between big bites of bread and cheese.

"What happened?"

"He slipped and cut himself."

"You weren't anywhere nearby, were you?" I asked.

"I was a few machines down." He looked like he didn't understand why I might care.

"So no one can say you did anything wrong."

"I was the one who shut the machine off."

"Good." I paused and felt vaguely ashamed of my complete lack of concern. "Did he—"

"Just some stitches and a scare."

"That's good."

He looked at me. "What's bothering you?"

I didn't want to explain what was really bothering me in the kitchen of an apartment where everyone could hear everything. But I didn't have to come up with an answer, because Comrade Lebedev started yelling. "You fucking bitch!"

Let me be very clear: Mrs. Lebedev never did anything that any reasonable person would consider wrong. No lovers, no shoe habit, not even a cross word at the end of the day. Maybe she felt cross, but she never would have dared to show it. He'd always had a temper, especially when he was drunk, but it took less and less to set him off. I tried to help in any way I could, whether it was making a little extra if she hadn't gotten home in time to start dinner or watching their daughter so she could correct whatever tiny thing he might find fault with that day.

Once I suggested she leave him, but she just looked at me like I'd told her she should fly to the moon. "He'd make sure they found me," she said. I didn't have to ask who "they" were. Lebedev bragged constantly about his status as an informant. He must have been terrible at it because no one would speak freely in front of him, but perhaps he just made things up to please them.

Vitya got up. I grabbed his forearm. "You can't fix it," I said. But I wasn't sure he heard me. He started toward the door leading to the bedrooms. I wrapped my arms around him. I wasn't strong enough to hold him in place, but it did seem to surprise him enough to bring him back. It helped that Lebedev had made his unreasonable point and quieted down.

"What were we talking about?" he asked.

"Kaminsky's accident," I said and let him tell me the whole thing over again. I hoped he would never be home alone when Lebedev was getting started. I didn't want to think about what might happen if he hit one of their informants.

It all happened so stupidly. One little accident, like a thousand others that everyone had been willing to shrug off. I suppose in a workers' paradise, it was awkward to explain why men kept losing fingers, so someone decided every accident had to become sabotage. But they wouldn't stop with one scapegoat. Someone had to pay. Then everyone connected to that person, and everyone connected to them. I imagined that hateful drunk sitting alone in the building by the end of it all.

They started with Polzin, the factory's chief engineer. Vitya whispered the story to me as we laid in bed. The commissar had called everyone in to discuss Kaminsky's injury.

"I thought he was going to tell us to be more careful. But he stood up there and asked who could be responsible for sabotaging Kaminsky's machine. We all knew he'd been working too fast and slipped. But the commissar insisted someone did it. And Lebedev named Polzin because he was in charge of maintaining the machines. Then another guy said he saw him fiddling with it before Kaminsky got hurt."

"Was he fiddling with it?"

"No. I'm sure he wasn't." He paused. "But I didn't say it. All those other people were in the room too. They would have known it wasn't true. And I thought, could I have missed something? But I know he didn't do that."

We'll all march into the furnace if everyone else does. "You couldn't have done anything," I said.

"No. I voted against expelling him. A few other people did too. They didn't believe all that trash about helping the fascists. Just because he went to school in Germany. Where else do you learn engineering? But enough people voted yes for it to pass."

The next day, they expelled two other engineers who worked with Polzin. Then his secretary and a manager he was friendly with.

"I held out for the first three," he told me, sounding ashamed he hadn't voted against all four. "But when they got to the manager, I was the only one voting no. And I knew someone would say I was part of it. So I voted yes."

Maybe that was why he lost the ability to lie there and do nothing.

I'd stuffed cotton in my ears because that was the only way I got any sleep in that place jammed with people and their noises. So I didn't hear Lebedev screaming at his wife when he came home drunker than usual. If I had, I might have stopped Vitya. But he was already through the door by the time I woke from the mattress shifting under us.

He knocked Lebedev flat. I was afraid he'd killed him when I saw the blood on his hand, but it all came from that contemptible man's nose. Mrs. Lebedev looked like she wasn't sure if she was afraid or relieved. I led her to an old neighbor woman's room in case her husband came to in an even worse mood.

I found Vitya in the water closet, face in his bloody hands. I got a towel and cleaned him up. There was no point in telling him he'd condemned us. He knew that already. So I just put my arms around him and laid my head between his shoulder blades.

"If you want a divorce ..." he said. But I just held him tighter.

You'd think the thing he'd actually done might come up at his expulsion. Some mention of assaulting a government agent. But it was all sabotage and fascists. And they somehow managed to turn it against him that he was the only one who kept his head enough to shut off Kaminsky's machine before someone else got hurt.

Maybe it didn't matter that he'd hit that man. I wish he hadn't. But I was also proud that he'd done it. That poor woman didn't deserve what her husband gave her, and no one else had the courage to even look askance at the miserable informant. If he had to be arrested, at least he'd done something of a little value.

I went to work the next day, as usual, and he said he'd go looking for another job. We both knew it was hopeless, but being Vitya, he had to try.

When I came back from work, I found him lying on our bed, holding his head. The old injury rarely bothered him anymore, but strong emotions could still trigger enough pain to bring him down. I could imagine his thoughts. Without his job at the plant, we had no right to stay in the apartment. My job would keep us fed, but not much else, and we'd lose even that if I stood by him. He was probably hoping this headache meant a blood vessel in his brain had finally burst.

I lay down beside him and took his hand.

"I'm sorry," he said.

"You should rest," I said.

I told Sasha we were going to have supper picnic-style in the room because Papa wasn't feeling well. I didn't want to face the neighbors' eyes. Our son was prattling about a game of Reds and Whites, so the boys hadn't started to torment him yet.

I don't think either of us had gotten any sleep when we heard the knock. Not our door, but not far away. "Polzin!" Then there was shuffling, like the sound of people rearranging their furniture, and glass breaking. Then footsteps. Then silence.

I did the only thing I could do. I made the most of those last days. I noticed my husband in a way I hadn't in years. I held him and memorized the color of his deep brown eyes with little gold flecks, the scratch of his stubble, the scent of his hair. We made love in the courtyard, and I remembered a little bit of what it had felt like to be that young ballerina the first time she let herself fall. They might kill him, but they couldn't take those memories from me unless they killed me too. We all have our ways of bearing things that no one should have to.

Vitya kept trying to find another job, even though we both knew no one would hire a man dismissed for sabotage and counterrevolutionary activity. But no one moved to evict us. That was how we knew it wouldn't be long before the arrest.

I've wondered ever since if I should have told Sasha the truth about what was happening. He came home in tears and hid under the bed. Vitya waved me off. I didn't know what to say anyway, and I couldn't deny him a moment with his son.

"Are you an enemy?" Sasha asked between sniffles.

"No."

"They said—"

"It's a mistake." I suppose there was no other way to put it, not to a child.

On that last night, we had our dinner and told our son a story. Not long before, he'd decided he was too old for Baba Yaga and Aesop. I'm grateful he changed his mind that once. Once he was asleep, we stole away to the courtyard for a few minutes alone in the dark. When we came back, we both lay awake, holding each other, trying to savor each moment and not to think about why we were savoring them.

When they came, they made us all sit on the bed while they searched. Sasha was crying and I was shushing him. We had nothing of interest. I'd taken Vitya's old notebooks and hidden them among some ledgers no one checked at work. I couldn't imagine there was anything in them that a reasonable person would find incriminating, but these were not reasonable men. And if they killed him, I wanted to hold on to every little piece that I could.

When they didn't find anything, they told Vitya to pack a bag. I whispered hints, though I had no idea where they might take him.

"You'll need socks." "Take a coat, just in case." I should have thought to tell him to take a picture of us, but I didn't until they'd walked him out. He wasn't even allowed to kiss us goodbye or to stop for a last look. Maybe that's for the best. None of us would want to remember that night.

All I could do was grab a few clothes before they threw us out and sealed the apartment. Evidence. What a joke that was.

I didn't know who to turn to—there was no one—so Sasha and I rode the streetcars for the next four hours, until it was time for work and school. He laid his head in my lap and cried until he fell asleep. I stroked his dark hair and tried to work out how we'd survive until the next day. I felt absurdly safe on the streetcar, as if the Organs—as the Russians call their secret police—couldn't catch us.

But we had to get off. I dried my son's tears as best I could and said I didn't know when his father would be back, but Papa would want him to do his best at school that day. Then I went to work. I fully expected to be arrested there, but I fully expected to be arrested wherever I went.

Nothing happened for the first week, though. I found us a pest-filled hostel because we couldn't afford anything better. I made my son go to school and myself go to work, and I put on the expected faces for every occasion when I wanted nothing more than to curl up in a corner and never move again.

On the eighth day, the new manager was waiting for me with a man I didn't recognize. He loaded me into one of their Black Marias and drove me to the Lubyanka, the central Moscow prison. I thought I should have left instructions for my son about what to do when I disappeared. But he'd be in an orphanage by nightfall, regardless of what I said.

The officer led me down halls and stairwells, like a rat in a maze. I heard thumping and screams behind some of the doors. A man in a butcher's apron covered in blood and a pearly white goo passed by, and I couldn't help staring until I worked out that it was brain tissue. The officer told me to keep my eyes on the floor, and I didn't want to raise them after that anyway.

We sat across a table from each other and stared for a moment. Then he leaned back in his chair and lit a cigarette. "Your husband was arrested last week for counterrevolutionary terroristic activity."

"Yes, he was."

"Did you know anything about it?"

"No."

"Your father was a Trotskyite."

"Yes. But he killed himself after the Party pointed out his errors."

"Were you a Trotskyite?"

"No." I'd initially thought Trotsky made the better arguments, but I'd never done anything more than try to explain them to Vitya, who had been perfectly indifferent to all of it. "I was a ballerina."

"Is your husband a Trotskyite?"

"No."

"Did he ever talk about wanting to sabotage the factories?"

"No."

"About killing Party members?"

"No."

"About killing workers?"

"No."

"About hating Soviet power?"

"No."

"About Trotsky?"

"No."

"What were his views?"

"He never talked about any."

"Not even with his wife?"

"I assumed he didn't have any."

"That didn't seem suspicious?"

"He came from peasant stock."

"A clever lady like you thought he was too stupid to have any ideas?"

"I'm not as clever as I thought." And it was true. I was sitting there answering questions with one word, like the stupidest of children, because I knew any wrong word could mean prison or worse.

"So that son of a bitch was attacking Soviet power right under your nose, and you didn't know?"

"I knew nothing about any plots."

"Of course you didn't." He smiled like he wanted to bite. "So, you'll help us, won't you? To make up for your mistake?"

"Yes." I could see where this was going. If I said and did what they wanted, I had a chance of going home to my son. "How?"

He handed me a stack of paper and a pen. "First, write a statement for the prosecution. One about your father. And one about your husband."

"My father's dead."

"But he recruited your husband. And how many others?" Then he handed me a form. It was a divorce declaration. "You'll want this. Then we'll talk about how else you can help us."

I stared at the blank pages for I don't know how long. I wrote, "My husband, Viktor Aleksandrovich Chekhov," then stopped. The worst thing I could think of to say was that his snoring had gotten louder as his belly expanded. I stared at the paper some more, trying to will myself to denounce my husband to save our son. I couldn't. So I crumpled up that paper, picked up another one, wrote "This mongrel" and poured out my hate for the informant, the men on top, the officer making me give this statement. I signed the divorce declaration without reading it—the grounds were false, so what did it matter what they filled in? My husband would never read any of this, if he was even alive. They didn't need my evidence to kill him or enslave him. It ultimately made no difference.

Bullshit.

We all have a moment. Sometimes many. The moment when we could have told the truth and died for it. When we could have stood by the ones we love and suffered the consequences. But we didn't. Oh, we all have our reasons. Good reasons, or just that we want to save our own skin. And how can purely material beings do otherwise?

That day I became an informant. The agent who had interrogated me would come by at the end of the week and ask what the Party wives who shopped at the store had told me. The first time I performed badly. All I said was that none of it was a crime.

"We prove the crime," he said. "You tell us who isn't reliable."

"Most of them are idiots. Their only interest is in dressing better than the others." They also wanted to be noticed by the men on top. It was ridiculous, like mice backstabbing each other to get closer to the cat. I almost pitied them, how little they understood about the trap they lived in.

"That doesn't mean they're reliable." He leaned in so our faces were only inches apart. "Anyone who can't be relied on to take a bullet for Comrade Stalin is someone who can't be around when the war comes. And we all know it will come. If you want to live under the fascists' heels, maybe I made a mistake in offering you a chance to prove yourself. Understand?"

"Perfectly."

I didn't disappoint him again. I told him all their empty-headed gossip about who was sleeping with whom, who they had lunch with, who they made jokes about, whether the jokes were cruel or naughty or gentle. But some days I could scarcely eat because I was so disgusted with myself. How do you listen to flies wrapping themselves up while you alert the spider? You tell yourself they'd do the same to you, or worse, and it's true. They hadn't troubled themselves over men like my husband or my father. This was revenge on the men that would go down with them. And if it got us a place to live that wasn't a flophouse crawling with prostitutes, well, so much the better.

Yes, I denounced and divorced my husband so our son wouldn't be sent to an orphanage where they'd turn him into a criminal or cannon fodder. I informed on silly, little women for the same reason. But I can never say I didn't have a choice. Neither can you.

I didn't completely betray my husband, though. Once a week, after work, I'd go line up with the other wives and mothers outside the Lubyanka. They kept accepting the letters and packages, which meant he was alive, at least in their records. I'd put in a jar of jam, which probably had some vitamins in it, and a few packs of cigarettes, as well as a letter telling him Sasha and I were alive and well. Another woman in line had suggested the cigarettes. Men who didn't smoke or could break the habit were able to trade them for food, she said. I hoped my husband's habit wasn't too strong to break.

I assumed my handler knew what I was doing. I'd become as bad as the Russians, believing they were everywhere and saw everything at all times. But if he knew, he didn't care. What was it to him if I counted my kopecks so I'd have something to send?

It was two months before I got a letter. It was addressed from a labor camp in Kolyma, which I had never heard of. The woman behind me in line gave me a look of pity when she saw it. "Put some warm things in the next package," was all she said. "And as many calories as you can."

There was no mention of my previous packages, but given the speed of mail across Siberia, they probably wouldn't have arrived before he wrote it.

My chere, it said:

> *Forgive me for bringing this on us. I don't know what they did to you when they brought you in. I don't know if you're alive to read this. If you are, do whatever you have to do*

to go free. You and Sasha are the only things in this world that matter.

If you are alive and free, don't worry about sending me anything. I will manage.

All of my love,
Vitya

I didn't initially understand what he meant about when they'd brought me in. And then it dawned on me, and I had to laugh, even though nothing could have been less funny. I would have given them what they wanted if we'd had that little chat in the back storage room. The trip to the Lubyanka cellar wasn't to soften me up. It was to break someone who could endure plenty of his own pain but couldn't abide the thought of me being hurt.

I was so angry I almost tore the letter up, but then I thought better, folded it neatly, and placed it in the pocket on the bosom of my dress. It was one of the last things I had of my husband's, other than that handkerchief with the curl, which I'd managed to slip in with some clothes before they sealed the apartment. I would guard it like treasure.

I had to go to a library to look up Kolyma. I'd always liked libraries, but I almost never went to them after settling in Moscow. It was humiliating, having to ask for a book like a child and being told whether they would let you have it or not. This time, I didn't say why I wanted a geography book, and the librarian must have thought it too mundane to be worth asking about.

Kolyma is about as far east as you can go without falling into the Pacific Ocean. Apparently, it has vast deposits of gold and platinum under the permafrost. Winter temperatures range from deeply unpleasant to unsurvivable. I made a note to find a thick pair of gloves and put them in the next shipment.

Awful as it was, I was grateful to have an answer when Sasha asked where his father was, a spot I could point to on the map, even if there was no possible way for us to get there. I also had an answer about when he theoretically might return—he'd been sentenced to ten years. But how can a child whose life has been less than ten years even begin to comprehend that? And I knew it was entirely possible he wouldn't survive. Not that I had any sense of what specific danger he might be in; I just knew the sort of people who work with the Organs and suspected they didn't take great care with their slaves.

His first letters contained increasingly desperate warnings about what I might face if I were arrested, as if he thought I might be foolhardy enough to challenge them. I felt a pang when I realized he might have thought my love was more all-consuming than it was, as if I'd failed him, which was nonsense. Getting myself arrested would mean effectively orphaning his only surviving child, not to mention leaving him with no source of packages. Still, some women would have done it, and maybe it should have been harder to do the rational thing.

My dear Diya,

I don't know if you are receiving these letters. There are so many ways they could get lost since I can't send them through the camp censor. But I must try to tell you.

The Lubyanka prison is bursting. There must have been twenty other men in my cell and only one bucket that the guards emptied when they felt like it. Each new man would start next to the bucket, then move further away the longer he was there. Five men came in after me in the three nights before they took me to question.

They wanted me to sign something saying I was part of a fascist plot with Polzin and the others. You understand why I said no, don't you? I never meant to hurt you. I thought they'd only hurt me.

First, they put me in a little space, like a cabinet. I had to put my head on my knees because it was too low. No room to move my arms and legs. I don't know how long I was there. I couldn't walk at first when they let me out. Then I could walk, but it felt like knives in my knees and my back.

Then they just made me watch the guards eat and drink. I was hungry and thirsty, but I wouldn't give in. Then they made me stand absolutely still for hours, so no sleep. I don't know how long that went. I couldn't see very well, or think. I didn't even feel it when they put out a cigarette in my palm. But I only needed to remember "no." They would kill me, but I wouldn't sign.

And then they brought you in. I signed as fast as I could. I didn't even read it. I pray it wasn't too late to save you. They wouldn't promise me not to hurt you. They just took the paper and threw me back in the cell.

There was no more space on the paper for even an "I love you." The next letter was much the same.

My dear Diya,

If you can't write, I understand. But this will be the last letter I send until I hear that it's safe. I could be compromising you right now.

I tried everything to find out if they set you free. But they lost interest in me once they had my confession. They didn't speak to me again until they were loading us up. First onto trucks, then a train. I thought it was a livestock car before, from the way it smelled. But maybe not. Dozens of men packed in for weeks smell about the same. Particularly when the criminals decided it would be fun to piss on us from the top bunks.

They didn't care whether we lived or died. All we had to eat was salted herring, and they made us drink from the same cup. I don't think anyone had syphilis, but how can you tell?

I tried to do the only good thing I could, helping the oldest prisoner. All I could do was talk to pass the time. About you and Sasha. He said to forget. That part of life was over. I thought it was just him seeing his own end was near. He died less than two weeks in, and they just threw him in a ditch beside the tracks. Not even a little dirt on top. And someone complained we shouldn't have told the guards, so we'd get an extra portion of herring.

Now, I think he might be right. I've warned you now. Anything I do after that is putting you at risk, for what? If you are reading this, know I love you always. That's why you won't hear from me again.

Yours,
Vitya

I sent him another letter promising we were well, in case the first one didn't get through. I debated with myself for hours about whether to admit that I'd agreed to divorce him. It would hurt him, but it might also let him sleep more easily.

"It's only a pseudo-divorce," I wrote. "We're waiting for you. Come back. Whatever you have to do, do it. Just come back."

I was never sure, day to day, how much danger I might still be facing. The little people tended to suffer when their patrons fell. My best hope was that I was too insignificant to be worth wasting a bullet.

My handler, who once told me to call him Vasya when he was drunk, had aligned himself with Yezhov, the new head of the Organs. He was also drunk when he told me what happened to the old head, Yagoda. From now on, if I mention that my handler said something that might have been true, assume he was drunk. They were all hopelessly dependent on the bottle to wash away any thoughts about how they were killers and probably soon would be killed.

Yagoda had been arrested for trying to poison Yezhov and diamond smuggling. The diamond smuggling might be true—I have no way of knowing. Maybe it made my handler feel important, trying to dazzle me with how much he knew. He said when one of his friends searched Yagoda's apartment, they found more than one thousand pornographic pictures. I suspect he exaggerated, but who knows? I pretended to be shocked, though, since that seemed to be what he wanted.

"You know what he said when they interrogated him?"

Ridiculous question—how on earth would I know? "No, what did he say?"

"That there must be a God, because he deserved punishment from God and honor from Stalin." Then he laughed, as if it was the best joke he'd heard in years. I faked a little giggle because I didn't dare let him think I found the whole thing disgusting.

That's how I knew about the plans for the last trial months before the defendants did. It was to be Yagoda; Rykov, who'd been premier until 1930 and commissar of communications after; and Bukharin, an Old Bolshevik who'd helped write the Soviet constitution. My father had hated Rykov and Bukharin—"rightists," he'd called them. But of course, none of what they might have believed came up in the trial. It would have been awkward to admit they were being killed for that. So it was all assassination plots (with a remarkably low success rate), spy games, and sabotaging railroads.

My handler had asked me about Bukharin's wife. Anna Larina was a child who was the mother of a one-year-old. She and her husband both had already been arrested, and I had nothing to offer about either, other than her love of Western dresses.

"Come up with something," Vasya said. "We need something good for the trial."

"I never served her," I lied. He looked displeased. "You want me to invent something?"

"She won't be on trial, but we'll need something."

I made up some absolute nonsense about how she'd been promised all sorts of fine things when her husband restored capitalism. This was repeated, with a few changes, twenty times over, so they had one more bit of rubbish testimony against every woman who'd loved the wrong man.

I suppose, theoretically, I could have refused. But they shot people for far less than that. In some cases, the regional Organs shot them for nothing at all, just to fulfill a quota handed down from the center. A quota, like they were making machine parts. I wondered if any of the factory wives or ballerinas I had known were killed or sent to Siberia, but I couldn't risk asking. If someone had been, I'd be condemning myself with even that little bit of curiosity.

It was especially bad for foreigners, most of all Germans and Poles—even the ones who were born behind Soviet borders. I thought that might finally destroy me, the fact that I was born in Paris. But I escaped, and I have no idea why. Someone might have protected me or forgotten to put me on a list. I might be breathing and writing this just because someone was careless.

I don't feel responsible for what happened to the women I lied about. Unlike some people, I never denounced anyone who wasn't already doomed. But I do wish to say now that it was all lies. I've heard that Anna Larina has been campaigning to clear her husband's name ever since she came back from the camps. Whether he was guilty of anything, I don't know, but neither of them did any of what Vasya got me to say they did.

My dear Diya,
You can't know how much joy your letter has brought

me. I'm sorry if I worried you. Really, I'm doing fine. I spent five days in the transit camp before they sent me inland. I thought about you and Sasha the entire time. When they lined us up for transport, men in one line and women in the other, I thought I saw you. Thank God I didn't.

I'm in a gold mining camp now. I got lucky. The doctor agreed to take me on as a feldsher. Maybe they didn't have those in France. It's kind of an assistant. I guess he thinks I can learn. Mostly, I just watch them at night so he can sleep. Maybe give them a little codeine if the coughing keeps the other patients awake. It's not too bad. Don't worry about sending me any food if it would stretch you. I get by on my feldsher's ration.

Give Sasha my love. Tell him to be strong.

Yours,
Vitya

I did tell my son that his father loved him and to be strong for him. For him, being strong meant getting into fights with boys who called his father a traitor. So I got a dressing-down in front of the other parents at the fall class meeting.

I wasn't the only one to be singled out. Everyone's child did something wrong: wiggling too much, pinching the girls, gossiping during class, carrying a pocketknife to school. Still, I could feel all their eyes on me when that smug bitch harangued me.

I looked her straight in the eyes, to watch her squirm for just a moment. "You can't tell children not to love their parents."

"You can and you must," she said. "Your son must accept that his father is a traitor, or he'll grow up to make the same mistakes. Only an unfit mother would let that happen."

I wanted to wrap the cords on the blinds around her neck and pull until she turned purple and died. Obviously, I couldn't do that. I told

Sasha he would have to stop getting in fights when the other boys said his father was a traitor. "There are other ways to be strong than fighting," I said. "Papa would want you to do well in school."

I wonder if that was when it all started to go wrong. But really, what else could I do? He couldn't give a black eye to every hateful human being in the country. No matter how much I understood why he'd want to.

My dear Diya,

I am well and safe. You and Sasha are in my thoughts always. I think Dr. Bogomolov is getting sick of hearing about how wonderful you both are. Maybe because he's unmarried. He says he has a girl in Magadan, but I don't think so. I was a young man once. I know anyone who has a girl would shave before going to town.

Magadan is the regional capital, if you don't know. The guards get to go on leave there a few times a year. I don't know if they ever go back to the mainland. That's what we call it here, the mainland. Siberia might as well be an ocean. Any news we get here is months old.

It's summer now. Don't know what season it will be when you get this. I think I'm writing at midnight, but the sun hasn't set for a week, so who knows? Army life gets you used to sleeping and working when you have to, no matter what the sun says you should be doing. I don't think Bogomolov is used to it, though. He's out of sorts.

Don't worry about sending me anything, unless you happen to find some powder for killing lice. If not, we'll be fine. You can always boil laundry.

All of my love,
Vitya

I should have been more worried than I was. I should have known he was downplaying it all so I wouldn't worry. I'd seen those posters, with Lenin's quote that either socialism would defeat the louse, or the louse would defeat socialism. But I'd never seen firsthand what they could do when people were jammed together and couldn't bathe. I did send some powder, but knowing what I know now, that they were battling typhus, I wish I'd sent more. Not that it would have helped much. The epidemic must have burned itself out before my package arrived, maybe even before I got his letter.

Yezhoz lasted about two years.

He didn't fall all at once. I knew it was starting when Vasya asked me about Mrs. Yezhova's lovers. Everyone knew the woman had made it her mission in life to fuck every writer in Moscow. Not that I blamed her for that, after my Italian artist. I don't know if they would have cared if her husband hadn't disappointed Stalin. But he did, and her lovers were going to pay. I never understood it. How did it hurt him, punishing the men she'd run around with?

Vasya wanted to know if she'd ever mentioned sharing any of them with her husband.

"No, but maybe she wouldn't know who he sleeps with," I said. "Or doesn't care." He noted that carefully. Interesting. Usually a 'no' was met with an order to turn it into a 'yes.'

Sex between men had become a crime again a few years before, but I doubted that was the sort of thing that would make it onto the list of things they ultimately charged him with. The men in the Organs, or whoever they were trying to please, had that strange mix of puritanism and prurient interest that tends to show up in priests and others who want to believe they're better than they are. It was probably the men on top—Vasya seemed under no illusions about who and what he was.

I don't know why they drew it out the way they did. It was clear Yezhov was doomed in 1938, but they kept slowly shifting responsibilities away and gradually increasing the viciousness of their criticisms, for two years. Maybe they wanted him to drink himself to death for them; as I understand it, he came close. Not that I had any sympathy for him after what he and his henchmen had done to my Vitya. But if they'd done it at once, just killed him instead of first getting rid of everyone who'd slept with him or his wife, Mrs. Yezhova might not have committed suicide, and their daughter might not have grown up in an orphanage. I don't know what good destroying a silly woman and a child did them. But they must have thought it did some good because they kept repeating that grotesque pattern, over and over and over.

My dear Diya,

Tell me: are we at war with Poland? I haven't seen any news in months. But we've had shipment after shipment of new men, and most of them are Poles and Lithuanians. Not Russians with Polish names, people who can't speak Russian. Or maybe they can and don't want to. They look like they want to stick daggers in every one of us. Well, they haven't seen the best of our country.

Dalstroi has another new head. Dalstroi's the company that runs the mines and everything out here. I can't remember if I told you. Grisha (that's Dr. Bogomolov) was worried. New heads tend to clean house. But it doesn't seem to have made any difference so far. I can't for the life of me understand why the boss would care who's stitching up wounds in a little camp like this.

No new disease with the latest batch of arrivals. Maybe because it's winter. Summer is always worst for disease here. It's bad for them, though. No time to get acclimated. Poland could get cold when I fought there, but not like this. They only let the men stay inside when it's below -75C. I'm a lucky man, working in a warm hospital.

The Silence that Remains

Send a picture of you and Sasha, if you can. Otherwise I don't need anything else.

Yours,
Vitya

I wasn't entirely sure if we were at war with Poland. Hitler and his men had invaded from the west, and we had invaded from the east, but we didn't seem to be at war with the Germans. The official line was that we were defending the Poles and the Baltic countries from the Nazi menace. I wasn't sure I believed it—why wasn't there at least a bit of fighting along the dividing line?—but they told us so little that I wasn't sure what the truth could be. Maybe there was fighting, and they just didn't want to explain why Russian boys were dying there. Who knew?

I don't excuse the Germans for anything they did. Their whole country could have been bombed to bits, and I wouldn't care. But I blame the Russian government too. For telling so many lies that people couldn't see what was in front of their face in time to save themselves.

1940-1944

Annushka

I saw the newspaper reports about great men confessing their crimes, but I never quite knew what to think of it. I knew that the Communists were my enemies. So their enemies should have been my friends, but the problem was that the accused and the accusers were all Communists, and I had no idea which group had destroyed my family. It may have been both. But I didn't know whether I was supposed to weep or rejoice, so the news they'd been executed was rather anticlimactic. Since none of us had families, we hadn't lost anyone, and I didn't fully understand that other people had. A few new children arrived in those years, but they'd never speak about their parents or about whatever life they'd known before.

I graduated from the orphanage when I was sixteen, like everyone else. Only the best completed the last two years of school to prepare for university. And I had no interest in being one of the best.

I went to the prison to ask about my parents on my first day of freedom, before I even had a job or a place to sleep. I got in line by 9 a.m. and didn't get to the window until mid-afternoon. Thank Heaven they had the records. The woman there said they'd both been sentenced to ten years without right of correspondence. Ten years, without even the right to send a letter, for a little grain when we were starving.

Sometimes I've thought about what I could have done, if I'd decided to break faith with my parents. All the teachers said I had potential.

Maybe I could have been someone in the Writer's Union, earning prize money instead of scribbling on scraps. Maybe I would have done that if they hadn't assigned us to write about the successes of the kolkhozes. I wrote about the woman who ate her child's liver. The teacher didn't say anything, just wrote a failing grade and the word "LIES" across the top. She was Ukrainian too. She knew I wasn't lying. But no one mentioned my potential after that.

Dima helped me through those first days, until I found a job. He was making good money forging documents, but he never seemed to have more than a few rubles in his pocket. There are three possible jobs for a boy after the orphanage: factory worker, soldier, and criminal, and it was always clear which Dima would choose. I knew enough to know that I didn't really want to know more about his life or where the money went. And I think he liked the idea that he was somehow protecting his little sister's innocence, as if I hadn't seen with my own eyes what people could do to each other.

I couldn't stay with him, and the only thing I knew how to do was bake, so I got a job in a bread factory, which had barracks for the girls without husbands or parents. It was nothing like baking with my mother. The goal was to make the bread as quickly as possible, and never mind if it would have been better with a few more minutes of kneading. I could imagine her tutting over my shoulder that the Communists couldn't even make bread right. It was better than imagining her emerging too broken to care about bread or anything else.

Sometimes, visions of her and my father leaving the camp as living ghosts, skeletal and unable to remember they ever had a daughter, would crawl out of my imagination like maggots. Would they know me in three more years, when their sentences were up? Would they know me even if they were released that day? If they were somehow released early, would I pass them by on the street and never realize it?

I prayed. Every time an awful thought entered my head, I prayed that my parents were well and would return. I don't know if God heard me, but I like to think He did.

In my free time, I walked up and down the street where Mrs. Liebowitz had found me seven years earlier, trying to figure out which building it might have been. They all looked the same. I remembered there was a tree in front, but none of them looked quite right. I didn't want to draw attention by asking the women who watched the doors, but I eventually decided there wasn't any harm in it. All I had to say was that she'd helped me when I was a little girl. Everyone knew door women were informants, so I wouldn't dare to say why I'd needed help.

The door woman had no interest in helping me. Yes, there was a family named Liebowitz. No, she wouldn't tell me which apartment or allow me to ring them. I was arguing with her, maybe a little too loudly, because a girl about my age stopped to listen. The door woman tried to wave her on.

"Do you know where the Liebowitzes live?" I asked.

She cocked her head. "Who's asking?"

"My name's Annushka. Mrs. Liebowitz ... helped me ... when I first came to the city. It was about seven years ago. I wanted to thank her. For the bread." Bread didn't have to mean anything other than that I'd missed one meal. It was all very deniable.

She kept studying me. "I can ask her if she wants to see you."

"Thank you."

The door woman made me wait on the steps outside until the girl came back down to get me. As we climbed five flights of stairs, I learned her name was Polya Liebowitz and she was studying for university. It wasn't a bad building, overall, but clearly, the residents weren't important enough to have a working elevator.

"My mother wondered what happened to you," she said. "She'll be happy to know you're—alright." The pause told me a great deal. The word she had in her head was "alive," which meant she knew the truth and knew not to speak it.

"I owe your mother so much," I said, which told her something about me too.

Mrs. Liebowitz smiled at me from a chair in the corner of their main room. Her feet were splayed, each propped on a pillow sitting on top of a stack of books, and a girl a few years older than Polya was sitting between them, holding a doll while her mother brushed her hair. "My, time passes quickly," she said. "I wouldn't have recognized you, and I don't suppose you'd recognize me."

"I did remember you being taller," I admitted. She also seemed healthier in my memory—I couldn't imagine her walking to the orphanage on those feet that looked like fruit about to burst out of its skin. But it would have been rude to say that. "I just wanted to thank you."

"You're more than welcome."

I hadn't really prepared anything else to say and was getting embarrassed. Mrs. Liebowitz asked me to help Polya make tea, and we all sat and talked for much of the afternoon. The older daughter's name was Leah—she could hear but had never talked and seemed happy ignoring the new person and playing with her doll. There was a son, named Zalman, but he was at work. Mr. Liebowitz had died some years before, and I could tell she was proud to tell another person how she'd raised three on her own.

They didn't ask about my past. It wasn't rudeness. They gamely listened to everything I could tell them about life in a bread factory. I don't know if it was to avoid bringing up bad memories for me or to ensure the conversation wouldn't drift to topics that we all knew were off limits. Maybe someday it will all seem absurd—that we all knew what had happened, and knew the others knew, but still couldn't touch the truth in case the other person might be the kind to report on conversations. We didn't form friendships easily, especially then. That made the ones we did have so much more important.

Polya and I really had nothing in common, other than being the same age and sharing a certain skepticism of what we'd been taught. In any other country or any other time, I don't think we would have been friends. Acquaintances who said hello and not much else, probably. Not friends.

But as it was, we were. Once, we were riding a streetcar to go see a film on a day off, and two people were talking about how the Jews were responsible for all of their problems. I started to open my mouth to tell them off, but Polya shook her head. We'd probably never see them again, and the odds they'd find a way to punish either of us were not high. But they weren't nonexistent, either. You never knew who was with the police.

"How nice to live in a country where there's no more hatred," I said instead as we got off.

"And where no one goes hungry," Polya added.

"We must be the luckiest girls in the world."

"Oh, without a doubt."

We had an arrangement, where I borrowed some of Polya's textbooks on Friday and returned them on Sunday. She preferred not to study on the Sabbath—that was the only time everyone was home in the apartment—and I'd always bring a loaf of bread to share at Sunday dinner as payment for renting them. Of course, then I'd generally be invited to stay and eat more than I brought.

I had already learned all the math I was likely to need, and I had no patience for what they wrote in the history books. The chemistry book did give me some interesting perspectives on baking. But mostly I learned German.

Polya was studying it because she wanted to be an engineer, and if engineers read foreign publications, they were generally in German. I was studying just in case we'd have a new government in a few years.

I don't dare admit that now, and it may seem unforgiveable to you, reading this and knowing what was about to happen. But we didn't know the truth then. The newspapers and the radio talked about the evils of fascism, but they never clearly explained what it was. All I knew was that the Germans were our rulers' enemies, so I assumed they were my friends.

I've never understood why they didn't tell us. If we'd known about their ideas on master and inferior races—that they believed Slavs should be slaves—maybe we would have fought back sooner. If I'd known that they wanted to kill all the Jews, I certainly wouldn't have been willing to welcome them. Maybe some people still would have. No, certainly some still would have. But not everyone.

They could have told us when the Germans invaded Poland. They never did explain what it was all about, why our soldiers were in Poland but didn't seem to be fighting the Germans. Polya and I had a long debate going on whether there really was a war that they just wouldn't admit was happening, or whether there was some kind of deal to split it. I don't suppose we'll ever know. It seems like the sort of thing we should know, after everything.

Diana

I found out the Nazis had invaded while standing in line outside the Lubyanka.

It was my forty-eighth time in that line. One package a month for four years. Four years. Our son had gone from thinking girls were a plague upon the earth to trying to comb his hair in a way that would catch their eyes. The city had continued to build up, imploding the old to make way for the new. And I felt aged and drained. If Vitya returned, would he recognize me? Would I know him? But I didn't often let myself think about it. They kept accepting the packages, which meant their records showed he was still alive. I pitied the women who lined up with us all day, only to hear their loved ones had been sentenced to ten years without right of correspondence.

Vasya had told me that meant they'd been shot, one night when he was not only drunk but in a self-pitying mood, going on about how I couldn't imagine how hard their work was, the pressure to produce results. I felt I had an inkling, but I nodded sympathetically. I could always tell what his standing was when he came in. If all was well, he'd sneer and threaten. If he was afraid, he'd stagger in and expect me to listen to all his troubles, like a wife or a bartender. It's strange to think that I probably knew more about him than his own family did.

The first thing I did after I learned about the invasion was write another letter to Vitya. I told him the Nazis had crossed the border, but that Sasha and I were safe. I wanted to tell him not to sign up if they came to get more warm bodies from the camps, because I knew Vasya and his kind well enough to be sure the police would promise the prisoners their freedom and then send them to clear land mines with their feet. No one's freer than the dead. I was sure the camp censors would shred my letter if I wrote that, though, so I told him to keep himself safe and hoped he understood what that meant.

The Russians are strange people. The men on top had crushed them, over and over, but they still signed up to die in droves, like bees willing to disembowel themselves for their hive. And Vitya was like that too. I knew it was entirely possible he'd sign up, even knowing that if he survived, it would most likely be an accident. But there was nothing I could do other than remind him that he had a family waiting for him.

The shop where I worked closed the day after the invasion. No fancy shoes for anyone while Hitler was on the march. It wasn't hard finding new work. They were rounding up the men to fight, and someone had to keep the machines running. Ballerinas aren't built for factory work, but I needed to feed my son, so I took a job in a textile plant churning out uniforms. Soviet factories were more manual than ones in the West, so husky ex-peasant women tended to be the ones building tanks. Well, the men needed something to wear, and someone had to make it.

I quickly made friends in the factory. Some of the other women had men in the camps, too, whether husbands or brothers. Those that didn't had someone at the front. Some had both. I'd never told any of my colleagues at the store where my husband had gone, but it seemed perfectly natural to talk about it while we scarfed down our sandwiches in under ten minutes halfway through a twelve-hour shift.

We worked six days a week, then "volunteered" to help with civil defense on our days off. That usually meant digging ditches to try to stop the Panzers from getting past the outskirts of the city. Callouses erupted all over my hands, and I'd be so sore at the end of the day that I could barely sit up straight. I suddenly understood why peasant women were so uniformly disagreeable.

The Germans were within firing range of the city by October.

There were rumors the Politburo had already fled to Siberia or was about to. For the only time in my life, I wished I would run into Vasya, so I could find out if we were all done for. The authorities insisted everything was fine, which was somehow worse than telling the truth. The factories ran out of cash but ordered us to keep working. Quite a few people just stopped showing up. Frantic men and women were looting everything they could carry and practically throwing each other under the trains' wheels to try to get a spot.

I didn't exactly decide we wouldn't go. I just kept working and waiting. If Vitya had been with me, I think we would have taken Sasha and fought our way onto a train. But I wasn't confident I'd do well in a mob trying to flee, or even one smashing store windows. If I couldn't push back hard enough, my son and I would both be trampled, maybe to death. So we stayed.

Instead of digging ditches, the boss had me take overnight shifts on the roof of the factory to douse any small fires set by German bombs. I'd walk from the apartment to the metro and from the metro to the factory each morning and notice where the bombs had fallen the night before. Sometimes, it was just a crater in the street or the steeple knocked off an old church. Sometimes it was a smoking hole where a building housing hundreds of families had stood. I didn't cry the way I had when that girl had died in the Paris church. If I'd done that for every innocent killed that summer and fall, I never would have stopped crying. If I thought about anything, I'd wonder if it was finally time to run.

Sasha wanted to stay. He was only thirteen, but he and his class had helped place barricades at strategic points and were practicing fighting with wooden guns. That might have been the best preparation, since we didn't have any real ones to give them. I told myself it was a game, to make the children feel important, or just a bit of overzealousness in training them early. I didn't want to believe they might actually throw children into the fight if they ran out of grown men and women.

I didn't tell Sasha that, though. He felt he was part of something important, finally stepping out of the shadow of his father's arrest. I didn't want to take that from him. Maybe I should have.

Annushka

They never called on us to prepare defenses. Maybe they thought we were too strong for the Germans to consider attacking us. Even on that beautiful June day when bombs started to fall in Poland, we went to work and came home as usual.

That summer seemed endless. The newspapers said nothing, and the radio said less. I learned to read between the lines—when a city dropped out of the news, it had fallen. We stopped hearing about Kyiv in late July, as if it had never existed.

As far as I could tell, the front was moving closer every week. The city was bursting with people trudging in with whatever they could carry. There was nowhere to put them. No one was in charge of that.

Some of the girls from the bread factory joined up as laundresses and radio operators and machine gunners. I worried I'd be ordered to evacuate with the bread factory, but they forgot about us. Or perhaps we weren't important enough, or they ran out of time. All I know is that I was still in Kharkiv when the Germans marched in with the autumn rains.

We heard the battle creeping closer every day, but since the order to evacuate never came, I never had to decide whether to disobey it. I think some of the important Communists left, and maybe they had time to remove some equipment, but not much. The bread factory commissar had told us to stand firm behind our fighting men but couldn't tell us what to do when our men retreated and left us to the Germans.

The first few days of the occupation were quiet. The Soviets hadn't started organizing partisan bands yet, and most of us weren't in the mood to die for the people who had starved us. Then the Germans started coming for the Communists. They took our factory foreman and commissar and put someone they trusted in charge. He was Ukrainian, a frightened little man just following orders. And the main order was to keep turning wheat into bread. The next time I saw our commissar, he was twisting in the wind, dangling from a hotel balcony. I never knew what happened to the foreman, but girls who lived at the edge of the city said they'd heard shots. Not a battle. Just shots. I'd prayed for the end of the Communists, but it never occurred to me that the Lord would take little people who had just joined the party for a promotion and let the ones who'd ordered His church destroyed continue to live.

Next it was the Jews. It wasn't all at once. The police went from factory to factory, and people denounced their Jewish coworkers. Then they put them on trucks and took them outside the city. I don't know if people told themselves it was just for forced labor—just—but who could have believed it, when they took old women and little children? And they didn't let them bring anything, not even a change of socks. I knew. We all knew, if we wanted to see. I suppose it was like the city people turning away from the starving peasants in front of them.

Polya and her family stayed home, hoping they'd go unnoticed. I remember, after the first roundup of Jews, how frightened she looked when she opened the door. She seemed a little less scared when she saw it was me, but only a little. We'd been friends, but she knew I could easily become part of the mob they'd always feared more than the Communists or the Germans. That's what they called it, the mob. Individual people wouldn't drag them out of their houses and beat them in the streets. But when power approved or looked the other way, all those people let their hate feed off each other until they did things that seemed impossible a few days earlier.

I'd bring them bread, though it was getting harder to find an extra loaf. The Germans weren't willing to tolerate a certain amount of food disappearing, the way the old management had been. I also brought some news, but not all of it. I didn't want to tell them they might die. I think they knew, though.

It was too late to run. The Germans had the city surrounded, and they were checking papers on all the roads. I have to imagine any Jew who tried to leave was loaded on a truck right there, never to return. If the Communists had told us the truth about what Nazism was, she and her family would have run. Anyone who wasn't bedridden would have. But they never got that chance.

On the last night I spent in Kharkiv, I was saying my evening prayers when I got the overwhelming sense I needed to go to their neighborhood. It was like I had received an urgent message from a king, or someone even more important. I went, and I saw the German police going door-to-door just a few blocks away. There was a curfew, but I walked quickly while they were busy raiding someone else's house. They never noticed me.

"It's time to go," I said after Polya hurried me in the door.

"You said they had the city surrounded."

"There's no moon tonight. If you keep to the shadows, you might be able to get out. People can live a long time in the forest." I took her hand. "There's no more time. Now or never."

Mrs. Liebowitz asked me to help her pack some bread, while Polya threw some clothes together. She pulled me close and whispered, "Drag her out the door if you have to, but make sure she goes."

"You need to come too," I said. "You'll die if you stay. It's only about twenty kilometers."

"I don't think I could walk one on these feet," she said ruefully. "And Leah won't understand. If she makes a sound at the wrong moment..."

Leah couldn't talk, but she would respond with little moans or yelps if she didn't like something.

"When you're a mother, you make a commitment that you'll do everything to protect your children," she said. "Zalman went with the army. I can't help him. I can't save Leah, and I'd slow down Polya. So I'm going to give her a chance to live, and I'm going to make sure Leah isn't alone when … when it happens."

She took me by the shoulders, stared into my eyes, and made me promise to get her out. When I had run almost a decade earlier, I had thought my family was right behind me. I didn't know how we were going to leave, knowing Polya's wasn't coming.

"Don't you dare cry," she said. "You're going to save your sister."

I don't know if she was just telling me what lie to use, or something deeper. Polya could pass for my sister, particularly in a dimmer light. I could prevail on villagers for help, which they might give a fellow farm girl, and my sister wouldn't have to say anything. I nodded and said I would take care of her.

Polya tried to argue with her while I watched the street. They were only one block away when Mrs. Liebowitz literally shoved us into the hallway. "Live," she said.

We slid through alleyways, pressed close to the buildings, until we reached the edge of the city. A sentry saw us and took a few shots, but maybe his heart wasn't in it. There were people like that. Some raced to join up, to get their revenge on the Jews, who they thought were the ones pulling the Russians' strings. But others were just trying to survive.

We walked toward my old village. I had hoped the Germans had disbanded the kolkhoz and we could just slip in and last out the war as milkmaids or hired hands. But they must have decided that big farms would produce more wheat. A woman I met at the edge of the village told me that they were good with records, and if anyone with city papers showed up to work on a farm, they would want to know why. She probably saved my life, or at least Polya's. Even if they hadn't killed us on the spot, their plan was to work their "inferiors" to death. Bring in a harvest and clear the land all at once. It was the same as the Communists, except more efficient.

Winter was setting in, and we had no idea how far we might have to walk to get out of the Germans' net. I could keep us safe while we were on terrain that I knew, but I'd be as lost as Polya was once we crossed into the Russian side. But we couldn't survive on pine nuts, so we started walking east.

I think we would have frozen or starved to death if some partisans hadn't seen our campfire a few days in.

The commander told us they weren't in the business of sheltering civilians. We could join them, or we could try to make our way to safety. It was a choice that was no choice at all.

Polya was eager to join. She was ready to kill, and who could question why? She would go with the men and a few other women who were disrupting supply lines and doing anything else they could to wear the Germans down. I didn't want to fight. I couldn't imagine ending another human being's life myself. As much as I'd wished for the Communists' deaths, I knew I didn't have the stomach for killing, as soon as I saw them swinging from the hotel balcony. But I was perfectly willing to cook, bandage wounds, and do whatever else they needed me to do. Finding food might have been the greatest contribution I could have made anyway. It was almost like I remembered, except people were dying at their plows instead of on city streets, because the Germans wouldn't let anyone escape.

The commander said we were fighting for our freedom. I didn't believe it. But we were fighting for our survival. Sometimes, that's the best you can hope for.

Diana

The battle for Moscow lasted four months. I don't know how much of the credit belongs to our men's resolve, the enemy's stupidity, or whatever chance made that December unusually cold. Maybe they still could have hit the city with shells by New Year's, but we knew the momentum was on our side. The factory let discipline lapse just that once, and we threw a party that rivalled any I've been to, even though all we had was cheap vodka and whatever scraps we could bring from home.

Just a few days later, I finally got my first letter from Vitya since the war had begun.

> *My dear Diya,*
>
> *No one has come to recruit soldiers here yet. The commandant said our role is to dig the gold that will pay for tanks and planes. I guess it's nice to know that.*
>
> *Our doctor is gone. I'm not surprised. Grisha is still young, and young men don't like to sit safely behind the lines when their country calls. The polite people are running the hospital now, so I'm back at general work. But don't worry. I've had three years to get strong and fat. I can work.*
>
> *I think of you and Sasha every day. Keep yourselves safe,*

whatever that means, and write to me when you get the chance.

All of my love,
Vitya

The "polite people" was a euphemism for professional criminals. They were probably raiding the alcohol- and opium-based medications and leaving the prisoners to fend for themselves. Not that there was much Dr. Grisha (apparently, he and Vitya were now close enough to use nicknames) could have done for them under the best of circumstances, if I was reading between the lines of the letters correctly.

My dear Diya,

Forgive me for taking so long to write to you. Normally, we'd work fewer hours until the sun returns, but the Motherland needs gold. So I don't have much time when I'm not sleeping, working, or eating.

It's not all bad, though. I actually found a friend I haven't seen in years. No one likes to see an old friend in a prison camp, of course, but it makes the work a little easier. You remember Kostya, my old sergeant? Well, he's here too. I don't think it's anything to do with me, but he won't tell me what happened.

I hadn't noticed him for a long time. I wasn't looking for him, and everybody looks the same with a shaved head and a padded jacket. But then some men tried to take his bread, and I stepped in. Then he recognized me.

You wouldn't believe how much easier it is to work with a friend. We always seem to get the full ration. (It's like a job where they pay you based on what you produce, except with bread instead of cash.) And it's nice to have someone to talk to, even if he's getting bored with hearing about you and Sasha.

All of my love,
Vitya

I did remember Konstantin Fyodorovich. I'd met him once, and it had been absolutely clear he despised me. Nothing I'd done—he would have despised any woman on Vitya's arm. I could overlook it because I felt sorry for him. It must be terrible to love someone who can never love you back. But Vitya had no interest whatsoever in men and was completely oblivious to why his former sergeant kept helping him.

When Vitya had gone to order more drinks, Konstantin Fyodorovich looked me over, as if appraising me. "You think you can handle his spells?" he asked. "The times when he's almost crazy."

"I was friends with modernist painters. I've seen every type of crazy a man can have."

"Have you?" he sniffed. "Well, we'll see."

"Yes, we will. Whenever you meet someone, we can all get supper together and you can see how I've done." He eyed me. "I know. I won't say a word."

He barely spoke to me for the rest of the night. Vitya sensed the awkwardness but had no idea where it came from. He thought his friend wanted me for himself. I said he hadn't been anything but gentlemanly, but we never had drinks with him again—whether Vitya's decision or Kostya's, I don't know. But I kept my promise and never said anything. So I wrote back and said how pleased I was he had a friend with him. And I was. Kostya might have the good sense needed to keep him alive in that place.

"I'm going to join the Komsomol, Mama," Sasha told me on one of the rare nights when we could share a meal. That was the youth league, a sort of preparation for Party membership. I wasn't surprised. My son wasn't a genius, but he was smart enough, and people who wanted to be something someday joined the Komsomol. I assumed it would be a slightly more grown-up version of the Pioneers, where they just sang songs about Lenin and Stalin and painted banners for holidays. I had no objections.

Until he wrote the essay denouncing his father.

It was the price of joining, of following the only path upward. I wanted my son to succeed. And his essay wouldn't add a day to his father's sentence. And holding back wouldn't take a day off. It ultimately meant nothing.

Bullshit. I wept and pleaded with him to tear it up.

He'd stopped crying for his father a few months in, then stopped asking when he might return after about a year, then stopped fighting the boys who called his father a traitor maybe a year after that. But this … this was unbearable. I couldn't tell if he truly believed his father was sabotaging factories as part of some grand conspiracy, or if he'd decided we no longer mattered. I couldn't decide which possibility frightened me more.

I was a ballerina; I can understand naked ambition—though, obviously, I wasn't pleased to see my own son display it. I would have respected him more if he'd simply said his father had become an impediment to his future. But to act as if he believed it all, as if Vitya deserved whatever was happening to him in that camp run by thieves and murderers (the prisoners and the guards)—how could he?

I told myself it was the fever of war and it would pass. I almost believed it. But I knew they'd taught children it was their duty to inform on their parents. I didn't know anyone personally who that had happened to, but I remembered how the papers eulogized that boy Pavel Something-ov who'd denounced his father. And it occurred to me that if the Komsomol leaders demanded my son make up evidence to sentence his father to another prison term, he likely would do it. He might even denounce me, though he'd be good and sorry after a day or two in an orphanage. But I'd be lost by then, as irrevocably doomed as a woman falsely accused of witchcraft three hundred years earlier. You could easily make accusations, but you could never take them back. He was fourteen—a spindly, shrimpy fourteen—but I was still afraid of my own son.

    I'd said I wouldn't lie to my child, and maybe I didn't. But I certainly watched my tongue closely whenever we were in the same room.

Annushka

I found my way to the front accidentally.

I'd gotten closer to the Germans than any sane person would. All for mushrooms. When I got back, the partisans asked me where I'd gotten such a haul. I showed them the spot. We almost got our heads shot off when one of them made too much noise, but since the Germans hadn't heard me the first time, our commander decided I could be a scout.

It wasn't the exact spot of forest I'd hidden in, but it was enough alike that I could move without leaving much of a trace. Even though I was risking death every time I went out, I smile when I think of that forest. No one ordered me not to say my prayers there. As long as I saw something and got back alive, that was enough.

I wore my faded dress and my kerchief and walked with no shoes on my feet. I looked every inch a half-starved peasant hunting for anything edible. My gamble was that if I needed to get close, the Germans wouldn't see me as a spy. They might shoot at me for sport, but they wouldn't torture me for information, or so I hoped. They fired warning shots a few times, or just shot badly. Either is possible.

I don't know if I was skilled or just lucky, but our commander trusted me enough to have me show our men the best way to the village east of our camp. They were going to get food and medical supplies from some peasants who supported us. We got to the edge of the village and found the right hut. I did my part. What happened next wasn't my fault, or so I keep telling myself.

The Germans had laid a trap. Maybe they held the woman's children hostage to get her cooperation and deliver the partisans. But it doesn't really matter how they did it. They came from the house, shooting at anything they saw. The only reason I'm alive is that they didn't see me at first. I hid behind a haystack while the bullets flew. I knew a haystack wouldn't protect me, but there was nothing else that would. My only hope was that God had something else left for me to do and would keep me alive long enough to sneak away.

A man—his name was Tolya, and he'd been a Komsomol organizer—fell near me. I dragged him behind the hay. He was bleeding from his head. So much blood. I don't know anything about wounds, but I sensed he was beyond help. I took his gun, which I didn't entirely know how to use, and prepared to run. But once I crawled out from behind the haystack, there was a German standing over me. He smiled. I know, because the little bit of light in the sky reflected off his gold teeth. I'm only alive because he must have been an evil man. The only reason to not kill me immediately was if he wanted to rape or torture me first. If he'd been a good man, I wouldn't have had the time to shoot him.

I don't remember deciding to shoot. I just saw him looming over me and did the only thing I could to save myself. And I ran, and kept running as I heard their gunshots cracking behind me. I slid down in a ditch in a field and tried to breathe. What to do? I did the only thing I could think of, which was run back to the camp.

I told our commander everything. He stared at the fire for a moment. "They knew the risks. We all do. At least one made it back." He pulled out a bottle—I don't know where he'd gotten it—and we all drank a toast to our lost comrades. I'd never had vodka before, and I've hated it ever since.

I didn't weep. Maybe I should have. I don't know if any of us let ourselves cry when the people we had walked out with didn't come back. Or if anyone did, they never let the others see. I said a prayer for all their souls, and the German's, too, even though I was sure he'd earned his way into Hell.

I didn't kill anyone other than that man, and I'm not certain I killed him. At least, I never killed anyone directly. I did help the partisans lure out a man who was working as the Germans' enforcer. I understood why so many people kept doing their jobs, repairing railroad tracks and such, even though it helped the Germans. They just wanted to save their lives and feed their families, and if that meant other people died … they learned to live with it, I suppose. And how else could they keep their children alive when the Germans had taken every last potato and grain of wheat they could find? But this man was different.

My village contacts told me how he made everyone stand at attention whenever he walked by and beat anyone who didn't, including a woman too bent by years of working in the fields to stand straight, even if Stalin or Hitler himself had commanded it. If anyone was caught stealing, they spent a few hours with him before the Germans hanged them. I happened to be nearby when they hanged one girl. I only knew she was a girl because she still had on something like a dress. Her face was … It was still a face in the same way that the baby birds I'd killed and cooked were still birds.

So we arranged for him to overhear that I was sneaking around and cutting grain, knowing he'd want to deliver me to his masters himself and claim the credit. And the whole brigade of partisans was waiting for him.

We didn't shoot him. The village would have been punished if the Germans had found out we'd killed one of their enforcers. I don't know whose idea it was to do it the way we did. I just know it wasn't mine. The men subdued him and held him down. Then they took some gasoline someone had syphoned off a German truck and poured it down his throat, with a little bit in his flask to make it look like a suicide. I didn't watch. I got as far away as I could while he screamed for mercy. And when it was all over, they dumped the body under cover of darkness.

I didn't know the entire plan, but I knew enough to turn my stomach. I also knew how completely he deserved his death. I've never come to a conclusion on whether that added up to a good or a bad act.

I prayed constantly. Not just for my life. Have you ever heard the Our Father? As a girl, I'd never understood asking not to be led into temptation. Why would God tempt me? But during the war, I understood that I was asking for the strength to do the least bad thing out of all the terrible options when there was every temptation not to worry about it. I'm not sure if I succeeded.

I never spoke about the war after I got back, not until I was sitting in Grisha's office and we were desperately trying to talk about anything other than what we really needed to. The men decided the victory was theirs and theirs alone. And the women who'd stayed behind whispered about the whoring we must have done with their men at the front. There was no one to talk to but the other women who'd been there, and we already knew it all.

There was one man I loved, but I was too shy to do anything about it. I was just a girl. He wasn't exactly handsome, but I loved his dark eyes. Not tall, but taller than me, and strong, like a country boy. His name was Petya. I thought I was doing a good job hiding it. I didn't want to seem like a silly child, not among all those men. And besides, I wasn't sure if he liked me. He never said more than a few words to me, though he did give me a piece of chocolate he'd somehow gotten hold of—just walked up, handed it to me, and walked away. I thought I saw his ears turning pink under his cap, but I couldn't be sure. That piece of chocolate gave me hope.

The Silence that Remains

Why didn't I marry him? My love was no more sacred than anyone else's.

Two of the other men dragged him back from a mission. The lower half of his leg was mutilated beyond fixing. They gave him samogon—that horrible homebrew that people make when vodka is too expensive or unavailable—to knock him senseless and cut it off with a saw, right there in the forest. The men were there to restrain him if he came to and fought back. Our surgeon told me to hold Petya's hands. Not pin his arms down. He was so much bigger than me. Just hold his hands in mine. I kept my gaze fixed on his eyes, which were glassy and seemed to see nothing. When it was over, I helped the surgeon with his bandages.

After Petya came to, I brought him water and the little food we had and reassured him our commander had sent a message up through our connections to Moscow, and a plane would be there to evacuate him soon. I even changed the bandages. He didn't want anyone else to do it. He said I had the gentlest hands. So I knew before anyone—maybe even before him—when the infection set in.

The surgeon amputated further up the leg to try to stop it. I risked my life sneaking to beg for iodine from peasant women who supported us, and when they didn't have any, to steal some from the Germans' supply warehouses. It didn't matter. We cleaned and cut and cleaned and cut until we were at his hip bone. And still no one came for our wounded.

When he started breathing like a man running full speed, the surgeon told me to do whatever I wanted. And I understood that they'd all known.

I lay down beside Petya and told him I loved him. He said he loved me, too, before his mind clouded and he couldn't remember who I was. He called me Katya, his sister the Germans had killed, then Mama. And I just said yes to all of it, that I was here, and he was safe. I kissed him—lips, forehead, cheeks, everywhere—until he slipped away.

I took a button from his coat before we buried him. All of our dead were buried in a clearing not too far from our camp where wild kalynas grew. I wonder if it's still there. So many things were lost to the bombs or the tanks. The only thing I know is that I still have that button, threaded onto my rosary. It reminds me to pray that those I lost are at peace. As if I could ever forget to.

Diana

Vasya showed up at my apartment only once, near the end of the war, when I'd finally started to forget him and hoped he'd forgotten me. "You're going to do something for me," he said.

"If it's taking the blame and a bullet, no, I'm not."

"It's not that, bitch. Come on. Now."

I didn't really have a choice in the matter. He put me in the back of one of their black cars. I assumed he'd wanted to arrest me without a scene, and I didn't really feel like making one. It was bound to happen someday. When you work for them, you know you can be pulled down just as easily as the people you betrayed. And my son was almost a man. He'd manage, somehow. I watched the rain on the car's windows. I've always liked rainy nights. It wasn't the worst thing to see before you died, light refracted in a thousand little drops.

The car didn't pull into the Lubyanka, but in front of an old mansion from the tsar's time. I knew whose mansion this was—the only Central Committee member to have one. Everyone else contented themselves with Kremlin apartments. This might be worse than the Lubyanka, if the rumors were true.

A man in a uniform was there in the foyer. Vasya pushed me toward him and left. I just stood there. I'd already worked out what this was most likely about. Vasya, or maybe this other man, was in trouble, and I was going to be either a sacrificial lamb or a gift to win their way back into their boss's good graces. The man said nothing but nodded toward a chair. And we sat there, with no sound but the ticking clock, until four in the morning. Then the drunken idiots who ran the country came home.

Lavrenty Beria was a fat little man with a pince-nez that made him look like a man trying to look like an intellectual. The head of the political police was red-nosed, but he spoke clearly enough.

"What are you doing here?" he asked the man. He didn't seem to see me. I thanked any god that might exist.

"I brought you a present," he said, gesturing toward me.

"This old nag? She must be at least 35." I was 44, but it wasn't the time to be flattered.

"She used to be a ballerina."

"Are you going to dance for me?" he sneered.

"If you want me to." I'd been a wife, store clerk, and factory worker for years—hardly conducive to spending hours training in ballet each day. Peasant dances are for a circle—you can't dance them on your own without looking ridiculous. Would he kill me for dancing badly? A dance I'd seen at a disreputable café in Montmartre popped into my head. It would have to do. I didn't look at him and pretended I was onstage, where men could leer at me all they wanted, and I could safely ignore them.

"That's not ballet, is it?" I looked over and saw he was smiling. Was that good or bad? He looked over to one of his attendants and gestured toward the man who was saving himself at my expense. "Take him home."

Beria took me into the study. A walrus of a man wearing too many rings stood guard at the door. It wasn't a bad study. The chairs looked comfortable, though I doubted he did much reading in them.

He slapped his desk. "Bend over," he said. I did. "Lift up your skirt." What else could I do? He fondled me through my underwear. My husband had liked to feel me, too, like he wanted to touch every inch of this body he couldn't believe was his to touch, even when the body was saggy and worn out from childbirth. This wasn't like that.

Beria tore my underwear and raped me, right there on the desk, with his hand over my mouth. Were there children upstairs who might have heard me? I wanted to bite him. It probably lasted only a minute, maybe two, but I thought it would never end. And then he stood in front of me with his penis still hanging out of his trousers. "Clean it," he said. I looked for my handkerchief. He forced my head down and made me lick my own shit and blood from it. I didn't cry. I refused to give him that.

The walrus at the door gave me a bouquet. It wasn't even a nice one. Mostly greenery and a few gaudy yellow blooms. But I took it. I was afraid not to. I limped back to the streetcar and rode home, and no one thought a thing of the blood seeping through my skirt.

Annushka

My war ended early, with a bullet.

I was gathering information so we could mine the tracks and destroy the next German supply train. I looked like a girl taking a walk along the rails, plucking petals from a daisy to divine if her love returned her feelings—or more likely, if he would return alive. I never heard the shot. I assume the Germans were amusing themselves with target practice. If they'd known I was with the partisans, they would have had a public hanging.

I don't remember any of what happened next. It wasn't until later that I learned how the others found me and brought me back to die among friends. I kept breathing, though, and Polya persuaded the commander to radio for one of the small planes that sometimes brought us supplies, when they could get through. She never demanded credit, but it had to have been her. I don't know why one was available, why I was lucky when Petya and so many others weren't.

I woke up in a hospital. I saw two of everything, and the walls had a pale green cast. I felt sick to my stomach when I tried to follow the twin nurses with my eyes. They told me to sleep.

Eventually, everyone merged back with their other self, and I could see the room was white, not sickly green. I touched my head and found the bandages. They'd shaved my hair. I wondered if my braid had gone on the same pile as the soldiers' arms and legs. You think strange things when you have a head injury.

I was awake, but I couldn't do anything for myself. When I tried to use my hands, they went in the right general direction, but I couldn't make them grasp anything. I had expected to care for my parents when they returned from the camps. Would they have to care for me like an eternal infant? Sometimes I cried. The nurses hushed me, but I think they understood what it was all about.

After a few days, the surgeon came to see me. Her name was Dr. Medvedeva. She asked me some questions. I tried to answer, but I could tell it was gibberish. She sighed, patted my hand, and started to go. I reached for her. I don't know how, but I sensed that it was important that she see that I still had a mind. She sat back down.

"Give me some sign you understand what I'm saying to you," she said.

I couldn't speak or make my fingers work well enough to signal anything. I lifted my hand to my ear, and hoped she understood.

"Touch your mouth," she said. I think I actually got my chin, but it was close enough. "Hold out your hand." I did.

My intuition wasn't wrong. They sent me to a different ward. An old doctor with spectacles was in charge there. He must have been a professor of something. His name was Dr. Sanin, and he told me that he was studying how people might recover from brain injuries. He would try to teach me to speak, to walk, and to care for myself again, if I was willing to work hard. Of course I was.

But it was dreadful. Every day, I had to do something new, and if I failed, I lived with the consequences. When he decided I could feed myself, I had to do it, even if most of the food never made it to my mouth. I would learn, or I would starve.

Slowly, my arms and legs started remembering how to function, then my hands and feet, and finally each finger. It was strange. I had to learn how to speak again, but I remembered how to read and write, once my hands would obey me.

After a while, they let me work in the kitchen while Dr. Sanin kept notes on my progress. My hands weren't as strong as they had been, but nothing felt better than sinking them into a ball of dough.

Once, Dr. Medvedeva called me from my kitchen shift to her ward. She and a man in one of the beds were glaring at each other.

"Ah, Anastasia Georgiyevna," she said. "Tell this coward about how you came to us." I blushed a little, because I wasn't used to hearing anyone talk like that, but I told him and showed the surgical scar under my hair. "Now tell him about your therapy." I said as much as I could, though I stumbled. Speech was my biggest struggle. "Thank you, Anastasia Georgiyevna, you may go."

As I left, I heard her yelling at the soldier. "If that child has the courage to pull herself back together, what excuse can you have?" I didn't know whether I should be proud or embarrassed.

The doctors did their best for me. But they also were the ones who decided I was mispronouncing my name as Kolisnychenko instead of Kolesnikova, and insisted I practice speaking in Russian, first and foremost, rather than my "country dialect." I could speak Russian reasonably well before I was hurt, though I never thought of it as my language. Almost everyone in Kharkiv can speak both. I don't know if they thought their words were better than Ukrainian ones, or if they feared I'd be in danger when the people in power started looking for collaborators as the war wound down. It doesn't really matter. I couldn't tell them I didn't want my new name. That would make me a nationalist and buy me at least five years in the camps.

I remember that I would sometimes get overwhelmed by everything that had happened, and by the sense that none of what we'd sacrificed would matter. The people on the top would keep enslaving us, like they always had. "Excessive negative emotionality," Dr. Sanin called it in my chart because nothing seemed wrong to him. Sometimes I wonder if other doctors who learned from him were confused when their patients failed to produce as many tears as expected. I certainly set a high threshold for them to meet.

1945-1951

Diana

I will give the Russians this, if nothing else: they know how to celebrate.

Someone had a friend who got a group of us factory ladies onto the roof of a building overlooking Red Square. We brought our children with us to watch the Victory Day parade. The weaponry was less impressive than what you've probably seen, but there's never a victory parade like the first, when we were still absorbing that the whole thing was over. The sky was metal gray and hurling down a frigid rain, but we just huddled under our umbrellas and passed around a bottle of vodka to warm ourselves. I let Sasha have a sip, but just a sip. How bourgeois I had become.

By the end, though, even the vodka wasn't enough, and nothing sounded better than soup. We almost left early, though I'm glad we didn't. At the end, they threw down all the captured Nazi banners. Maybe they were going to set fire to them, but watching them turn into a waterlogged mess of red and black was satisfying in its own way.

We went to a workers' canteen, a dingy little place like all the others, with another vodka bottle smuggled in under someone's coat. Not that the people running it cared what we did. As long as we paid and didn't ask for an extra portion, we were of no interest to them. And so we proceeded to get rip-roaring drunk and tell our war stories, which were mostly about times that sparks hit the factory roof. Everyone already knew those stories, but we needed to hear them again on that day.

Eventually, they threw us out for taking up a table and we went back to the closest apartment, which was mine. I made tea, because I didn't make a habit of keeping vodka at home, and none of us needed more anyway. Our children scattered to amuse themselves, and we gradually got quiet as the edge of our intoxication started to wear off.

"Think we'll finally get paid for all those extra hours?" I can't remember who asked that.

"We can dream," I said.

"You won't have to worry about money. Your man will be home soon," Tonya said. Tonya's husband had left years before, and her son was with the army. I never heard if he made it home. "Everyone says there's going to be an amnesia."

"Amnesty, you drunk," slurred Lara, who had been to university and reminded everyone of it as often as possible.

"That's what I said, you—"

"Who's everyone?" I cut in. At one point, everyone had said Stalin had fled and was handing the city to the Germans.

"Everyone," Tonya emphasized. "Bet your man is home by New Year's."

I wanted to believe it, but I wasn't even sure "my man" was alive. They kept accepting packages for him, but the letters had stopped. In almost eight years, I'd never gone more than a few months without a letter, and the last one I had was from October. I almost would have been comforted if I thought he was alive and had found someone else, but it was a men's camp. And even if there had been women, that wasn't Vitya's way.

"If you talk about it, it won't come true," I said. This made perfect sense to them, and the conversation moved on.

It was dark by the time everyone collected their children and stumbled home. I started making scrambled eggs because I already felt a bit like an unfit mother after the amount of day-drinking I'd done. Sasha wolfed them down, then kept tapping his plate with his fork, the way he had when he'd wanted a few kopecks to take a girl to the cinema.

"Just say it, whatever it is," I said.

"He's not really coming back, is he?"

"Who?"

He made a face. "'Your man.'"

"I don't know. I hope so. I've missed him."

"He's a traitor."

"Just because you wrote something in that damn essay doesn't make it so." I took a breath to steady myself. "If he's alive, he's coming back. He's your father, Sasha."

"No, he's not."

"I would know, wouldn't I?"

He looked horrified, the way kids do when they consider how they came to exist. "He's not really my father anymore," he finally responded and slammed the chair against the table as he got up. "I'll run away if he's here."

"Hmm, that so?" I knew he wouldn't, or if he did, it would only last a night. My son was not made for living on the streets. "That's too bad. I'm sure he'd like to see you. He asks about you in every letter."

"He hasn't sent you a letter in forever," he said, which cut deeply because it was true. "He doesn't care about us."

I sighed and lit a cigarette. I tried not to smoke much, but sometimes that boy drove me to it. "I'll never understand why you so badly want your father to be a monster," I said.

He made a frustrated sound and went to the water closet, which had the only door available for him to slam. I splashed my face in the kitchen sink and started another letter I knew wouldn't be answered. I'd been lying by omission for so long I hardly even considered if I shouldn't.

Meg Wingerter

My dear Vitya, we went to the victory parade today. You would have loved it …

Annushka

My therapy was over, but I stayed on at the hospital as a baker. Mostly, I baked bread, but my joy was making something out of nothing. Shortages or no shortages, there are occasions which require dessert. I found substitutes for everything—sugar, eggs, milk. And I got very good at layering flavors to hide what was missing. I'd tell the soldiers they were old family recipes because that seemed better than admitting their government didn't care enough to issue them some butter. But I was content there.

Polya had somehow survived all the way to Berlin. She must have had an angel watching her. She sent me letters along the way, mostly filling them with anecdotes of the absurd things that happen during a war. She wouldn't have been allowed to tell me anything else, and I knew enough from my time with the partisans to fill in the rest.

> *I bet Berlin was beautiful before the war, she told me. It makes me hate them even more. They had everything they could want. Why did they come?*
>
> *We were in a house, arresting a policeman, and his wife came down in high-heeled shoes with pearl necklace, pearl earrings, pearl rings, and diamond rings. Oleg Vladimirovich (I think I told you about him, he's a good comrade) asked me if I wanted to take any of it. I didn't*

want to, though. It would have felt like wearing something that had been floating in sewage. But let me know if you want anything. I'm not taking everything people have to live on. We're better than them. But I'm not above sending my friend a wristwatch, especially from a house where everyone has three.

Some of the men aren't controlling themselves. You know how war is, the way the Germans used women here. It's not right. But I don't have much sympathy for them, not after what they sent their men to do.

I kept those letters hidden in my pillow, more out of habit than because I thought she'd actually said anything wrong. The letters had gotten through the censors, hadn't they? So I never expected the note that came at the end of the war, postmarked Arkhangelsk. It's a little city on the White Sea with a bay where they can break the ice for enough months to make it worth having a port there. I couldn't imagine what Polya was doing there, because I didn't think the Navy took women. Had she gotten married? Relationships happened fast at the front. I tore the envelope open and one little scrap of paper fell out.

Did you turn me in?

Only then did I look at the envelope more closely. It wasn't Arkhangelsk. It was Arkhangelsky, and it was a camp.

I'd never shown her letters to anyone or seen anyone looking in my pillow. Whatever ridiculous charges they'd come up with may have had nothing to do with what she wrote to me. I swore my innocence and put together a package with heavy socks and gloves. I didn't know much about Arkhangelsky, but one look at the map told me she'd need those.

I was allowed to send one parcel a month and as many letters as I wanted. I'd tell her about the mundane incidents of my life because if

I wrote anything that annoyed the censors, they might take away mail privileges. Mostly I asked what to send in the next parcel. She'd ask for vodka and cigarettes to trade. I'd stuff in any warm clothes and food that wouldn't spoil that I could scrounge together. I made some matzah once, though it must have had the consistency of granite by the time it got there. Polya said she dissolved it in the soup they got every day, and it was the best meal she'd had in camp.

It was a logging camp. I couldn't imagine Polya was big enough to chop down great evergreens, but if you put one small woman on each end of a saw, you'll eventually bring down a tree, or so she told me. All of her studying mathematics and engineering hadn't completely gone to waste, she said, since she was the one everyone checked with to ensure they weren't about to crush another pair. I wouldn't have had the courage to even pretend to see a bright side.

She'd say, from time to time, that she understood if I couldn't send anything. She'd couch it in concerns about whether I was earning enough to keep myself fed. I knew the real message was that I didn't have to stand by her if the pressure became too great.

I'd long since learned the uselessness of speaking. And who would I appeal to, who would possibly care that they'd imprisoned an innocent woman—not just innocent, heroic? So I did the only thing I knew how to do. I fed her.

After the war, they tried to return everything to normal. The stores, the ice cream shops, and everything else reopened, as if we could all just forget what we'd lost. The nicer bakeries reopened, too, and Dr. Sanin recommended me to one of them.

I believe it was done with the kindest intentions, but I didn't want it. But once you've been recommended to someone near the top, you can't say you'd rather be a little mouse in your hole. Because then they wonder why—who would give up the perks they can offer to work in a hospital kitchen or a bread factory? And I knew enough about them to know what they'd conclude about me. I thought about bungling my pastry audition, but I'd promised Dr. Sanin I would do my best. I didn't want to make him look like a fool after all he'd done for me.

I'd never seen a bakery like that, and I probably never will again. All the treats were custom-made, and they had every spice, dried fruit, and nut that a person could desire. We didn't bake for the Kremlin, but for the people a step or two down. I wondered if maybe the Kremlin bakers had ingredients I didn't even know existed—not that I would ever be curious enough to want to work there. This was bad enough. Not the work itself—there was joy in trying recipes I'd never tasted before and experimenting when the customers wanted something new. But I had to pretend to be stupid about everything but baking, and that's tiresome. If I'd returned to working in a bread factory, no one would have known or cared what I thought. In that bakery, the only way to be safe was to convince them I thought of nothing but flour.

I must have put on a good act because no one I worked with ever asked me anything or told me about themselves. Maybe they were all playing their own version of my game. That was a godsend because I'd decided there were some lines I wouldn't cross: I wouldn't denounce anyone. I wouldn't stop doing everything I could to help my dearest friend. And if anyone asked, I wouldn't deny God.

It felt good to set those rules. Because I am Annushka, there are certain things I will not do, and if I do them, I am no longer Annushka. But what the rules really do is give you permission to do everything else. I can act deceptively, or keep my mouth shut when I shouldn't, or any number of other things because that doesn't break the rules. And once you've done everything else, what do your rules even matter anymore? I thought my rules proved I was different, but maybe they just showed me how people do the appalling things they do—one small step at a time.

Diana

We won the war, and they rewarded us with more arrests.

I would have liked to stay in the factory. But Vasya came and brought me back to the ladies' store. The war was over, and they'd need new shoes.

I'd really thought something had changed during the war. Hadn't we all proven we could be trusted to do the right thing? Or at least the thing our leaders wanted us to do? We'd saved them when they didn't deserve it, and it seemed like they'd acknowledged that by not crushing us for a few years.

But they were just busy crushing other people. Vasya told me they'd deported the Tatars from Crimea to Siberia in case they were ready to welcome the Nazis, and they'd cleared the Volga region of anybody who'd had a German relative in the last few hundred years. Now they were certain everyone was an American or British spy, and I needed to listen for any evidence that the wives might carelessly drop.

After a while, I, too, was arrested as a foreign spy. Vasya must have fallen out of favor. I suppose he was shot. Occupational hazard. The last time I'd ended up in their hands, his boss had been trying to save himself by bribing Beria with flesh, and apparently, it wasn't enough.

Since I'd been an informant, they passed me up the chain. Or perhaps they had a note somewhere that I was a compliant lay for their boss. Whatever the reason, I found myself in front of that man-shaped pile of excrement again. I wanted to spit on him, but this could be my only chance. Everyone knew what happened in these cellars. You crawl, you confess, you die. The only way out was to change the script.

"Do you remember me?" I asked. He looked surprised. "I danced at your mansion. Your men brought me there. I guess at least one of them was a traitor. But how was I to know that?"

"You stand accused of spying for the Nazis."

"I'm Jewish."

"And Britain." That must have been the accusation of the month.

I leaned in. "Do you believe that? Of me?" He slapped me. I waited a beat and looked back. "Punish me," I said and hoped I'd live long enough to regret it. And he did. But they let me limp out.

A few days later, a policeman picked me up again. I debated whether a bullet in the brain was preferable to sucking that monster's dick again. My son had joined the Air Corps, so he'd likely have the chance to denounce me and get on with his life. But the car didn't stop at the Lubyanka—it pulled in front of a slightly better than average residential building. The man took me to the top floor and let me into a furnished apartment. The furniture was good quality, foreign-made, and obviously chosen by a man who'd never learned to match colors. "You'll stay here," he said, and locked the door as he left.

I looked around. There was a kitchen, bedroom, living room, and private bathroom. I moved with absurd caution, like I expected a man with a knife in every cupboard. I saved the wardrobe for last because I knew what I would find there: all types of obscene clothing.

Then I waited for something to happen. When nothing did, I ate. It was pastries and fruit. There was wine, but I wasn't inclined to lose my wits yet. Then I waited some more, and still nothing happened. So I tried on some of the clothing. It was too big in the chest, and all of it left some vital part uncovered. I tried to piece a few items together to produce something that a self-respecting whore would wear but gave up and crawled into bed.

My job was to entertain his guests. I was a combination hostess, burlesque dancer, and concubine, for whomever he told me I had to please. I didn't mind the other men so much. Most of them just wanted to fuck and get it done with. I gave a few hand jobs because some were too embarrassed for anything more. But then there was Beria.

The first times were the worst, when I thought he might actually strangle me or beat me to death. But after a while it all became … boring. I shrieked and writhed as expected, but inside, I wondered: How could the head of the police have so little imagination? I would imagine myself doing his job better. My favorite, of all the tortures I'd concocted, was to come in, administer a paper cut to a prisoner's finger, promise "Tomorrow will be worse," and go away until the same time the next day, when I would bend back his thumbnail and promise, "Tomorrow will be worse." This would continue until I ran out of nonfatal tortures. And then I would make him sit in a room, bring in his wife, give her a paper cut and promise her, "Tomorrow will be worse." And he would break.

I had a great deal of time on my hands.

Most days, there was nothing to do but fill up the time any way I could until midnight, when I got dressed in something obscene in case he dropped by. I made myself get dressed in ordinary clothes when I got up, which admittedly was around noon, but nonetheless, I got up and cleaned up the place, ate my meals on a schedule and practiced dancing, not that there was enough room to exercise much. I plumped up rapidly, which Beria liked. Only a very powerful man could feed his whore so well.

Sometimes a policeman took me out and let me shop for clothes. Maybe I should have felt ashamed for people to see me, but I didn't. I felt fascinated by the most ordinary things. I watched people and made up lives for them when I had to go back to the apartment—anything to pass the time. Not that anyone's life was very interesting in this damned country, but I gave them great loves and daring adventures just the same.

I imagined a life for my husband, too, for just a few minutes a day. It was riskier now, trying to get away long enough to send him a package. I still hadn't received a letter, and I half-wondered if they were just accepting the boxes I put together so they could resell the contents at a steep markup. But I couldn't bear to think that, so I would tell myself that, for that day, he was safe and well-fed, and that he had a friend with him. I couldn't fill in any more detail because I knew nothing good happened in the camps. And I knew he was too decent a man to rise up through them. So I reassured myself that he was well and would return when his sentence was up, even though I knew he was most likely already dead. It's possible to hold two entirely contradictory things in your mind, if you're motivated enough to do it.

The highlight of the day was when the pastry girl came. She brought a selection each day in case the pile of excrement wanted to have a party. She was nothing like any daughter I would have raised—we once spent more than an hour trying to catch a mouse before she conceded yes, we would have to poison it. But I enjoyed her company. She was one of the few people I saw who wasn't contemptible.

Annushka

I know she's protecting me by only talking about the mice. Because there might be trouble if anyone knew I told her things like how everyone fought like animals to get into the new apartments the German prisoners were building. I've heard they were sturdier, though I don't know if that's true.

My job gave me the right to a room in a communal apartment, but there were so many people and so few spaces that I ended up sleeping in the kitchen. It was nicer than you might think, because it was always warm. I felt like a bird with a little nest of blankets, surrounded by sheets hung from laundry lines instead of leaves from branches, high enough up in the trees that hungry little hands could never reach me.

Every day was much the same: get up well before sunrise, breakfast and morning prayers, take the metro to the bakery, work my shift, and go to sleep to the smell of whatever my apartment mates were making for supper. Except for the afternoons when they needed me to make deliveries. Dropping off pastries wasn't technically part of my job, but we were always shorthanded. There were too few people with functioning arms and legs to do all the work that needed to be done in Moscow. And I didn't really mind. It usually meant a few extra rubles in my pocket, which I could use to get some nutritious canned food to send Polya.

I rarely went into the customers' apartments. I didn't really want to see how they lived, not when I passed homeless children begging me for crumbs on the way there. I can only imagine what it must have been like in my village, when the Moscow bread factories had been ordered to mix in fillers because the wheat harvest fell short. I was never in serious danger as a bakery worker. The boss just accepted that everyone would skim off the top. I think she built it into her calculations of how much flour we would need. But when I couldn't get something, I'd stand in line to buy a loaf so I could hand out slices. No child should go hungry.

But I understand why everyone wanted to look away. They didn't seem like children anymore. Not just because there was so little flesh on their bones. They had gotten this far, which meant they were survivors, and who knew what they were prepared to do. My parents always took care of me, or tried, but I remembered that some homes became battlefields, everyone fighting for the last crumbs. You could hear it, the younger children wailing when the older ones took every morsel. Even the parents who didn't eat their babies sometimes went mad and smothered them. I wondered if Mrs. Liebowitz thought about any of that when she saw me. If she wondered whether everything human in me was gone. But she hadn't looked away, so I couldn't, no matter how much I suddenly understood why the city people had wanted to.

There was a building a few metro stops from mine where I often made deliveries. Beria owned an apartment there and rotated women through it. You're surprised I'd just say his name? He's not God. I assumed they were favorite mistresses because it was a nicer building than most. I don't know anything about the first few ladies. They never talked to me. But Diana Sergeyevna was different.

It was obvious she was desperately bored. I admired that. I would have been too frightened to be bored. She immediately saw through me and told me not to play stupid in front of her. We talked about all sorts of things: her parents and mine, her Vitya, my Petya, Polya, her son. She'd ask me what was in the papers, then ask me my opinion. I'm not sure anyone had done that before. I started wrapping newspapers around the wax paper the pastries came in so I could sneak her some information. She even trusted me enough to give me a little money to put together a box to send to Kolyma for her husband the next time I took a package for Polya, because she was sure she was being watched. That was dangerous for both of us, but I never considered saying no.

She was a fashionable Parisian with firm opinions on everything, including that there was no God—nothing like my mother. I still latched on to her and told her everything that was bothering me, even though there was nothing she could do about it.

I remember once she decided she was going to fix my hair. It was half out of the braid after I'd wormed my way into a particularly overcrowded car on the metro. I didn't care, but she insisted that I sit down while she rebraided it, French style. No one had brushed my hair since we'd been thrown out of our house, and I'd forgotten how soothing it could be. Then she added just a dot of rouge on each cheek. My mother would not have approved of that.

"Now the young men won't be able to look at anyone else," she said with a naughty smile.

"I've had my love," I said.

"You say that now," she countered. "But sooner or later, someone will catch your eye."

"I don't know about that."

"I know."

There were only two options if a girl like me wanted to marry. Be honest with what might be the wrong man and accept the consequences. Or live as strangers on intimate terms until one of us died. Neither appealed to me. But I didn't say that. I just thanked her for making my hair look so much better and walked home alone, like I always did.

I met Viktor Aleksandrovich when he stole my bread, which I'd bought to give to the street children. If I'd stopped to think, I wouldn't have chased him, but it had been a long day, made up of petty annoyances that I'd ignored until this one broke my composure. I thought about beating him with my grocery sack full of potatoes, until I got a good look at him. He was at least half starved. I'd intended that bread for the children, but I could hardly argue he didn't need it.

"That wasn't nice," I said. He looked confused, and I wondered if he didn't speak Russian. He looked like he could be Georgian or Armenian. Well, I wasn't getting the bread back, so it didn't really matter if he didn't understand what I was saying.

He turned away from me and vomited. That happens when a person who's been starved is allowed to eat too much at once. His jacket was filthy, but I rubbed his back anyway because it felt strange standing and doing nothing while someone got sick at my feet. He finally stopped heaving, but his shoulders kept shaking. It took me a moment to realize he was crying. Not a hardened criminal, then.

"I'm sorry," he said, and handed the remains of my bread back to me. He wouldn't meet my eyes.

"It was just bread," I said, and was surprised to hear myself say that. Bread is never a small matter. But what else could I say? "If you want to follow me, I'll make you some potatoes."

I didn't have a good reason for why I decided to do it. He reminded me a little of my father, though of course it wasn't the same man. I also don't know why he followed me. I could have led him straight to the militia, the ordinary police who dealt with crimes against individuals. Maybe the promise of food was worth the risk. Or maybe he was so disgusted with himself that he thought he deserved to be turned in.

"Wait here," I said when we got to the front steps. He looked too tired to take another step anyway. I went upstairs and cooked some potatoes with butter and milk. It was dark by the time I came back down. I'd never seen a man look more embarrassed, until I brought the food.

Hunger is stronger than shame.

The bowl was only about half-full, and I brought a small spoon, like you'd use for tea. "Eat it slowly, with this," I said. "Your body needs to learn how to eat again." He still ended up gulping it down, spoon or no spoon. "Now wait. I'm not punishing you. It'll hit you." And it did. I could tell. "I know a thing or two about this."

"Thank you," he said.

"You're welcome." I wrapped my sweater tighter against the cold and wondered what I should do next. I doubted he'd do well on the streets overnight, but bringing a stranger into my kitchen home was no small matter. "Who are you?"

I was shocked that he actually told me his story. If I'd been the type of person to turn him in, he'd have given me everything I needed to do that. But I wouldn't. And then he told me about his wife. I excused myself to go refill our glasses of tea.

It took me ten minutes to come back, mostly because I spent the first five staring at nothing and trying to calculate the odds that Diana's lost Vitya should stumble into my life. They were too small to calculate, which meant one of two things: it wasn't true, or God had laid our paths with His own hand. Maybe this was the reason I hadn't died when the bullet pierced my skull; I still had something good to do. I should have been overjoyed, but fear set in. I knew who controlled her life. To get involved was to tease death. So I prayed for the strength to do the right thing, and I refilled the glasses and invited him to rest in my little nest.

"If you can behave, you could sleep on the floor in the kitchen," I said. "But if you try to steal anything or hurt anyone, you'll be caught, and I'll be in trouble." He stared at me like I was crazy or playing a game with him. "I hope someone would do it for my father."

I found a bar of soap and a razor and told him to wash himself and shave as much hair as he could after the others had gone to bed. I shaved the parts of his head he couldn't reach. Everyone in those camps has lice, no matter how clean they might have been at home. There was no hope for his clothes, so I gave him a blanket to use for the night. He swaddled himself like an overgrown baby and laid next to the stove, which was still giving off some warmth from supper.

"I get up early," I said as I retired to my blanket home. "You can spend the day in my room. I'll try to get you some clothes. Now rest."

"Thank you," he said again. He sounded vaguely dazed. I really think he might have believed he was dreaming but was being polite just in case he wasn't.

I bought some old clothes in a secondhand shop. They were threadbare and too big, but free of lice.

"I feel like a prince," he said when he put on clean socks. I smiled, even though I felt a little like weeping at the thought that my parents might be this broken.

The building supervisor didn't like it. People were always inviting friends and relatives to sleep on any spot of floor that wasn't occupied, but most of them didn't look like they'd just gotten back from Hell.

"Your uncle's a smelly mongrel."

"He's had a hard time."

"I'll get a job," he promised her.

"And keep your hands to yourself," the woman added. Did she think we were lovers? He was more than old enough to be my father, though I suppose that doesn't always stop people.

"I'll get a job," he repeated to me after she left. "I'll pay you back."

"Don't worry about it now. Just get your strength back." Officially, you needed a permit to live and work in Moscow, but the construction crews were so desperate for men healthy enough to work that you didn't even have to pay the bosses to look the other way. I had no doubt he'd find a way to live, once he was healthy enough.

It was two days before I could see Diana again. I ran up the stairs, because I couldn't hold still long enough to find out if the elevator was working. I must have looked wild when I arrived, because she hurried me in and whispered, "What's wrong, chérie?"

"What did your Vitya look like?"

She was taken aback, but she described him. Average height, dark hair and eyes, more a Mediterranean than a Slav, from that gypsy blood. "Pudgy, the last time I saw him, but I imagine not after … everything."

I mostly told her the truth. I lied about the bread, though, and said he'd begged me for some. I didn't think she would understand, since she'd never been starved herself. I could tell she was trying to decide whether to believe me, but it wasn't a long struggle. And so we cooked up a plan to bring them together.

It wasn't as hard as you might think. The doorwoman watching Diana's building liked me, and I brought her rolls with seeds on top when I could get them. She believed I was good and, therefore, trusted me when I said my poor uncle was too. It was all off the books, because they needed someone to fix things before the Last Judgment, and I needed them to not look too closely at the documents Dima was going to forge.

Yes, I'd found my old friend from the orphanage again. He'd made a successful living by avoiding the draft and replacing Party documents people had burned when the Germans were marching on Moscow. I had no interest in joining his band of thieves, but I wasn't averse to doing business with them for someone who deserved help. It was toward the lighter end of the gray area, in my mind. You can't be too concerned about your company if you ever hope to get anything done in this world.

Diana

My first inclination when the girl told me she'd found my husband was to believe she'd turned informant. I studied her for a long moment and almost said I had no husband. But hope won out.

The next month passed at an even more glacial pace than usual as we arranged to get him into the building without arousing suspicion. And then I had to wait until the others had gotten accustomed to seeing the new handyman walking around. Finally, I lost patience waiting for something to break and jammed a fork down the drain. Then I fixed my hair and makeup and agonized over what dress to wear. Something becoming but not overtly sexual. It was ridiculous, trying on outfits to meet my own husband, but it let me put off deciding what I would say. When I'd settled on a light blue dress with a floral pattern, I called the doorwoman to send up the handyman. Then I made some tea and tried not to vomit.

When the knock came, I answered it without really deciding to. It felt as if fate had brought me to this moment, and there was no choice but to follow where it led. Which is absurd. We'd both taken any number of risks to get to this moment. We couldn't pretend there was no other choice.

I greeted him like a handyman, but in the exaggerated voice that was meant for the neighbors. He understood. At least, I hoped with all my heart that he understood.

I don't know if I would have recognized him if we'd passed on a Moscow street. He'd lost all of his excess fat and much of his muscle. His hair was gray and short, like it had been shaved not long ago. His cheeks were sunken and his eyes ... they were the same shape and color, but they no longer belonged to the same man.

He went to the sink and started working at getting the fork out. I watched and felt strangely like we were in a room filling with water, slowly rising to drown us.

"I had to have something, in case anyone came," I said as he struggled to get the fork out of the drain. He nodded but didn't speak. I said a few nothings and tried not to panic as I felt this one chance, this moment I'd dreamed of, slip further and further away. All those years that seemed like nothing when he was on the far edge of Siberia were back, long and deep like a trench.

"Why thank you, comrade, I have no idea how that got in there!" I chirped for the neighbors when he finally wrenched the fork out. "Let me get you a glass of tea for your work!"

"I'll need to wash up, madame."

I laid out the tea and some fruit and pastries. It felt ridiculous, immoral to have such things here while he'd been starving in a camp. But there was nothing else to do. I could imagine him, looking at the size of this place, noticing that I'd gotten plump and was wearing makeup and perfume, and concluding I'd happily betrayed him.

The only thing that gave me hope was how embarrassed he was. If he still cared about what he looked like in my eyes, then I wasn't hopelessly corrupted in his. He wiped his hands on his shirt, so as not to dirty a towel. He stuffed down one croissant—a "moon roll," as he'd always called it—and then forced himself not to take another. I could see him looking at the food and trying to master his hunger.

"Please eat," I said. "I wish I could feed you every day."

The silence stretched. I pulled out a cigarette and handed him one. He smoked with the same movements. That hadn't changed, but it just seemed to highlight everything that had. And then he asked the question I hadn't expected.

"Are you happy?"

The answer was simple: No. But what good could come from saying it? Knowing about my pain would only increase his. But to lie and say I was happy would rip out his heart. So, I didn't really answer.

"I've never loved anyone but you. But this is a dangerous game we're playing." There. I gave him the choice to leave. The Vitya I knew would never make that choice, but this one might.

"I endured ten years in the camps—"

"And now you're free!" I hadn't meant to yell. "Are you sure you want to risk that for ..." A used-up whore? A bloodsucking informant? A worthless mother who couldn't keep her own son faithful?

"You're the only reason I survived. You and Sasha."

I got up and stubbed my cigarette out in the sink. I couldn't turn around and face him, not knowing what our son had done. I tried to stand straight, but I could feel my shoulders starting to shake. He put his arms around me, and I could feel that he was shaking too. I leaned back against his chest. He turned me around and he kissed me, tentatively, like he wasn't sure he remembered how. We were both crying and then we were in the bedroom, still crying as we undid my dress and his belt.

It was all someone else's play, and we were acting out our assigned parts. There was no other possible end. We hurried about the work of sex before the moment burst like a soap bubble. Then, only after he rolled off me and was catching his breath, did we begin to explore each other's skin again. We were both crying as we touched each other, searching for the one we knew and loved buried in a decade of history.

"What happened?" I asked as I stroked a scar on the side of his abdomen. It looked like he'd had some kind of minor operation.

"Knife," he said quietly. "On the ship between the transit camp and the gold fields. The thieves were ... they were at the women prisoners.

I tried to stop them."

"That was very brave."

He shook his head. "I'm only brave when I can't think straight. It was pointless. They knew it would happen when they loaded us onto that boat. Loose, in the hull, like buttons in a jar. There was a partition between the men's and women's areas. I knew it wouldn't hold if anyone really wanted to break through. They must have known too. They just didn't care about the women getting hurt. About how many people died on the way. They just tossed the corpses in the harbor when we got there."

"You cared," I said.

"My caring never helped anybody much, did it?" He looked away. "Sometimes when I sleep, I think I hear them. All those people I couldn't help. The ones I had to denounce in my confession. I destroyed them."

"Those people were already marked for death," I said. "I've learned a thing or two about how they work."

"I wanted to protect you."

"You did. The only way you could. And you came back. That's the only thing that matters." I turned his head to face me. "Listen to me. You came back. I don't care what you had to do to survive. You're here, with me."

"I'll never leave again," he said. It was a lovely promise. We both knew he'd likely be powerless to keep it. But we made many promises like that.

When a few days passed and I didn't land in Beria's dungeon, I let myself believe I'd gotten away with it. It had seemed reasonably safe, since the idiot never visited unless it was the middle of the night. I wasn't sure if he had anyone watching my apartment during the day, but there was no way to be certain, except to risk getting caught.

The question was how to get away with it again. I never seriously contemplated not seeing Vitya anymore. If I were an unselfish woman, maybe I would have. He knew something about Beria, but not how much that monster loved to cause pain. I don't know if he was truly prepared to face that. I wasn't. If they came to arrest me, I'd throw myself out a window. I always kept one unlocked, in case the day came today. But I was going to risk it, if it let me see my love again.

And even if it would have been unselfish to set him free, it might have killed him. He was so sure that he was too old, too broken, or too corrupted. Every time he came to see me, he asked if he should take a shower. Even if it was first thing in the morning and he hadn't been doing sweaty work yet. I finally realized that he thought I could somehow still smell the camp on him.

My days finally had something to fill them. I spent hours working out ways to see my husband without the stranger I was fucking finding out. I couldn't see him often. I'd draw a playing card from a deck after he left, to avoid getting into a pattern. Ace, and I summoned him the next day. King, I waited almost two weeks. Could it keep us safe? I didn't know. But it felt like I was doing something.

The building manager gave him a small room, so he'd be available whenever the tenants needed repairs. But sometimes we went a week or longer with nothing more than a glimpse and a furtive smile as I walked to a waiting car. We couldn't risk anything more. And I would spend the rest of the day imagining conversations that might have been and how we would have lost ourselves in caresses if we were free.

I never hated Beria more than when he threw off an upcoming rendezvous. I was one day away from waiting out the king of spades, then he showed up and left me with a black eye and rope burns, all because Stalin had given someone else control of his beloved police. So I had to wait even longer. I could never let Vitya see me like that.

Maybe I should have been more concerned by a sign Beria could be losing favor. They had a habit of killing the mistresses of the men on top right alongside them, or at least that's the impression I'd gotten from overhearing him talking about others who'd fallen from grace. But I'd accepted my brains would soon be splattered either on the street below or on the walls of the Lubyanka. There's a strange clarity when you don't expect to wake up the next morning. I knew what I wanted, and that was as much time with my husband as possible.

I spent the time when I wasn't plotting ways to conceal our meetings coming up with interesting topics we could chase around for hours. For instance, how on earth did mankind develop vodka? Distilling is hardly intuitive, and it must have blinded quite a few drinkers along the way. His first response was that it was a gift from God, but then he played along. Debates like that let us lose ourselves in the present, kept the fear at bay after we'd made love and were lying there in bed.

He'd tell me little anecdotes that meant nothing, acting out the consternation of the drunken man who stumbled into the girl's corner of the kitchen, thinking it was the lavatory. I insisted that he tell me more about Ivan the Dyspeptic, and all the other things he'd made up to get me to laugh twenty years earlier. It wasn't that I wanted him to amuse me. I wanted him to remember the man he had been. I wanted to see that man again, just for a moment.

And anyway, we had to laugh. We couldn't reclaim the past. We had no future. I accepted that. But I was going to squeeze every second that I could out of the present.

They were never supposed to meet. Damn that vent.

For once, I hadn't sabotaged anything. I was wrapped up in a fur coat when the drunken idiot brigade arrived. They called the night watchman to get the handyman and then proceeded to get even drunker while I mentally implored Vitya to be anywhere else. Visiting the pastry girl. At a beer hall. In some strange woman's bed if it came to it. But he came up and started to work while Beria fondled me.

I was sitting on that monster's lap, in some flimsy thing that barely covered my privates. He stopped, and one of Beria's men pushed him, thinking he was just ogling. "You're not here for the show."

I suppose he cleaned the vents or did something to make the heat work while I pretended to be amused by these animals with their butterknife wits. He stopped again when the officer was showing him out. Beria was making some sort of joke about my barely covered breasts. I could see Vitya breathing heavily, and I tried to implore him with my eyes to keep moving, not to try to save me this time.

Beria finally noticed him. "Who are you?"

"I fixed the heat."

"Do you know who I am?"

"I've seen your picture in the papers."

"And you're looking at my woman?"

"I didn't think it would hurt anything. Sir." I knew it killed him to call Beria that.

"What do you think, Frenchie, should I let him look at you? Let him see what you can do?" He spread his legs and showed his thoroughly unimpressive erection. What they say about Georgian men must not be true, or at least it didn't apply to him.

I laughed and spoke in the girlish voice I only used when there was an audience. "I don't think he did that good a job on the vents."

He laughed. "Well said, my little whore." He tossed a few rubles in front of Vitya. I knew he didn't want to pick them up, but I tried to signal that he should. Even the slightest display of dignity wouldn't be tolerated. Vitya bent and picked them up. Beria laughed like it was the funniest thing he'd ever seen.

I really had thought that we would die that night, that my husband would attack and we'd both end up with bullets in our brains. The man I'd known couldn't have endured it. But he was different now.

That was the worst of all those nights. Not because Beria's cronies were especially sadistic. Most just wanted blowjobs or to fuck, and a few were so drunk they couldn't do anything more than crawl on top of me and grunt. No, it was the worst because I felt ashamed. I'd always known that I was only doing what I had to do to stay alive and that most women would do the same. But knowing that is one thing and defending it when your husband sees you playing the whore on the devil's lap is another. He'd known, yes, but now he'd seen.

It was only an hour before dawn when the last man rolled off me and out the door. I locked myself in, threw the fouled clothes in the corner of the wardrobe, cleaned my vagina with vinegar and turned the shower as hot as it would go. I scrubbed until my skin turned red. And I cried. I wouldn't cry, no matter how much they hurt me, but I cried that night. I wanted my husband that moment, but I also couldn't bear to ever face him again. When two contradictory feelings decide to crush you at the same time, you cry. There's nothing else to do.

The water turned cold, and I put on a nightgown. It had matched my eyes years ago, but most of the blue had faded out. I wrapped myself in a blanket and waited for the sun to rise.

Then he knocked. I answered. He had a hammer in his hand. It wasn't bloody. They must have all gone down in a group. If Beria had been alone, I had no doubt he would have struck.

I couldn't bear the thought of another man inside me again so soon, even a man I loved more than life, but I also couldn't say no. I would hate him for it for a while, yes, but I'd rather hate him than lose him. The girl I'd been wouldn't have understood that.

But we just laid in each other's arms on the bed, and he whispered about how he would take me away, where no one would hurt me again. It was a fairy tale, just like my mother's stories had been, but I let him weave it. I knew how those stories ended. But I let him lie, because I knew he needed it at least as much as I did.

A few days later, he came to see me. I hadn't drawn a playing card. He'd been kind enough not to make me talk about that night right after it happened, but I knew we would have to talk about it eventually, and I wanted more than anything to postpone that as long as possible.

"I need to tell you something," he said. I led him to the table and made tea. He took a deep breath. "I need to tell you why I stopped writing."

"I know you must have been exhausted," I said.

"That wasn't the reason, though." He shook his head. "I told you that Konstantin Fyodorovich was in the same prison."

"You did."

"I—I was so stupid. When we worked together, we always got the full ration at the end of the day. How much you got was based on how much gold you dug. I didn't know how we did it. I thought maybe having a friend to talk to made it that much easier.

"Then this one day, we were close to getting the full ration, but not quite there. He went to relieve himself, and I stayed with the gold to make sure no one took any. Then I heard him talking, the way you'd talk to a small child. There were some kids in the camp, but they got hard so quickly that they weren't kids anymore after a week. But he wasn't talking to them. He was talking to two men who were—what's the word?—they had flat noses and no idea what that place was all about. I saw him take out a little bit of bread. Just a crust. He gave it to them and took their gold.

"I said, 'Tell me you haven't done that before.' Because they couldn't understand about the ration system. Trading like that was killing them. He asked if I knew them. I didn't. And he said, why couldn't we kill them to save ourselves. That you weren't waiting to give me a medal for staying pure. That you weren't waiting for me at all. That you wouldn't want a bent old man who'd strained all his organs out of place."

I took his hand and kissed the knuckles.

"I didn't believe it, but I got angry. I hit him. He hit me back. The two men with the flat faces came over and were buzzing around, and we all ended up in the punishment cells. They were just holes in the ground. One of the men, he was scared to jump in. So the guard shot him. Didn't even bother to pick up the body. Just left him there. And then someone …" He shuddered. "I can't tell you that part. Those things happened, but I can't talk about it. I tried not to hear it, to think about you and Sasha, but I couldn't not hear it. I don't know how long it went on before someone shot him from the watchtower.

"They made me carry the bodies to the grave in the morning. They just threw everyone in a pit and let the rats have them until it was full and they covered it over. I couldn't get close to it without vomiting, even when there was nothing inside me.

"The boy—man—he reminded me of something. Something about my daughter. They looked nothing alike. But … after that other man had taken parts off him … there was something …" He shook his head. "You can imagine my friendship with Konstantin Fyodorovich was never the same. But I didn't want him to die." He looked at me like it was vitally important that I believe that.

"Of course you didn't," I said.

"We left the other man alone," he said. "I stole scraps to help us survive. I didn't know what he did. Assumed he also stole and was better at it."

I could see where this was going, but I nodded that he should continue.

"They said we'd be rewarded after we won the war, but they just brought in new prisoners. Some were Germans, some Russians who couldn't get out of Hitler's way fast enough, some even Red Army men who'd been captured. I never understood that, how they could imprison men who'd fought for them, but they did. And then there were the nationalists. I don't know if they were all nationalists when they started, but they hated all us Russians by the time they reached Kolyma. And they talked about it. They'd been wronged, and they wanted everyone to know it. And then they started disappearing.

Sometimes into the punishment cells. Sometimes into the graves. The guards weren't grabbing men at random. They knew who they wanted, who was stirring up trouble. There was an informer. I didn't think too much about who it was. I just kept quiet.

"The 'polite people' didn't mind. They were sort of in league with the guards. Both tormenting the politicals. But one of the new guards didn't know that and confiscated the cards and homemade betting chips from their hiding place. Then the thieves had to find the rat.

"I was trying to sleep. Konstantin Fyodorovich was somewhere. And suddenly a thief had his hands around my neck and dragged me onto the floor. The other thieves each held a man. They killed the first two when they said they didn't know who the rat was. Then their leader stopped in front of me. I couldn't get out of the chokehold, and no one was standing up to help me. So I told him it might be Konstantin Fyodorovich. I didn't really believe it was. I just thought maybe he'd be smart enough to talk our way out of this. So they took me and we went to find him. I really thought he was stealing or doing … something else."

I don't why he thought I'd be offended by the notion of someone performing fellatio for food.

"But he was just talking, in their office. It was him. And I'd gotten him killed."

"He got himself killed," I said.

"I could have named some stranger."

"It all would have ended the same."

"They just left him in the snow. I covered him up, up to the neck. Gave him a little dignity. I couldn't do anything else."

"No, you couldn't."

"And they … after that, they decided I'd work for them. I don't remember most of it. They somehow got samogon. Like vodka, but stronger, and it kills you if you make it wrong. I didn't want to do the things they made me do. But I had to survive. I had to come back. To you and Sasha. So I drank. So I wouldn't quite remember what I did.

"I don't know how long it went on. It might have gone on forever if they hadn't brought a shipment of women prisoners. The thieves played cards to decide who would own the women's barracks. I told the women to barricade themselves in. Then I threw a cigarette in the samogon shed and blew it to the sky. To buy the ladies some time. No one saw me, but the leader somehow knew. They beat me, then had the guards assign me to the hardest work. I don't know why the guards took their preferences so seriously. To ensure the thieves wouldn't turn their knives on them while they slept, I guess.

"I couldn't work. Not really. I was shaking too much. I'd taken beatings before and never felt like that, but I guess it must have just been the way they hit me."

I had a pretty good idea why he was shaking, based on my time with the artists, but I didn't want to sound accusatory. He'd always prided himself on not letting his drinking get out of hand.

"It would have killed me, fast. The work and the bare minimum ration. The new doctor agreed. Said they couldn't get anything more out of me. I was close to dying. They said Moscow wanted a lower death rate that quarter, so they just took me and the others and dumped us in town.

"It had been ten years since I'd seen a town. I felt like a visitor from another planet. I found a step and sat down. I didn't beg, not with words. That would have invited the militia to take me. One kid—" He laughed. "One little boy pointed at me. Like kids do. He said, 'Mama, what's wrong with that man?' The mother grabbed his hand as if he'd been about to burn himself. 'That's not a man. That's a prisoner.' I didn't really disagree with her.

"There was no help, so I stole garbage to eat. But I could never fill my stomach, not when I had to rest after walking only a few blocks. I needed food, real food. So I found a rock, broke a store window, and took some cans. Not many. Just a few. I went down to the railway station, found a bit of metal, and opened the first can of meat. I rested and waited for a westbound train, where I could sneak into a baggage car. And that's how I came back. I'm sure the girl's told you the rest." I nodded. "So you have absolutely nothing to be ashamed of, before me. I've done ten times worse than you could even dream of doing. You'd be right if you threw me away."

He looked at me, waiting for my response. "I told you I didn't care how you managed to survive," I said.

"Yes. But you didn't know how bad it was. How bad I was."

"None of it matters," I said, and tried to make myself believe it. I don't mean that it mattered to me, but it mattered to him. It's so unfair, that bad men can do anything and feel perfectly fine about themselves, and good men drive themselves mad with remorse for doing only what they had to. But this world never was fair.

I spent the long nights of that winter trying to tell Vitya the truth about Sasha without actually telling him. Have you ever done that? When you know a person simply must accept the truth, but that truth is too bitter in your mouth? So you sweeten it enough to get it out, and hope he hears what you can't say. But men never do.

We agreed that the time was not yet right to tell him his father had returned. What I couldn't say was that I feared the time would never be right. Still, I promised to break something so he could see our son when he came home for the New Year holiday.

I regretted that promise almost immediately. It was the first morning Sasha was back, and I had yanked the kitchen faucet loose so Vitya could listen while we talked at the table. We were already arguing by the time he arrived. I suppose it was my fault, but I couldn't smile and nod when my son said he was joining the police. The people who'd tortured his father, who let that monster imprison me, who'd killed how many others for no reason at all.

"I thought flying was the goal."

"Goals change, Mother."

"You wanted to serve the country from the time you were a little boy—"

"Well, I'm not a little boy anymore, Mother. And anybody can learn to fly a plane. Only the best can serve the country this way. Your friend chose me specifically."

My jailer, my rapist, my horror. How could he be so blind? Because it suited him to be. It's always that way. He wanted to be an important man, and the people who could make that happen tortured his father and raped his mother. So his father was guilty and his mother was just a loose woman. "You know he isn't my friend."

"I don't care if you sleep with him. Just don't lecture me about him."

"Men like that sent your father to prison."

"Do we have to go over this again?"

"Is that what you want to be?"

"There's no reasoning with you." He grabbed his coat.

"Where are you going?"

"For a cigarette!"

"You can smoke here."

"Too much hot air!"

He slammed the door. Vitya put his arms around me.

"He's gotten worse," I said.

"Just give him time. I've waited ten years. I can wait a little longer."

Vitya followed Sasha down and somehow talked him into meeting "his niece." He said it was an excuse for us to chaperone them and spend more time together, but I think he really hoped they might like each other.

She stopped by at the end of her shift to deliver a cake so she'd have an excuse to leave if she wanted. I actually thought she might, after all that talk about having had her love. But she was still so young, so much younger than she seemed to think she was.

I knew it was hopeless within an hour. When he talked about his devotion to the Party, she answered in kind, but in her stupid voice, like a slow child repeating an answer that's been drilled into her head. Sasha didn't notice. Most men wouldn't. His father was rare in his respect for female intelligence.

"He isn't right for her," I said to Vitya when Sasha had left to walk her to the metro station.

"They got along beautifully."

"Because they didn't talk about anything that mattered."

"There's time."

"Just don't set too much hope on it." He said he wouldn't, but I knew he already had. He was imagining a little family, that she would somehow reach Sasha in the way he believed she'd reached him and started to pull him out of the shadow of the camps. We would replace her lost parents, and everything would be perfect.

Somewhere along the way, he'd developed an optimism that produced visions of the future bearing only the slightest resemblance to realistic possibilities. But how could I blame him for that? How else would a person survive the camps, where the realistic options were death by a bullet, starvation, or typhus? And we had no future, but we were not yet dead, so we had to live somehow.

The next time I saw the pastry girl, I asked her how she liked my son. She blushed and looked away.

"I like him," she said, and I knew that meant she liked his dark hair and broad shoulders, "but I'd be a bad wife for a policeman." I shrugged my agreement. "But … it doesn't hurt anything to see him when he's in Moscow? As a friend?"

I should have warned her off, told her that getting close to my son would be the worst mistake of her young life. But I couldn't bring myself to believe he'd hurt such an innocent little lamb. Maybe Vitya and I are more alike than I like to believe.

Annushka

I told myself I was humoring Vitya, and that I'd had my one great love in this lifetime. But I think I secretly hoped this boy would sweep me off my feet and make me forget how many people I'd lost.

He was handsome. He should be, with such a beautiful mother. I never saw Vitya in his prime, but I suspect he was a good-looking man too. I know a handsome face and a sturdy frame mean very little, and I knew it even then. But no matter how many times I told myself I was resigned to living and dying a spinster, that little hope was still there, ready to attach itself to the next handsome man I met.

I could have refused to meet him, if I'd really wanted to. But it seemed so right, marrying into Vitya and Diana's family, that I had myself prepared to fall in love with almost anyone.

When I stepped back and thought objectively, I knew we couldn't ever succeed as a couple. When we spoke, I reflexively fell back into my stupid persona. The fact that his mother was so intelligent, but he didn't think he was wasting his time with a girl who claimed to have no idea we were blockading Berlin, should have told me everything. He was one of them, through and through, even preparing for a career in the police.

But I went to see him again. Yes, because he was handsome. But also, because the rest of it felt right, sitting there at Diana's table and seeing Vitya so happy. I knew it would never come to anything, but it can be nice to imagine an alternate life, where my great love wasn't taken from me and I was part of a family. It felt like a game at the time, playing house until he went back to his life and I went back to mine. It was foolish. There's no way around that. But we can all be fools sometimes.

Diana

It was a terrible idea to see each other while the young people were at the May Day parade, but we'd had nothing but terrible ideas for a while, so it didn't stop us. I pretended to have a headache, for Sasha's benefit, and Vitya agreed to look after me while our son's class and the bakers' unit marched. Then they'd come back for dessert.

"First time in history a woman faked a headache so she could sleep with her husband," I said.

We didn't immediately jump into bed, though. The building was so still. We had to be sure everyone was gone before we dared make any sound above a whisper.

"We could run away," he said, as quietly as he could. "Leave a note or find them later."

I shook my head. "Where would we run?"

"Siberia?"

"Siberia?"

"No one would look for us there."

"You think a person can just leave the head of the police?"

"You said he didn't love you."

"Of course he doesn't love me. He owns me. I'm alive because I've never challenged that."

That sat a moment. He finally spoke. "We could make it. All four of us."

"He wouldn't come." I said it gently, like I was telling a child his dog had died.

"Someday he will."

I touched his face gently. It was useless to try to make him see reason. "Let's not argue, my love. I want to go to bed." We crawled into the sheets.

People always think the best sex of your life is when you're young, trim, fueled by reproductive drive, and too stupid to think twice. But for me, those stolen moments with my handyman husband were the closest thing to perfection this side of Heaven. Who cared what our bodies looked like, if we'd probably be dead by morning? We were older, more tired, yes, but we wanted to move slowly. Each moment had to last a lifetime.

I started off on top, sweeping forward and back so our chests and stomachs brushed. That any part of our flesh should not be touching seemed like a sinful waste of nerve endings. He pulled me down, trapping me to his chest, and rolled me over, then kissed along my jawline up to my ear. I moaned, because it felt good and because I knew it would make him hard, and I squeezed my thighs around his hips. I'm thankful that, after everything, I could still go wet and tingle between my legs with the only man I love.

I wish the gas stove had been leaking and we'd just died there.

But he came home.

Sasha pulled Viktor off me and beat him. I tried to grab his arm, but he shook me off.

"He wasn't hurting me!"

"You whore!"

"He's your father!" He stopped. The only sound was Vitya trying to breathe. I was the first one to remember how to move. I brought my husband his trousers. "He came back from the camps. To find us."

"And you let him back in."

"He wasn't guilty. You know he wasn't."

"Mother!"

"I love him, Sasha. That's all."

He pulled Vitya to his feet and grabbed his head so they were only inches apart. "If you ever come near my mother again, I'll make sure they splatter your brains on the cellar stairs," he whispered. "You understand?" And he pulled his hands away, like his father was covered in filth. "Get out."

I wrapped myself in a robe and sat down at the kitchen table. Sasha stood by the counter.

"You've put me in an impossible position, Mother," he said.

"I didn't mean for you to see me sleeping with your father."

"No, you just meant to lie to me. That girl's uncle. Did you have to pay her off to string me along?"

"Leave her out of it. This is you, me, and your father."

"My father is a traitor. And you're just as bad for protecting him."

"You know that isn't true."

"I have to report this!"

"No, you don't. The only other people who know won't dare to tell. No one would ever know."

"I have a duty."

"What about your duty to the parents who raised you?"

"He didn't raise me."

"He didn't choose to leave." He scoffed. "I did raise you, and I'm telling you now, if you betray him, I will be dead by the next morning."

"Don't be dramatic, Mother."

"Dramatic? My only son is going to send his father to his death, and you say I'm dramatic?" I lit a cigarette and took a few drags to calm myself before speaking again. "They will come for me if you report him. And I will kill myself before going to their dungeons. You know what they are, even if you won't admit it." He didn't respond. "I can't stop you. But is it worth it, betraying both your parents so they'll let you into their club?" Maybe I should have kept the disdain out of my voice, but I couldn't. "I promised myself I'd never lie to you. And this is the truth. Do with it what you want."

He started to argue with me again, but I showed him the door. I'd said everything I could say. You can't control what people will do, not even your own children. Before he left, I turned his face to look at me. I tried to find my little boy, who'd wrestled on the floor with his papa. I didn't find him in that young man's hard eyes. So I let my hand fall from his cheek and watched him go.

I knew my son had betrayed us when a stranger came to deliver pastries.

I asked her what had happened to the girl with the brown braid. She didn't know. Of course, no one did.

I paced for hours. My fingers kept finding their way deep into my hair. I had to light a cigarette so I wouldn't rip it out. I smoked one, then another, then another, until the saucer was overflowing with ashes. Beria didn't come that night. I wished I believed in God so I could pray and feel like I was doing something to protect her.

I mentioned that the pastry girl had gone missing when he returned for the next party. No one cared enough to even ask what she looked like.

Except his driver.

The driver kept a list of Beria's women. It had hundreds of names, addresses and telephone numbers. Why? I don't know. Maybe the boss liked having a way to summon submissive females any time the mood struck. Or he just took pride in how many pelvises he'd bruised. But whatever his reasons were, the driver had all the evidence if he ever got the opportunity to use it. And he asked me if I knew her name.

I told him. He nodded. I felt as if he'd punched me in the lungs.

"She's smart," he whispered, while the others cracked open another bottle of vodka.

The Silence that Remains

"What do you mean?"

"Because she left town after her first … interrogation." I tried not to shudder. "No one knew where she'd gone when they came to take her in formally." He looked at me. "You don't know where she'd go."

"No."

"No." He met my eyes, and we understood each other. He'd find a use for that list when the time was right.

***

Going from having no allies to having one is like being stuck in a pit, only to glimpse a narrow outcropping where you might grab hold, too high for you to reach. It doesn't do you any good at the moment, but it gives you hope that something might change for the better.

Beria was too powerful for nonentities like me or his driver to challenge. But that could change. Why, just then, the heroes of the Battle of Leningrad were being killed, so they couldn't distract from the top hero. Beria could be disposable, too, under the right circumstances.

It did cross my mind that, when important men fall, their followers go with them. I hoped my cooperation would be enough to save my son, even though I couldn't stand to look at him. I wrote him a vague letter, telling him to be no one's disciple but Stalin's. I had no faith he'd listen to me. It was August, and I hadn't seen him or heard from him since May. But in this particular case, I don't blame him for not listening. After all, I was preparing to denounce his patron to save myself.

I had had some time to think about how it might play out that summer. Beria had gone to Kazakhstan on some project no one would breathe a word about. I figured it out, though. No one would launch an invasion from Kazakhstan, and if they'd been building labor camps or slaughtering the locals, they would have talked about it. They were building something to match the bombs the Americans dropped on Japan.

Of course, I wanted us to be able to stop the Americans from flattening Moscow. But I also hoped Beria would fail, so they would kill him. Maybe they could lose patience, kill him, and send someone else to finish the job. That would be ideal.

I thought about running, as the girl had done. But she was an anonymous, one-time amusement for him—not worth pursuing. I'd benefited from his riches, and he'd make me pay. Maybe it's a sign that I really believed that trash, that they were omniscient, even as I scoffed at their stupidity. I never doubted they would track me down and destroy Vitya in the bargain. Or that our son would help them, if asked.

My hopes came to nothing. A mushroom cloud rose over the steppes. He'd done it, or rather, the scientists had done it under his threats of death.

This didn't discourage me as much as you might expect. Yes, he was in relative favor, for now. He wouldn't be finished in one blow. But he was always only a few mistakes from death. They all were. They knew it, too, but they were so intoxicated by power that they couldn't do the sensible thing, which would be to plead ill health and retire to some backwater. It could have been a Greek tragedy, if they didn't so thoroughly deserve what they would get.

Annushka

We'd gone to the May Day parade while Vitya and Diana stayed behind. We were almost there when Sasha pulled me aside and suggested that after we marched, we find a hotel instead of going back to his mother's apartment for cake. He was so close that his hips brushed my belly. I'd never been that close to a man, except when I'd held Petya as he died. Part of me liked it and part of me didn't, and it was too much to sort out right there, when I was supposed to be taking my position behind the bakers' banner. All I could come up with was to buy time.

"Your parents are expecting us," I said, and I heard the fatal mistake as soon as it slipped my lips. My only hope was that he was too preoccupied with his flesh to notice it. But no. And I wasn't a good enough liar on the spot to brush it off convincingly.

"Who are you?" he demanded.

"Just Annushka," I said.

Vitya never told me exactly what happened after Sasha stormed away. I only knew things had gone badly wrong when I saw the seedy men in spotless uniforms lurking around Diana's apartment. It wasn't the time for detailed explanations. She gave me some money, and I ran to get him a ticket and a bag for the few things he owned.

"You have to go now," I told him.

"Where? Why?"

"Because it's dangerous here."

"I have to see my wife."

"They're watching her apartment. More than usual. They searched me when I came to deliver baguettes. The only reason they haven't arrested you is that they don't know to."

He was frozen. I touched his shoulder.

"I told her where your train would go," I said. "She'll find you when she's free. But you have to go. Now."

He hugged me and kissed my head. "Take care of yourself, child. And take care of her."

Vitya's train was going to Norilsk, a city that no one in their right mind would flee to. It's the northernmost city in the world and sits atop a gigantic nickel deposit. (I knew this because of a newsreel before a film I'd gone to see with Polya.) There would be work there, and no one would be inclined to question a man mad enough to sign up for it.

I'd hoped that would be the end of it. But then the police showed up at my nest. And I knew Sasha had told them about me.

I remember thinking that the Lubyanka would seem like a nice building if you didn't know what it was. I wondered who decided to keep painting the bricks yellow, over and over, so it would look more like a university building than a prison. I don't know why I thought about that. Maybe it was easier than thinking about what was sure to happen next.

I went over the list of things I would not do. I wouldn't stop trying to help Polya—well, that was a lost cause. I couldn't even help myself at that point. I wouldn't deny God, but it seemed unlikely they'd demand it, since my case wasn't overtly religious. And I wouldn't denounce anyone. That would be the difficult part. When they put me in an empty room, I prayed over and over for the strength to resist.

But my interrogation wasn't much. A young officer, who would have been handsome if he'd been a better person, asked me if I'd harbored a returning traitor. I said I hadn't done so knowingly. I played stupid and said the man looked just like my uncle, and I had no idea where he'd gone. It was a flimsy story that he could have pulled apart. But he didn't. He just left me there in the room, unhurt. I hoped that it was a miracle, the answer to my prayers, but something in the pit of my stomach told me it wasn't.

The young officer came back and told me to follow him. I kept my eyes on the floor because it seemed the safest thing. We went up the stairs, to the biggest office. And there was Diana's jailer, waiting for me. He didn't ask any questions.

I don't want to talk about what he did to me. I felt so dirty, as if he'd chewed me up and spat me out. The most humiliating part was the flowers at the end. I didn't want to take them. The man who'd taken down my information insisted. "Take them if you want to live."

I did, but I threw them under the metro train that would take me home. I packed only the things I could carry. They'd released me that time, but they would be back. I was sure.

I went to Dima to buy false papers. "I need to get away from here," was all I said.

He took my picture and assigned me a new name. Anna Georgievna Popova. "Just tell everyone to call you Annushka, and you'll have no problem," he said. "You'll have to give me your real one to destroy. No quicker way to be arrested than getting caught with two sets of papers."

Dima was really very good at forging papers. I knew no one would realize it was a fake. Still, it felt wrong, looking down at my face next to a stranger's name. I reluctantly handed over the only proof Anastasia Heorgiyevna Kolisnychenko had ever existed.

"Where are you heading?" he asked. "Back to Kharkiv?"

I shook my head. "No. If they wanted to look for me, that would be the first place they'd try."

"Then where?"

"I don't know."

I took the first train east. The further east, the more they needed workers and the fewer questions they'd ask. I got off in Chelyabinsk because it seemed as good a choice as anywhere. There was a bread factory, and it needed workers.

I didn't really get to know anyone during my few months there. I wasn't quite used to being a fugitive with forged papers, and friendships seemed risky. Every day, while I worked my shift, I planned what I would do if I had to run again. I assumed the underground life was taking a toll on me: I was so tired, and often too nauseous to eat.

It was only when I noticed it was getting harder to close the bottom button of my dress, the one below my navel, that I put together what it meant.

I'd always thought I might like to raise a child, but I assumed it was impossible. Petya was dead. I didn't dare trust some other man with my story, and without trust, there can't be real love. I'd expected to die a withered virgin, like a plant that had never flowered.

It was illegal to get rid of a baby then, though that never stopped anyone. I thought about it. It seemed kinder than sending him to an orphanage, if he reminded me so much of that man that I couldn't bear to raise him. But I decided not to do that. I decided to pretend instead. That when this child someday asked about his or her father, I would lie and describe everything I had loved about Petya. I'd know it was a lie, of course, but I thought it might be comforting anyway, to pretend that something remained out of everyone I'd lost. Diana had told me she used to do something like that, pretend that the camps weren't so terrible, knowing full well they were worse than she could imagine. Sometimes the truth is too much.

Notebook of Viktor Aleksandrovich Chekhov

21 August, 1949

My dear Diya,

I know I can't risk sending you these letters, but I'm writing them anyway. So you know I've never stopped thinking of you. And maybe you'll find them interesting when we're together again.

Hopefully when we're together again, it won't be in Norilsk. My mind is always far away, with you, but I can tell you wouldn't like it here. The air tastes bad and stings the throat even more than in Moscow. And there's the camp. I can't relax, knowing it's there, even though I'm on the other side of the fence. But there's nothing to do about it.

I live in the free workers' barracks now. Most of them started on the other side of the fence and had nowhere else to go when they got out. We work next to the prisoners in the nickel mine. We don't talk about any of it much. We don't talk about anything much. There's a lot of grunting. That's fine with me.

1 September, 1949

My dear Diya,

You'd never guess who I ran into. Literally. I almost put a pickax through his skull when I tripped on him. I said something nasty, like he'd picked a hell of a place to take a nap. But I could see he was sick, so I tried to move him out of the way, where nobody else would fall over him. Then he said, "typhus corner." And I knew it was my old friend, Grisha (the doctor from my camp). No idea how he came to be in the mines.

I told the guards he was too sick to work, and they had me carry him out to the camp infirmary. Lazy bastards. But I did it, even though it meant going back through that fence. I told him to drag himself to work the next morning. The camp doctor couldn't save him.

A guard stopped me on the way toward the gate. I got on my knees. I was sure he'd shoot me. Another one looked up from his card game long enough to say he'd seen me walk in. That was all. Nothing really happened. But I still vomited as soon as I got out of the gates. And I thought good and hard about whether to take the risk. You and Sasha have to come first. He's probably dying anyway. But having bread in your pocket isn't a crime. If another man steals it from there, that's just a thing that happens. There's no harm in that, is there, Diya?

Annushka

My worries expanded with my waistline. Little Petya or Polya—it hadn't taken long to decide on names—was starting to kick, reminding me that I was carrying a person, not just an idea of one. No one had come looking for me, as far as I knew, but that didn't mean no one ever would. And even if they didn't, it was entirely possible that I could someday be arrested for something completely unrelated, or just because someone needed to fill a quota. Diana had told me about how they gave policemen quotas, like factory workers, and that they weren't picky about how they filled them.

I wanted to go back to Diana, but I couldn't, and every other woman I trusted was dead or in a labor camp. So I went to the only person who owed me a favor, and who I believed was good enough to actually follow through with it. If anything happened to me, my son would be safe with him.

Norilsk was a mining camp first, and it mushroomed as prisoners completed their sentences and were transferred outside the fence.

Petersburg has its white nights, when the sun barely dips below the horizon at the height of summer. In Norilsk, the best you can hope for is yellowish nights, because of the strange smoke the refinery belches continuously. The snow was gray, and the air bit with something worse than cold on the night when I arrived. This is not a good place to raise a child, I thought, but the simple fact was that I had no other options.

I felt as if everyone was looking at me when I disembarked from the train. Maybe they were. I don't think I saw another woman anywhere in that station.

I spent the night on a bench, waiting for someone to open the information stall in the morning. When I woke, the clock said eight, but I had no idea if it was eight in the morning or the night, since the sun wasn't going to rise again for weeks. It turned out it was eight in the morning, and soon, an old man who'd evidently survived a bad case of smallpox opened the window. I pushed myself up to sitting and grabbed my small bag.

"I'm looking for a man named Viktor Aleksandrovich Chekhov," I said as cheerfully as I could.

"Prisoner? You'll never see him, little girl."

"No, a free worker."

"Oh, that's different." He checked his directory. "No listing. Must be in the barracks."

He wrote me clear directions about which bus to take, for how many stops, and where to duck in if anything went wrong. He impressed on me, over and over, that I could die if I were caught outside, particularly in what was starting to seem like an inadequate coat and hat. I thanked him repeatedly. I could see I was going to need every friendly stranger I could find.

I hadn't thought about what to tell Vitya. Just getting there was enough to worry about.

He almost crushed me in his arms when he saw me. Then he seemed to notice my belly, which wasn't so obvious under my coat, and almost crushed me again. Then he hustled me into the barracks and insisted I sit by the stove. The other men were all looking at me. Some lustfully, some curiously, like Vitya had brought in a pet monkey.

"How are you? What brings you here? Are you hungry? Did Sasha let you travel all this way by yourself? You must be freezing. Would you like some tea? Has anyone seen the samovar? It's so good to see you! Are you planning to stay long?"

"Damn it, Vitya, let her answer one!" someone yelled.

Did Sasha let me travel on my own? "I'm planning to stay, if you'll help me get settled."

"Of course I will. I'll need to have some words with my son, though, letting you travel all this way alone."

"Please don't."

"It isn't right, especially with you having his baby." Some of the men groaned.

I started crying. I should have just told the truth then, but I was so tired and hungry, and the truth was so bitter, I couldn't stop sobbing long enough to get it out. He wrapped me up in his arms again and stroked my hair until I shushed.

"Don't worry," he said. "I'm not really cross. Don't worry about a thing. I'll take care of everything. This is wonderful."

I hadn't meant to lie. I'd assumed he understood my relationship with Sasha, what it was and what it wasn't. And the fact that I was in Norilsk should have told him that something had gone terribly wrong. But he was overjoyed at the prospect of a grandchild. And I kept quiet.

When you don't confess something like that right away, you never can. Well, you can, but every passing day makes it harder and harder until it seems impossible. So I persuaded myself it was right. Vitya would get the grandchild his son would never allow him to love. My child would have a better chance at survival with two adults looking out for him. And I would be safe, protected from the other men by someone who considered me part of his family. Everyone would get what they needed. But I don't deny that it was cowardly and selfish.

Notebook of
Viktor Aleksandrovich Chekhov

30 November, 1949

My dear Diya,

I wish I could send this letter, to tell you our daughter-in-law arrived safely. Though I have some things to say to our son about letting his wife travel all this way alone. Especially with her pregnant.

I've taken to stopping at the store for regular workers on the way home. Usually there's nothing worth buying, but I never know when there will be something fattening for my prisoner friend. The clerk sometimes keeps something back. I like him. We trade jokes. So I thought he was setting up a joke when he said a woman had been looking for me and he'd sent her to the barracks. Once I believed him, I ran there without even thinking about food. I was sure it would be you, though of course I was happy to see her.

She's crying a lot. I think some of it's being tired from the trip. But pregnant women don't really need a reason to cry, do they?

I told the other men I'd kill them slowly if anyone lays a hand on her. So that's taken care of.

Finding a home was harder. There isn't any decent housing. Only Party members are expected to have families in a town like this. The only option I've found is an old dugout near the mines that one of the early workers must have used before there were barracks. I'm going to have to chase out the rats, but it has an old stove I can probably get working again. I've started grabbing broken shipping crates so I can make furniture. It's not much, but I think it will do. You always wanted a home with no neighbors, didn't you?

I hope you've told our son he'd better marry that sweet girl whenever he follows her out here. I'm going to. He'll never do any better than her.

Annushka

My son was born early, in the middle of a snowstorm. It was January, and he wasn't supposed to come until February. But there's no arguing with these things. Vitya and I were both home, because the visibility was poor enough that the buses weren't running. We had just finished setting up the shipping crate cradle when I felt the first spasm in my abdomen. I laid down and hoped it would pass, and it did, but then it came back, cycling over and over. Pain, relief, pain, relief, pain, relief.

Neither of us really knew what to do. Getting to the hospital was out of the question—we might make it alive if we walked just the right way, but it's more likely we'd get lost and freeze to death on the tundra. So Vitya followed the rope that connected our door to the gates of the camp. It was a precaution in case a storm blew in while he was underground. The workers could follow the rope from the mine to the camp, then the free ones could turn off and follow it to the barracks or to our dugout. Sometimes we had dozens of them sleeping on the floor because it wasn't safe to go any further.

I waited for what was probably a few hours, certain that Vitya was dead in a snowbank and that the baby and I would be stuck in this in-between space forever. But then he was back, with a guard and a prisoner following him.

"This is my friend, Dr. Bogomolov," he said.

He was half starved and looked more in need of help than able to give it. But he was alert enough to ask how far apart the pains were, so they must have fed him recently. I hadn't been keeping track, so the guard, who said to call him Misha, timed them on his watch. Six minutes.

"Could still be hours," Dr. Bogomolov said to the men, probably thinking I was too distracted to notice. "Better hope this storm lets up so you can get her to the hospital. There's nothing I can do if something goes wrong. I haven't delivered a baby since medical school. And unless you want me to cut her with a kitchen knife—"

"I can hear you!" I shouted.

"Sorry, sorry."

"Maybe you should sit down and rest," Vitya suggested.

"I don't think there's any harm if she wants to walk," the doctor said slowly. "Though—"

"Don't say it," I cut in. "Don't say anything."

"Alright, alright, we'll all shut up," Misha said. And they did, mostly. Vitya followed me as I paced the room, over and over. To catch me if I collapsed, I suppose. Misha kept calling out the times. Five minutes, then four, then three. The doctor would step outside periodically to assess the weather, then would come back and tell me to drink some tea, or to try to urinate or move my bowels. Any other time, I would have been embarrassed to try to relieve myself in front of three men, even though they turned their backs like gentlemen. But the longer it went on, the more irrelevant they became.

"We're not getting to the hospital," I said to the doctor when he came back, grim-faced, after Misha had counted only two minutes between pains.

"You're doing fine," he said. "It won't be much longer."

I think I heard the men talking about how there was no need to keep time anymore, discussing just how much blood was normal, and assigning each other new jobs. I didn't care what they said. I tried to pray but kept getting distracted with each new pain. After a while, Vitya and Misha held me up while the doctor sat at my feet to catch the baby. Maybe someone told me to push, or maybe the command came from somewhere inside.

And then it was done. I was surprised to see how small my son was when the doctor held him up. He hadn't felt small for all those hours. They did end up using a kitchen knife, to cut the cord, after sterilizing the blade as best they could. No one was quite sure what to do with the afterbirth—throwing bloody tissue out in the snow might attract bears. They must have sorted something out, but I didn't notice. Once they'd washed my baby and laid him on my chest, I didn't care about anything else. And suddenly they didn't seem like prisoners and guards and miners. Everyone around me seemed like an angel, sent to comfort me and ensure my baby would be safe.

"That's the hormones," the doctor said. "They make the milk come in."

"That's wonderful," I said, and snuggled little Petya against my breast, so we'd both be ready whenever his first meal came. He looked up at me with those big, grayish eyes, and I sobbed without really knowing why. He didn't seem to mind.

Notebook of
Viktor Aleksandrovich Chekhov

---

17 January, 1950

My dear Diya,

We have our first grandson, Pyotr Aleksandrovich Chekhov. He wasn't supposed to come for a few weeks, but I guess he got impatient. Decided to come in the middle of a blizzard. Fearless little bugger.

I thought for sure she was dying, with all that blood. But Grisha says that's just the way it is. Glad they told me to stay in the waiting room while you had Sasha. Wouldn't want to see that twice in a lifetime. She's doing fine, resting and nursing him.

I'll give Petya a kiss for you. He's perfect. Hopefully you'll see him for yourself soon.

Annushka

My son was so beautiful it took me a few months to realize something was wrong. I wore him in a sling on my chest to work, since there was nowhere to put him, and I nursed him during my breaks. He would fall asleep after a few minutes and fuss when I had to wake him to try to get him to keep feeding. One of the other bakers had a baby about a month after I did, and her boy was plumping up like a little cherub while mine had barely filled up his newborn wrinkles. Hers walked at eleven months, and mine was still crawling listlessly at one year.

He was always sick, with a runny nose and eyes. He was always fussing, like he was in some pain I couldn't see. His belly swelled, even though he took so little milk. He never made sounds like babies do, and he evidently didn't hear much, because he didn't respond to my voice when he couldn't see me.

I kept praying that he would outgrow some of it—the deafness was most likely there to stay—but he kept falling farther and farther behind babies his age. Some of the other bakers talked, when they thought I couldn't hear, about how he wouldn't last long. At first, I thought I was the worst mother God had ever unleashed upon a child, but gradually, I realized that even if I was, it didn't explain all of my son's suffering.

There isn't much medical care for the in-between people in Norilsk. There's a nice-enough clinic for the Party leaders and "responsible workers," and the prisoners have their infirmary where they go to die. The hospital will take anyone in an emergency, but if you're not bleeding all over their floors, you need to bring a gift to get a doctor's attention. All I had was bread. All of my pay went to feeding myself and sending boxes of matzah to my friend (who no doubt wondered who Anna Popova was but wasn't inclined to point out the mistake). Vitya's job supported him and bought some extra bread for his doctor friend. We had a few rubles at the end of the month, but it would have taken years to save up enough for a decent bribe.

That's the advantage of prison labor—it only costs a bottle of vodka and a few packs of cigarettes for the guards.

Dr. Bogomolov looked worse than he had at the birth a year earlier. His gums were bloody and swollen, and he moved as if every muscle and bone hurt. Vitya had been giving him all the bread he could spare, but bread can only keep a person alive for so long if he isn't getting any other nutrition. Still, he looked like he was trying to listen sympathetically as I detailed my son's symptoms.

"Vitya, could you ask the infirmary to lend a stethoscope?" he said suddenly. "I'll need one."

"Is it his heart? His lungs?" I asked after Vitya had gone.

"No. Get him to open his mouth." He turned to Misha, the guard. "Do you have a light?" He shone it on my son's baby teeth, then shut it off. "That's it."

"What?" I couldn't imagine what he saw in Petya's mouth.

"He's got notches on his teeth. That's syphilis. I didn't want Vitya to hear this way that his beloved daughter-in-law was whoring around—"

Misha hit him on the side of the head, just hard enough to make a point. "Don't talk like that, you piece of shit." Then he turned to me. "Don't worry, everybody here has it. Pretty girl like you will still have your pick." This did not help, but I didn't tell him that.

"Will he die?" I asked.

The doctor looked surprised. What else could he have thought would matter to me? "He'll probably live a shortened life. How much shorter, I don't know."

"Is there anything that would help him?"

"There's a drug that might help. Salvarsan. But it wouldn't undo what's already been done."

"Then I'll get salvarsan."

"Here?" He gestured around. "Maybe if you were someone important."

"I don't care. I'll find a way."

"Hmm."

"What hmm?"

"I guess I thought you'd send him away. Since he'll never be right. Especially since you're going to have to explain—"

"I don't care what anyone thinks. I don't care what I have to explain. He's my son. Don't you understand that?" I had to stop for a moment, because I was choking.

My son had started to fuss, so I picked him up and rocked him. I couldn't sing to him until I calmed down, so I hummed. I knew he couldn't hear me, but the vibrations in my chest seemed to soothe him. The doctor was looking at me like I was conducting some strange ritual from a foreign religion. Once Petya had drifted off to sleep, I could finally speak. "I suppose no one would consider that it might have been his father's fault."

I don't know if he believed me or if he just didn't want to tell Vitya that one of two people he loved had betrayed the other. He said my son had an infection but only talked about it in the vaguest terms. It was important to take precautions and wash his hands after cleaning my son's runny nose or touching his other bodily fluids. Anyone who got this infection needed to be careful not to let their blood or mucus get on things other people would touch or eat. I knew that warning was for me. There was a drug that might help, but it would take time to get it.

"It's no one's fault," he said. "These things just happen sometimes." He looked straight in my eyes as he said it, and I wondered what kind of implicit bargain we were making, and what this lie might cost me. I had said I didn't care what anyone thought, but that wasn't true. I didn't want Vitya to hate me. Because he reminded me of my father. But also because I needed his paycheck, as well as mine, if I was ever going to buy this salvarsan. And the doctor knew both of those things, or could guess them. Whatever the cost was, I'd have no choice but to pay it.

Notebook of
Viktor Aleksandrovich Chekhov

---

1 May, 1951

My dear Diya,

Happy May day, my love. I realized I haven't written a letter for you in over a month. Maybe there's not much point, since you'll read them all at once. But still.

We're starting to get good at sign language. I can't remember if I told you the dynamite man has been teaching us. Petya watches us. I can't tell if he understands that we're talking to him yet.

Every day is about the same. We get up early. She wraps him up in a blanket and goes to the bakery. I go to the mines. We work, we come home, I keep him busy while she makes dinner. Then we sleep. I'm always tired. But maybe that's good. Sometimes my dreams are bad. I see terrible things happening to you. If I wasn't so tired, I wouldn't sleep. But exhaustion makes me. And it's good to be needed. I think I'd lose my mind if I didn't have something important to do while I'm waiting for you to come back to me.

Annushka

It takes time to make connections in a place like Norilsk, but it can be done.

The first step was to make friends with as many of the other bakers as possible, so they wouldn't want to knife me in the back if step two succeeded. It wasn't all that hard. Everyone had either been exiled or followed a man who was in the camp. Not that it was a perfect sisterhood, but we looked out for one another, walking in groups so that it was harder to attack a woman on her own and covering for each other when a child was sick.

I brought in things I'd baked at home to share with the others until someone said I should really be working on the made-to-order side. There were fewer important people in Norilsk than in Moscow, but there were some, and they had birthdays and holiday parties too. I acted like I'd never given the idea any thought, but now that Katya had mentioned it, perhaps I would see if they had an opening.

The job officially paid the same, but you know how the world works. The person who bakes bread that goes on sale for the whole city never gets a tip, but the person who makes a cake for the family that can afford to buy it does. That was step two, moving into a job that would let me build up savings faster. It also won my son a coveted spot in the new kindergarten for free workers, meaning he received at least one well-balanced meal for free each workday. I appeased the other bakers by watching their children on my breaks and stealing sweets to share.

Even with the extra money, though, I knew I'd need to take step three. I had no idea what salvarsan might cost, let alone how big a bribe I'd need to convince a doctor to divert some to my son. If Misha was even close to right about how pervasive syphilis was, surely there would be many bidders for each chance at a cure. So I started trying to endear myself to anyone who might someday be able to do me a favor.

My best hope was Mrs. Shakmakova, the camp commandant's wife. I don't know if I've ever met another woman who was free and well-fed, yet as unhappy as she was. Every time she felt a twinge of pain, she was sure it was cancer and that she would die like her mother had. I don't think her husband was very sympathetic—at least, she said he wasn't. She sought solace in baked goods, which was better than alcohol or morphine. I listened patiently and tried to make myself believe I was genuinely concerned about her well-being. But I was a mercenary friend, just waiting for the moment when this connection might help.

It was through her that I met Dr. Grossman. Mrs. Shakmatova wanted to send her a bread basket, to see if it would hasten her next appointment. I connived to deliver it myself.

Dr. Natalia Abramovna Grossman was a little woman with graying hair, and every time I saw her, she looked exhausted. She wasn't a prisoner, but you'd be forgiven if you thought she was. She walked like a prisoner, plodding her way through the wards.

She was going to call an orderly when I brought the basket. I clung to it.

"If you take a look and tell me what you like, I can make the next basket special for you," I said.

She raised one eyebrow and half smiled, probably at the idea of being bribed with bread. But she let me into her office for a moment. "What do you want?"

I'd had some pleasantries and flattery lined up, but clearly, she wasn't in the mood. "Salvarsan. My husband ... was not loyal. And now my son is sick. I don't care if you don't have it for me. Just if you can get it for him. He's so small, it can't take much. I'll pay whatever you want."

"Salvarsan." She leaned forward. "How do you know that's what your son needs?"

"A prison doctor told me." I wasn't sure how she'd feel about that, but I didn't have a lie ready.

"That explains why he's so far behind the times. Salvarsan is out. There's something new, without all the risk of toxicity. Penicillin. Heard of it?" I shook my head. "Truly a miracle."

"So you don't have it in Norilsk."

"You catch on quickly."

"Couldn't you still give him salvarsan? It would still work, wouldn't it?"

"Not an option for a child. It's tricky enough to treat an adult without poisoning him. I'm sorry."

I took a breath. "What would it take to bring penicillin here?"

"Someone with connections higher up would have to pull the strings. Not you, and not me. So you can keep your bread."

"It's not mine. Mrs. Shakmatova sent it." She sighed at the name. "Would she be important enough to get something like that?"

"Her husband might be. But you're wasting your time if you think you can just ask nicely or convince her with bread."

"She's more of a pastry person anyway."

She snorted. "You can try anything you want. But don't bring me into it. And don't bother bringing me gifts again."

"There's nothing you want?"

"There's nothing to buy here with whatever money you bring. I like bread, but I can get it myself. So unless you can bring me a basket full of qualified doctors and nurses, no, there's nothing." She sighed and seemed to soften a bit. "I could take your money and give you some false hope. But I won't. Take care of your son. Love him while you can.

Maybe someday, we'll have penicillin here ..." She trailed off. "People can't move mountains, child."

"Then I'll have to find a way around."

Notebook of Viktor Aleksandrovich Chekhov

12 October, 1951

My dear Diya,

I wish you were here. I always wish you were here, but especially when I need advice. What do you do when someone gives up?

Maybe that doesn't sound like such a bad problem. But you weren't in the camps. You didn't see the difference it made. People gave up and then they died. It usually didn't take very long. You have to have some hope to hold on for. I had you and Sasha, so I could endure anything. It must be hard for a man with no family. I promised him a grand feast when he's released, with one of our daughter-in-law's cakes. He smiled like it was a nice thought, the way a palace on the moon might be nice.

If it were just any stranger, it wouldn't matter. But Grisha making me a feldsher gave me a chance to survive. I was paying him back, bringing down the bread for him. It's helped. But now he's giving up. Told me there was no sense in me wasting my money trying to save someone with a twenty-five-year sentence. It's been five or six years, depending on when you start counting. And he's sure that even if I keep him from starving, he'll freeze to death, get typhus, or be shot or beaten to death. He said to me, "If somebody survives this camp, it's an accident." He actually said that.

I thought about just washing my hands of him. If he's determined not to live, what can I do? I could put the money from that bread toward my grandson. But it's not a small thing, to let a man curl up and die. Not one who helped you.

Silly to write this to you. He'll be better or dead by the time you arrive. But it makes me feel close to you, writing. Too bad I can't hear your answers.

All of my love,
Vitya

Annushka

I suppose I could say that I was acting from entirely pure motives when I hinted to Mrs. Shakmakova that the understaffed hospital could be bolstered with a good doctor who was stuck behind the fence because of a misunderstanding. But I haven't lied so far in what I've told you.

I couldn't bring Dr. Grossman a basket of qualified people, but I was confident I could deliver one, and that might be enough to put my son at the top of the list, should she ever get an order of this penicillin. (I hadn't figured out how to trick Mrs. Shakmakova into ordering that.) It seemed like the best sort of influence trading: my son might be cured, Dr. Grossman would get the help she needed, Dr. Bogomolov would no longer be wasting away in a mine, and the other patients might do better with one more doctor to take care of them. Who loses there?

It was at least unkind to prey on Mrs. Shakmakova's fears, but she wasn't the sort of woman who would take up a prisoner's cause if there was nothing in it for her. She couldn't have stayed married to the commandant if she were. The idea that the hospital might not be absolutely ready when she inevitably needed it was horrifying to her, and she badgered her husband into releasing Dr. Bogomolov.

I was ashamed of my machinations, though, when Vitya helped him back to our dugout on the day of his release. The hospital was where he belonged, but not as an employee. "We'd better tell Dr. Grossman there's been a delay," I said to Vitya.

"I can work," the doctor insisted after collapsing onto one of the crates we used as chairs. "Tell me where to go, and I'll work."

I thought of those people who fled to Kharkiv, insisting they could earn their bread until their hearts gave out. I wanted to push that memory far away, but there it was, sitting in front of me and catching its breath. "Yes, of course, but you'll need a bath and some rest first."

Vitya filled the discarded basin we used as a tub and laid out his good set of clothes, which he never wore down into the mines. I wrapped the camp clothes into a bundle and hung them outside to let any bugs in them freeze to death. The doctor did his best to scrub off the worst of the dirt, and my son glanced over at this new person in his world, then decided the change wasn't important enough to stop rolling the crude toy car Vitya had made from scraps.

"When did they last do the shaving?" I asked with my back turned, because I didn't want to assess his body hair for myself.

"About a week ago."

"So not much for lice to hide in?"

"No, not much."

I'd hoped never to see a grown man less than fully clothed again, but I did have to make an exception in this case. I waited until I heard him working the belt on Vitya's trousers before turning around.

"Will those clothes work?" I asked, because I didn't want him to know I was trying to calculate his odds of survival. He pulled the shirt on as quickly as possible, but not before I saw that his belly was bloated and his arms were spindly. "Yes, looks like they will, for now." I knelt down and checked his feet, which were also bloated. "Don't think we have any shoes that will fit. You'll have to wear the camp boots, once they're clean."

When people swell up, it's not good, but it's better than just wasting away. He could still bathe and dress himself, though slowly, which meant both that he had a bit of strength and that his skin wasn't too fragile to endure scrubbing and rough fabric.

Not like the boy whose belly was weeping yellow tears.

I tried to push that boy out of my mind. The person in front of me was not hopeless. He'd even turned his back to get dressed, so something more than animal instincts remained. Perhaps he might be ready to work in only a few weeks, if I was careful about scaling up how much he could eat at once. I'm ashamed to admit it, but what I thought was: this could still work.

Then the fever hit.

I shouldn't have been surprised. Malnourished people can't fight off infections, and some little bug can take them out just as they seem about to recover their strength.

I had to keep waking up in the earliest hours for work, so I tried to give him something to eat every few hours when I was home and hoped he slept while I was at the bakery. It was almost like my son's first year, except I was caring for two people, and the other women didn't understand my exhaustion. Vitya helped, of course, since his shift started a few hours after mine, but he'd never seen anyone brought back from the edge. I'd seen it a few times, and seen the best efforts fail far too often. It was December 1951, and I didn't expect the doctor to see 1952. I started to think about how I would explain it to my son. Though he was so young that he might not make anything of it, especially if I didn't let him see the body.

Petya did notice something was different, though, and didn't understand why the stranger was getting so much attention. "He is sick," I signed. "We must take care of sick people."

The thought occasionally crossed my mind that my plan had failed completely, and that we were worse off than before, trying to keep an incapacitated adult alive. I didn't let myself think about that for long.

I suppose "I will not use other people and abandon them when they no longer serve me" was not one of my rules, but it should have been. I never thought I'd be tempted to do that, but I also never thought I'd be a mother to a sick child.

A few days in, the doctor startled awake as I sponged his forehead. "Hold still," I said. "You need to rest, comrade."

"Grigori," he murmured. "My name is Grigori Nikolaievich. Nikolai the tsar."

"Mmm, is that so?" I hummed a bit to soothe him, and he fell back to sleep.

A few days later, the fever broke. His eyes lost their glassy sheen, though he still didn't leave the bed. He was a bit like a baby, waking and sleeping unpredictably. Occasionally, I'd notice him watching me. Sometimes he half-smiled when I sang to my son. Sometimes I saw the animal in all of us, ready to rip the bread I was cutting from my hands.

Not that he could have, at that moment. When he could stay awake for more than ten minutes at a time, he tried to get up, but his legs wouldn't work to raise him. "Stay there, comrade, I'll bring the porridge," I said.

"You could call me Grigori Nikolaievich, if you want. I don't know if I said that."

"You did, but you also said you got your patronymic from the tsar."

"Did I?" He rubbed his face. "Well, it did come from him, but he wasn't my father. Obviously. Everyone in the orphanage had the same patronymic. Until the revolution, when they switched from everyone being the tsar's children to everyone being Lenin's."

The word 'orphanage' interested me in spite of myself. My son was happily playing with his wooden car, so I sat on the floor beside the mattress while Grigori Nikolaievich ate the porridge. "What happened to them?" I finally asked. "Your parents," I added, when he looked at me blankly.

"Oh. I never knew them. I was only a few days old when someone left me with the church. My mother, I guess, unless she died in the birth."

"I can't imagine what it would be like, giving up a child," I said. Which isn't true. I could imagine it, but I didn't want to, because it's like imagining your heart being ripped out of your chest.

He shrugged. "Must not have been too bad. She never came back, even after the revolution. Didn't even leave a note. But maybe she couldn't read."

"No one would leave their child like it was nothing," I said, feeling some strange protective anger for this woman I knew nothing about. "She could have died. Or she couldn't come back. You couldn't bring a child back to a village, no matter what the laws said. She probably saved your life." At the edge of my village, there was a well no one used. They called it the children's well, and I overheard people talking about how babies used to go down and never come back. I lived in mortal terror of falling down that well and being lost forever, because I didn't yet understand that an adult might harm a child on purpose.

He started coughing again, and I couldn't be angry anymore. I rubbed his back until the fit subsided.

"Rest, Grigori Nikolaievich," I said.

A week or so later, he was walking a few meters, mostly to relieve himself outside. "What do you want me to do?" he asked while I made supper.

"If you feel strong enough, you could set the table," I said, gesturing with my head toward the plain earthenware plates next to the stove. "If not, I'll do it."

He got up and carried the plates to the table, then sat down to rest again. "I meant, what do you want from me? I can't help your son."

"I know that." I shook my head. "I don't want anything from you."

"Then why? What are our terms?"

"Dr. Grossman needed help. You needed to get out of the mines. Everyone gets what they need." I could feel him looking at me. "And it helps to have friends."

"You'll get something too."

"Yes."

"Your son will be first in line for treatment."

"I hope so."

"Hmm." I could tell he was tabulating whether that in some way reduced his debt to me and how that weighed against my debt to him for keeping the nature of Petya's illness a secret. He said almost nothing for the rest of the evening, but that wasn't unusual. I kept up the conversation, and Vitya had no hint that anything was amiss.

The next morning, he got up while I was preparing for my shift.

"People don't die if no one wipes the sweat off their faces," he whispered.

"You're still dreaming," I said, though I checked his forehead all the same. It was cool.

"You promised this doctor you'd get her another doctor. As long as I don't die, you get what you want."

"What are you getting at?"

"It didn't matter if I was comfortable, so long as I don't die. Not to her. But you wiped off the sweat yourself. You sang."

"Yes."

"Why?"

"Maybe I don't like seeing people in pain. Maybe I felt guilty."

"Guilty? Why?"

"I helped you to get something for myself. For my son."

"Still got me out of the mine. No sin there." Our eyes met, just for an instant, before he quickly looked at the floor. "You must be a very good person. I see now why you're so important to Vitya."

"I'm not as good as you think I am."

"Better than his son deserves anyway," he said, and I felt a chill come over me.

"Don't ever say that. Not around him."

"I won't. I won't ever say anything that would hurt you."

"I believe you," I said, even though I wasn't sure if I did. Not because he was any different from anyone else. Because he was probably the same, and gratitude doesn't mean anything when people have to choose between protecting you and getting what they want. I'd learned that lesson well.

1952-1955

Notebook of
Viktor Aleksandrovich Chekhov

18 Feb., 1952

My dear Diya,

I now have two people fussing over me. Annushka fusses over everyone, and you know how doctors are, always thinking every sniffle is the beginning of the end.

I'm fine, though. Just a little cough, maybe a little tiredness. It might be a touch of influenza, but I don't think so. Probably just a miner's cough. I'll put a wet rag over my face when I go down, and it'll be alright.

I hope by this time next year, they're fussing over both of us.

All my love,
Vitya

Annushka

Dr. Grossman had put Dr. Bogomolov to work in the infectious disease ward. I don't know if that was where she most needed help, or if it was a small favor to me, putting him in the position where it would be easiest to steal a vial of penicillin, should any ever come.

It had taken until February to get him healthy enough to work. Which was long enough that my son went from asking why this person was here to wondering where he'd gone when he moved into the hospital. There wasn't any decent housing to spare, so staff who didn't have families lived in rooms that were probably supposed to be broom closets.

He rapidly developed a habit of turning up at meal times, though at least he brought something. The hospital had a cafeteria, where the doctors could eat for a pittance. As far as I could tell, he paid, loaded his plate until someone told him to stop, ate what he couldn't easily carry, and brought the rest. I usually didn't mind, though it became an inconvenience when my son wasn't well, which was happening more and more often.

"You make the best potatoes," Grigori Nikolaievich said, which was not true. They were just pan-fried on the stove with diced onion, sunflower oil, and a little salt. But everything tastes the best when you're recovering from malnutrition. "You have to show me how."

"But you don't have a kitchen."

"Hmm. I'd still like to learn." That's part of it, too, the obsession with food. Not just eating it, but buying and preparing it. Who knows if I would be a baker if I hadn't survived what I did? "If you don't mind. Maybe I could be helpful."

I wasn't really in a position to alienate an ally, particularly when he at least thought he was being helpful. The first time, I put him at the stove with strict instructions to keep stirring so nothing burned or stuck to the pan. Then I got busy with other things and almost forgot about him until I saw him grab the stove pipe for support. "Sit," I said. "I'll handle it from here."

He sat and buried his face in his hands. "I'm sorry."

"Don't be."

"I thought I could … I'm not getting better."

"You are. It's just slow." I left the potatoes for a moment and took one hand, without really thinking about it. "Look, your fingers were like sausages when you got out. Now they're alright." He was still a bit puffy, but if you didn't know, you'd assume he drank too much. "Your body's still trying to rebuild itself. Once it's done, then you'll get your strength back."

"How do you know about this?"

"A person picks up things," I evaded.

"You could tell me the truth, if you want."

I didn't want. "There's nothing to tell. Are you feeling steady enough to chop the onions?"

He chopped quietly for a few minutes. "I'd given myself up for dead, you know. I knew how it happened. I'd been a camp doctor."

"Vitya told me."

"Yes. So I knew how it goes. When your heart starts fluttering, the end is close. Then you saved me."

"I didn't—"

"You did." He coughed. "Dr. Grossman says salvarsan is out."

"She told me that too."

"That's bad. Not the new drug—that's the best thing in medicine since I've been alive, if it does what she says. But there are things you need connections to get, and things you need a bribe to get. I think this is both."

"If someone important enough got sick, could you pad the order? And just … lose those extra vials?"

"That's called theft of state property."

"That's called daily living," I snapped.

"A person could go back behind the fence for that. I can't risk that. I was going to die there. I would die if they put me back in the mine."

"I'm not asking you to die," I said wearily. "But … there must be something. I can't just stand by while my son gets sicker and sicker. We have to think of something."

"We will," he said, though without much conviction.

We didn't say much of anything to each other over supper. My son ate well, for once, but Vitya didn't, which was unusual. Miners always have an appetite.

"Just not hungry tonight," he said with a shrug when I asked, then coughed into his sleeve.

Grigori Nikolaievich gave me a glance that I couldn't quite read. "That'll probably be better in a few days, but if not, come see me. I can always squeeze you into the clinic."

Vitya waved him off. "Not necessary, not necessary. I'm as healthy as I ever was. Just not hungry tonight."

"Of course," Grigori Nikolaievich answered, no more convincingly than when he agreed we'd save my son.

I was cooking sausage on a rare day in April when I could let my son out without his tiny fur coat and hat. It was so unseasonably warm for Norilsk that the snow and the top layer of the earth had turned into a deep brown quagmire, which I didn't doubt my son was at least knee-deep in. "Wipe your boots," I said and turned to sign when I heard the door open.

Grigori Nikolaievich dutifully attempted to scrape off the mud on the door sill. He held out a loaf of bread—maybe one I had just baked for sale this morning. I took it and set it on the table.

"I wanted to talk to you." He gave up on cleaning the boots and left them at the door.

"Alright, but I have to keep making supper."

He started quietly, barely audible over the hissing of the grease. "I want to tell you something I've never told anyone." I looked over my shoulder. He had his eyes trained on the floor, like he was confessing to it. "I was an informant. At the university. It wasn't something I really planned. This was in '34, right after Kirov was killed. Do you remember?"

I had some memory of the Party boss for Petersburg being shot by a nobody, black crepe being hung everywhere, and everyone having to act as if their favorite uncle had been killed. I remembered being angry, but not being able to explain why, even to myself. "I think so," I said, keeping my own eyes fixed on the sausages, "though I was pretty young."

"You probably don't understand, but the city hadn't mourned like that since Lenin died. We all wondered if there were more men with guns, lurking all over, ready to kill us or hand us over to the fascists. Well, not all. The boy—man—I was paired with for dissections, he laughed at the rest of us. Yura. His father was someone important, so he never did much, except talk and play around with the organs.

"Anyway, after Comrade Kirov died, he decided he was going to prove how much more worldly he was than the rest of us. 'Don't you know the old fox in the Kremlin arranged it all,' he said. He was accusing Comrade Stalin of murder."

Whoever could believe that, I thought, but I didn't say it. I made some little sound to indicate I heard.

"I'd always ignored what he said. But that was too much. What if someone believed him? So I went to the political instructor. I thought he might think I was being silly or telling tales. But he didn't. They expelled Yura. He hadn't done any work anyway. And the political instructor said I'd done a service to the country. Some people he knew asked me to listen. Just listen and tell them if I heard any counterrevolutionary talk. They gave me a little money for the trouble." I could feel eyes on my back—he was gauging my reaction. I didn't turn to meet his gaze. "I never told them much of anything. Just suggested they could pull a few people aside and do some education about why making jokes about our leaders was harmful. But now you know, and you can do whatever you want with that."

"What would I do?" I finally turned.

"I've never told Vitya. I don't know if he'd have forgiven what I actually did, but I doubt he'd forgive me holding that secret for this long." He sighed. "He's the only friend I've got, Annushka, and you can take that away, if you want to. So you don't have to be afraid of me. Not that anyone would listen to a denunciation from someone convicted of terrorism."

"What is it you want?"

"I don't know. Not …" He blushed and made some embarrassed gesture, which I took to mean, "not sex." "I just don't want you to be afraid of me."

I could tell that what he really wanted was for me to like him. Orphanage kids can be that way. Either they push everyone away or they cling to everyone. Sometimes they cling until they push people away. They can be the most loyal friends you'll ever find, though, if you can handle their quirks.

"I know about starvation because it happened in my village," I said, and I could feel something cementing between us. "But I can't talk about it now, not when I have to look happy for my son. Don't make me, Grigori Nikolaievich."

"Grisha. Please, call me Grisha."

Diana

If I could have asked our great leader one question, it would be whether he believed any of it.

An elderly doctor had spoken a little too frankly about Stalin's health in a bugged office, was beaten into naming co-conspirators (what the conspiracy was, I don't know), and died when they overestimated what his heart could handle. Then someone said the new head of the police, Abakumov, had him killed on purpose to cover up his own crimes. As if people didn't die of "heart paralysis" in their custody at least once a month. And then Abakumov was arrested and accused of some Zionist conspiracy, never mind that his conscience hadn't troubled him when he was pulling out old Jewish men's teeth.

That particular doctor had somehow escaped arrest when they'd rounded up the members of the Jewish Anti-Fascist Committee back in 1949. Most of them were artists of some sort, though they had a few scientists in their ranks. During the war, they drummed up support among the Jewish communities in the West to send equipment and eventually, their boys. But now they weren't needed anymore, and those contacts abroad became a sign of treason. They finally went on trial in spring 1952, after most of them were so broken they would have admitted anything.

The whole case never made any sense. The central defendant, Solomon Lozovsky from the foreign information bureau, pointed out that if he'd wanted to overthrow the state, he probably could have found better co-conspirators than a few actors and poets. I suppose by that point, no one believed the lie that they'd be spared if they confessed. The whole charade was so embarrassingly bad that the judge tried to send the case back for further investigation. That had never been done, not in any trial that mattered to Stalin.

It didn't matter what Lozovsky said, though. There's only one possible verdict in the Soviet Union. They shot thirteen of the fifteen that went to trial. One was already in a coma because of a stroke. They sent a scientist into exile, maybe just in case her research on keeping geriatrics alive ever came to anything.

I understood why they killed people close to the top. Couldn't have them getting any ideas they didn't need the old man, though I think most of them were so cowed they wouldn't get rid of their worn-out shoes without direct orders. And of course, ordinary people like my father and Vitya had always gotten swept up when the great went to war on themselves. But why bother putting poets and doctors at the center of a show trial?

I hoped he believed it, though. Because the alternative was worse. If the defendants' only crime was being Jewish, I could be put on trial as easily as anyone else. So could Sasha, for that matter, even though he'd used the right to have "Russian" printed as his nationality on his passport. (Apparently his disdain for his father didn't stop him from claiming the parts of his heritage he found useful.)

Beria was against that trial. He was a monster in so many ways, but somehow also managed to be one of the few near the top of government who wasn't an anti-Semite. (Only a handful, really, if you didn't count the ones who were Jews themselves or married to Jewish women.) Though I don't doubt that if it had been his responsibility, he wouldn't have raised any objections to killing them all. He certainly didn't do anything to stop it when they started jailing more and more Jewish doctors that fall.

"Be glad you're not a Jew, dearie," he said to me one night after playing his games. He was the sort of man who said "dearie" as an insult. Was he warning me to hide it, or had he just never cared to look at my passport? Either seemed possible.

"Why? Are the fascists back?"

"Don't be stupid. The fascists are all dead."

I knew that wasn't true. Some of them had helped him build the bomb. "Oh, that's wonderful."

"Yes, yes, but it's a bad time to be a Jew. Stalin will have them all killed."

"Why?"

He shrugged. "Too cosmopolitan?" But he said it as if the answer didn't really matter, and I suppose it didn't. You might as well ask why tsunamis happen; the answer would be just about as useful for someone in the way.

Notebook of
Viktor Aleksandrovich Chekhov

30 May, 1952

My dear Diya,

It almost feels like there's a conspiracy in this house. Grigori Nikolaievich comes over for supper before I get back from the mines and whispers with Annushka, then shuts up and looks away as soon as he sees me come in.

I know Annushka isn't capable of anything underhanded. But Grigori Nikolaievich? Maybe. I wouldn't have thought so. I hope not. But he is a lonely man.

My cough hasn't gone away, but it isn't getting worse. Maybe it's not the same cough. Now little Petya has it. Maybe we keep passing it back and forth. Annushka never seems to catch it, though.

But don't worry, love. I'm sure nothing is really wrong.

Vitya

Annushka

I finally harassed Vitya into seeing a doctor when he'd been coughing for months. He'd lost weight but kept insisting he wasn't hungry.

"It's nothing," he said.

"If it's nothing, that's what the doctor will say," I countered. "Indulge me. Anyway, it's just Grisha. We don't even have to bring a gift."

He came back more irritated than worried. "Grigori Nikolaievich insisted on taking a radiograph," he said. "Can you see lungs on a radiograph? I thought it was just bones."

"I suppose they must be able to," I shrugged.

The next evening, Grisha came. He wouldn't look at either of us. "I'm sorry."

"How bad can it be?" Vitya said with a good impression of humor. "I worked in the mines all day."

"I'm impressed," Grisha said quietly. "I truly am. Most men couldn't have kept going this long."

"Am I dying?" Vitya asked. He said it so lightly that it was clear he didn't think the answer could be yes. I'm sure the whole conversation had already played out in his head: *Oh no, of course you're not dying, we just need to …*

That wasn't what Grisha said. "I don't know. It's a serious disease. But some people live a long time. You've always been strong. Your body might beat it back." He sounded like he didn't believe it but wanted to.

"What is it?"

"You see, the radiograph showed scarring—"

"Damn it, just spit it out!"

"Tuberculosis." It felt like he'd pronounced some magic word, bringing down a curse. "I'm sorry."

"That's not possible. I'm not that sick. Tell him, Annushka."

What could I say? The truth was that he was sick, and I knew enough to worry but not much more. "Are you sure?" I asked.

"I asked the radiologist to look at it again three times. The scarring is there. That and the skin test. I'm so sorry, Vitya." Vitya just buried his head in his hands. "We have a treatment for it. Sometimes it works. I've seen it. If you pack up tonight, we can start tomorrow."

"Pack up?"

"Yes. We have to treat you at the hospital. I'm sorry. I truly am."

"I have to work."

"You can't." He shook his head. "You can't be down in the mine, everybody breathing everybody else's air. Or here." The air in the dugout suddenly felt oppressively stuffy. "Please, Vitya. Don't make me go to them. Please, just come. Let me try to heal you. The sooner we start, the better. Please."

There wasn't much to pack: just some clothes, a toothbrush, a comb, a razor. Petya and I waved goodbye from the other side of the room, which felt like some kind of charade. We'd been breathing the same air for years.

Grisha dashed off a note excusing me from work the next day. "You'll need to bring the boy too," he said. "Just to be sure. You're probably alright. Most people never know they have it."

Tuberculosis bacteria spread like dandelion spores but only take root if the soil is prepared for them by other diseases or starvation. I knew that they'd think my son's lungs were the finest black earth in the world. I didn't want to know it, but I did, even before the radiograph.

"When can I see the picture, Mama?" my son signed to me, because

I'd told him he had to stand very still so the doctors could get a picture of his insides.

"They have to develop the film first," I signed, forcing myself to smile even though I wanted to start screaming. Hadn't my little boy been through enough already? He'd been sick since the day he was born, then God sent this? Why give such a good, beautiful, brilliant child, only to take him away?

"The good news is that your lungs look fine," Grisha told me the next day. "Let me know if you start coughing or losing weight. Until then, you can work and go wherever you want."

"Is he dying?" I asked, because I didn't care about my radiograph.

Grisha sighed. "Not immediately."

"But he will."

"He might have a chance with only one disease to fight. From what I'm reading, it sounds like penicillin doesn't work on the bacteria that cause tuberculosis. But if we could knock out the other …" He trailed off. "I can try to adjust the treatment for a child. But I don't know where we'll put him. There's no infectious disease ward for children."

"Can't he stay with me?"

"You're already exposed, so he can't make it worse. But what about your work? You have to keep bread on the table. And he can't go to the nursery."

"Could I leave him with Vitya while I'm working?"

"There's a risk. I can forget to put him on the isolation list, and no one's going to notice that. But if somebody noticed you slipping him in and out of that ward and decided to report it, we'd have to lock him there with the others."

"Then what do you suggest?"

We agreed I would leave him at the hospital. He'd sleep while Grisha did early morning rounds, then they'd find some way of coexisting in his office. I wasn't terribly optimistic about the arrangement when I first handed my son off, because Grisha took the bundle of blankets as if I were handing him a bomb. But he gradually softened his arms and started to hold my son closer to his chest. It was probably against some rule, but no one noticed except Dr. Grossman, who gave me a knowing look every time I passed. I assumed she'd concluded we were having an affair but decided if it didn't interfere with hospital work, she didn't much care.

The only treatment for tuberculosis is a solution of calcium chlorate, and it's terrible. If the doctor misses the vein, it makes the flesh turn black and start to die. Grisha told me about how he'd quickly do the injection when he needed Petya to get up for breakfast. My son never seemed to figure out why he woke up with an ache in his arm when he stayed at the hospital.

He was always sticky when I got him back, so I knew Grisha was bribing him with sugar cubes. I think at first it was just about keeping him quiet, but over the weeks something shifted. I came to pick him up one day and saw him trying to bounce on Grisha's rock-hard mattress like a circus trampoline and Grisha playing along by lifting him higher and higher when he jumped. I knew my son could laugh, but I hadn't been so sure the doctor could.

At moments like that, I could forget how desperately ill my son was. Then he'd have a bad day, when he was too feverish and weak to even play with his toys. My Petya wasn't in the worst stage, but we didn't know how long it would be before he got there.

I tried to save up enough for a suitable bribe by skimming off the top, just taking a loaf when I thought no one was looking. The other women did it, too, so they just winked, but I couldn't let the boss see. She knew how the world worked, but she'd have to do something if she ever caught anyone in the act.

Grisha would get some sausage or cheese cheap from the hospital cafeteria, and we'd combine it with my stolen bread and eat together so we could both put a few more rubles toward the all-important bribe. I knew it wasn't a small thing, voluntarily eating less when your stomach demands that you fill it at least six times a day.

But we weren't saving nearly fast enough. It was a particularly bad day that made us face that. My son hadn't even wanted to get up, so Grisha had made him a little nest of blankets in the corner of his office. "I could try giving him a bigger dose of calcium chlorate, but I'm afraid I'd poison him," he said. "It's up to you, though. You're his mother."

I sat with my face in my hands, moving through the dark woods of my mind, looking for any possible way out. Then, a light. "Can penicillin do anything else?"

"What do you mean?"

"Could it treat cancer? Or prevent it?"

"There's no reason to believe it could. Though I suppose it's not impossible."

"Would a person who doesn't know much about it believe it could?"

I mentioned to the commandant's wife that there was a new theory that certain bacteria could cause cancer, and that doctors were trying penicillin as a way to stop it. I added that Dr. Grossman didn't think much of the theory, but the new doctor was interested in it. Grisha played his part, saying all sorts of things that sounded vaguely scientific but meant nothing. And her fears did the rest, pestering the right people until there was a shipment on the way.

"We'll see if we can lose four vials with no one noticing," Grisha said. "If not, we agree Petya's first. Then we'll have to decide who's second. Vitya might benefit more immediately, like your son. But you're young and have a lot of love—life—ahead of you. That counts for something too."

"Who's the fourth vial for?"

"Me. I noticed strange sores in the dry, cracked places on my hands not long after the birth. Once I realized what your son has, they made sense."

"I'm sorry." It's not really an adequate response to giving someone syphilis.

"You didn't do anything wrong. But I would like to be cured before it gets to my heart and brain. Even if there's no danger in me infecting anyone." He said the last bit with a strange bitterness.

"How long until it gets here?" I asked, because I didn't want to pursue that particular line of conversation.

"Months, most likely." He looked over at Petya's sleeping form. "There's nothing more we can do until then."

I wept. How could I do anything else? Grisha looked thoroughly uncomfortable but put his arms around me loosely. "It's going to be alright," he said, even though we both knew it likely wasn't, because there was nothing else to say. I'd been praying with all the force my soul could master, but I didn't doubt my mother was doing the same when she asked that I never know hunger.

"It will," I said through my tears, because I needed to at least pretend to believe it. Despair is a luxury mothers can't afford.

Diana

Denunciations are tricky. Act too soon, and the target can destroy you before falling himself. Wait too long, and you risk being arrested as his co-conspirator before your letter reaches the right people.

It was obvious Stalin had had his fill of Beria. Even after Abakumov was arrested for not doing enough to find this mythical Zionist conspiracy and the new head bungled the poets' trial, Beria still didn't get his beloved police back. Of course, my flesh had to pay for his disappointment.

And someone was telling Stalin how Beria's friends in Georgia were lining their pockets. Of course they were. Everyone did. The only way you'd get in trouble for it was if you'd fallen from grace, and if that happened, even the reputation of a saint couldn't save you. Not that there were any saints among those men.

But Beria was smart, in an evil way. Stalin wanted his corrupt friends in Georgia to die? He'd kill them himself! But that didn't stop him from talking, saying his boss was a senile old windbag and much worse. I suppose he thought no one was strong enough to use his words against him. I certainly wasn't, but I made up poems to keep track of it all so I could remember everything whenever the right moment came.

I don't know if Stalin had some inkling of Beria's disdain for him, or if the man's debauchery had finally reached levels even he couldn't ignore. His favorite mistress at that moment was a girl he'd started bedding shortly after she turned fourteen. I felt very sorry for her, though his friends made it sound like she'd somehow convinced herself she loved the old toad.

But whether that bothered Stalin or not, it was clear Beria would die. The question was when.

I bided my time until the Party Congress in October, to see if the boss led an attack on him. He didn't. That was reserved for Molotov and Mikoyan, two of the few old Bolsheviks who managed to survive that long. And he never killed more than two top men at once. Dozens of their friends, hundreds of their acquaintances, thousands of people who never knew them, yes. But only two top names: Kamenev and Zinoviev, Bukharian and Rykov, and now Molotov and Mikoyan. Maybe he thought if he tried to kill too many at once, the others would finally grow spines.

Whatever his reasons, though, the world would have to put up with Beria's presence at least a little longer. I kept refining the phrases of my denunciation in my head, but I didn't put a thing on paper.

It was bleakly fascinating, watching how it could all change in a moment. I wasn't there, of course, but I heard a story about a party where someone brought Stalin bananas as a gift. They weren't ripe. Stalin wanted the trade minister fired, and they all raced to do it. Beria got to it first. His entourage was very proud.

The one advantage I had in staying on top of the game was that drunken men who've just been sexually indulged will say anything. I was better informed than any of the Politburo wives. Sometimes I almost pitied Mrs. Beria and the others, sitting below a sword that was hanging by a thread while their husbands' rivals stood on chairs and played with scissors over their heads. But they knew who they'd married, and if they didn't, that was their own willful blindness. And what had they done to save any of their friends when it benefited them to stay quiet? I had at least as much reason as they did, living in that monster's cage.

Yes, I almost felt sorry for Nina Beria. But "almost" isn't enough.

Notebook of
Viktor Aleksandrovich Chekhov

3 Nov., 1952

My dear Diya,

I hope that they decide my treatment is done soon. The others' coughing keeps me up more than my own.

I can tell what their system is. I'm on the left side of the room, and most of the others on this side aren't so bad. The ones who are obviously dying are on the right side. So I can hope.

It's just Grigori Nikolaievich and a feldsher, no nurses or anything. So people have to wait hours for help. I try to help the weakest ones to the toilet, because otherwise the bedpans could be sitting there all day before someone changes them. Maybe the feldsher's lazy, I don't know. I don't think Grigori Nikolaievich is, but he often gets called to other wards.

We aren't allowed visitors, though Annushka stops by and waves to me most days. I hope I'm out by the time you come. I don't know what I'd do if you were standing outside and they wouldn't let me touch you. God have mercy on the doctor if he got between my family and me.

Annushka

"Vitya signed that he's mending fast," I said to Grisha one afternoon when I came to pick up my son.

"That's not true," he said without meeting my eyes. "Symptoms come and go, as you know. But I listen to his lungs every day. You can hear it there."

"Then it's staying the same." He shook his head. "Have you told him?"

"No. We never tell the patients they're dying."

That didn't seem right. "Would you tell me if my son was dying?"

"Is that what you want?" I couldn't speak, but I nodded. "Alright. If it gets to that point, I'll tell you. If you're sure."

I braced myself every time I entered that hospital, in case that was the day I'd hear those words I dreaded above all things. I tried to put on a good face for my son and for Vitya. I think Petya believed my fake smiles. Vitya didn't seem to.

Maybe I should have told him the truth instead of pretending everything was just fine. But I knew he'd blame himself for infecting Petya. Maybe I can't fault the doctors for lying to the patients and saying it was for their own good. I was doing the same thing.

Grisha and I gradually shared our stories on those winter afternoons that might as well be nights, when I was trying to delay the inevitable walk to the bus that would take me home. It was easier to talk about the past than about our helplessness in the face of a disease destroying the people we loved. We pretended it was about teaching him enough sign language to communicate with Petya, who bounced in and out of my lap if it was a good day but otherwise ignored us.

Grisha grew up in an orphanage in Petersburg. (Only officials call it Leningrad—to the natives, it's always Piter.) Not the nice one where they took the best orphans to train for state service, but a drafty gray building run by nuns with watery porridge and itchy blankets.

"Exactly like mine, except for the nuns," I said.

I felt bad when I asked if he'd been there when the people invaded the tsar's palace. I was just curious if it was anything like we'd been taught.

"How old exactly do you think I am?"

"Not old enough to have stormed the Winter Palace?"

"I was four."

"Sorry." I would not have guessed he was thirty-nine. He had fewer lines around his eyes than Vitya, but it wasn't as great a difference as you might expect. The hair that was slowly growing back was gray and lifeless, to the point that you couldn't tell whether it wanted to curl or lay straight. But one year in a camp is at least five on the outside.

"Still almost old enough to be your father."

"Oh, hardly." I was closing in on thirty, though people sometimes told me I looked younger.

"Anyway, I don't remember much of the revolution. One day they replaced the nuns. Sometimes we'd see soldiers go by outside. But not much else changed. There were hungry times. Because of the war, I guess. They sent the smaller children to another room after they got sick from not eating. I guess they died there. But I don't really remember."

"My parents lost their daughter Anna during that war," I said. "Like that."

"They named you for her?"

They didn't, exactly. But he didn't know my real name. I hesitated before whispering it to him. It was frightening, like confessing to a crime, but also such a relief.

"I've always worried the man who made us sick might be looking for me," I said.

"Well, he's not going to look here."

"No."

"And I won't tell anyone. Everything you say to me is safe."

"Doctor's code?"

He snorted. "Doesn't mean much to them, does it? You're not my patient, not really. My friend, though?"

"Of course," I said, because I didn't think it was really in doubt. It was a friendship even more unlikely than the one I'd shared with Polya, but it had the same glue. Maybe you, whoever you are that might someday read this, can't make any sense of it. But a long talk was more intimate than stripping naked and letting someone take his time examining every inch of your skin. After all, you weren't going to be arrested if that person found a mole he didn't like.

Diana

The ugliness that was always there had become steadily more apparent over time, like a blemish slowly growing and filling with pus. There had always been people who believed the most insane things about what the Jews were doing, but all of the talk about the brotherhood of nations had partially shamed them into silence. It had gotten worse after the war and especially after the creation of the state of Israel, when a drumbeat of articles about "rootless cosmopolitans" told the anti-Semites that their views were back in fashion. Still, it was mostly those who had already hated us that now felt free to spew their venom; most people just looked straight ahead in embarrassed silence when somebody decided to harass a Jewish clerk. It wasn't much, but it was better than the alternative.

Then Stalin said we were all American spies, and that Jewish doctors were being paid to kill Soviet people. "Killers in white coats," he called them. He was getting old and had developed a deep paranoia about medical poisoning, or so Beria's friends told me. Supposedly the police had had people killed under anesthesia or poisoned with medication, but I don't know if that's true. They bragged about all sorts of things that they might not have done. But it seemed somehow right, the most powerful man worrying his own tricks could be used against him.

"The new chief set up a torture chamber with tools from an operating room," Beria told me after I'd screamed enough to satisfy him. "Isn't that diabolical?"

He has more imagination than you, I thought, but I dutifully answered, "Oh, yes."

But they could have tortured the doctors to give whatever evidence they wanted without the public campaign against the Jews. One of his loose-lipped friends told me the rumor that the plan was to whip up the mob to attack us so prominent Jews would beg to be "protected" in a new colony in Siberia. It seemed possible, and I was very much afraid that it would work.

People didn't necessarily know what a cosmopolitan was, but everyone needs a physician sooner or later, and they were willing to believe the Jews were out to poison them. There were no official reports about it, but you'd hear of people at the hospital attacking their doctors and the verbal abuse in shops and on street cars getting dangerously close to physical assault. I was sure I was reasonably safe from the mob at that moment, with my blue eyes and unremarkable features. But I wondered if Aryan-looking Jews in Germany had told themselves the same thing in 1933.

Notebook of
Viktor Aleksandrovich Chekhov

---

3 Jan., 1953

My dear Diya,

I meant to write you a New Year's message, but my arm had to heal. Something went wrong, and it burned like hell. I could have stood that, but then the skin started turning black where he'd injected me. Dr. Bogomolov said the problem was the feldsher missed the vein and put the medication into the muscle. If that's what it does to muscle, I don't want to think what it does to my veins. But I can't refuse it, or I'll never get out of here alive.

Anyway, he gave me some extra codeine and cut out the dead flesh. It took a week before I could write again. So your New Year's greeting is late, my love. He promised to do it himself from now on and bawled the feldsher out for his clumsiness. But the truth is, I don't know if I trust him either.

How do I know it's medicine and not just poison? All I have is his word. I saw something in the paper about doctors acting as saboteurs, killing their patients. I don't know if I believe it. I'm not important enough for the Americans to want me dead anyway. But doctors can have personal, selfish reasons, same as anyone else. And I know he's got a reason.

I've seen the way he looks at her when she comes to see me. Once,

I even caught him hugging her. He said he was just comforting her because she was so upset about my illness. Good God, I'm not a complete idiot. I have eyes.

I reminded him she's as good as married, and locking me away won't change that. But I'm scared it might. Our son has taken so long to get here. Once or twice, in a bad moment, she said he wasn't coming. She sounded like she really believed it. I reassured her that he'd never abandon her, and especially not his own son. But I'm not there to give her strength now. And the doctor's no doubt feeding her fears and telling her to just give up and move on. Move on to him.

The worst is there's nothing I can do about it. He controls when I get out. He can keep me here until he talks her into doing something she'll always regret. And clearly, I can't shame him out of it. If he ever had any shame, the camps killed it. They do that. So there's nothing to do but hope he wouldn't go as far as killing me with whatever that is he's injecting in my veins. Nothing else I can see. Oh Diya, I hope you and Sasha get here soon. You could put this right.

Yours,
Vitya

Annushka

They didn't bother putting up a New Year's tree in the infectious disease ward. Granted, there are no trees for miles around Norilsk, but they could have at least hung some tinsel on a pole or given the patients something festive to eat or drink. The only sign there was a holiday was the kutia grain pudding I had brought. I wanted to put in more dried fruit, in case the vitamins would help Vitya and the other patients, but I didn't dare skim too much from the bakery. The patients seemed pleased with it anyway, even though it had partially frozen on the way.

That was long gone when Christmas Eve came five days later. But I stopped for a bit longer than usual to chat with Vitya through the glass before picking up my son. I would have liked to bring Petya to see him, but I didn't think he would understand why his grandfather wasn't coming home with us.

Vitya assured me that he was alright and feeling stronger every day. I pretended to believe him, even though I could see the color slowly fading out of his skin.

"You'll be with us by next New Year," I signed.

"Long before that," he answered.

My son was having a medium day, where he played with his toys in the corner between naps. But he jumped up when he saw me. There wouldn't be any gifts—I didn't have the money—but I had promised him kutia pudding and dumplings for Christmas. I felt safe telling him why we were celebrating, because so few people understood sign language. "Christmas now?" he signed impatiently.

"When we get home."

"What's that mean?" Grisha repeated the sign for Christmas. I spelled it out with my hands. "Oh. Well. You must want to get home for that."

It was painfully obvious he wanted to be invited, and while three people might be enough to qualify as an unsanctioned religious gathering, I was confident no one would know. It was the first time we had left the hospital at the same time, but since Dr. Grossman already assumed we were having an affair, it hardly seemed to matter. It wasn't until I felt Vitya's eyes as we left that I wondered if I'd made a mistake.

"Christmas," I turned and signed. "I'll bring some cake tomorrow. I wish you could come with us." I don't know if he noticed. His eyes were trained on Grisha with an expression that I couldn't quite read.

Ukrainian Christmas Eve dinners are supposed to have twelve courses, with no meat or other foods you wouldn't eat during a religious fast. The decadence starts on Christmas Day, when we can stuff ourselves with the perekladenets layer cake and whatever else we want. I didn't have a course for every apostle: just the pudding, dumplings, borscht, bread, and cabbage rolls. But it looked like a feast on the little table in the dugout.

My son scrupulously avoided the cabbage, and Grisha apologized profusely for spilling some borscht, but it was a joyous meal. I would have been happier if Vitya were there, of course, but I still felt closer to a normal family life than I had since I was not so much older than Petya. There we were, woman, child, and man, gathered around a table laden with everything we needed. It was so easy, and it occurred to me that if it weren't for sex, we could make a decent life together.

I don't mean that Grisha was physically repulsive to me. Gray, a little worn, getting a bit pudgy as his body tried to protect itself from ever starving again, yes. But none of that would have bothered me if the whole idea of being touched by a man hadn't been poisoned. I pretended to understand when the bakers with husbands behind the fence talked about how they longed to not just see their men again, but to hold and be held by them. I had held my forest love, but only as he was being taken away from me forever. The idea of being with someone who would want to do more than just lie quietly beside me seemed unbearable. So I pushed it away. And anyway, there was no particular reason to believe he even wanted to be with me that way.

After we ate, I told my son the Nativity story. This was probably illegal. Officially, you could believe whatever you wanted, but telling it to the next generation was a different matter altogether. They'd stopped persecuting the church during the war, when they needed anything that would rally people, but the war was long over. Even if it wasn't illegal, they could come up with some reason to take my son away if they knew. They could say my dugout was unsanitary for a child, or that his illness was proof I was whoring around instead of taking care of my baby.

But my son couldn't accidentally spill anything, since he couldn't speak, and Grisha understood what we could and couldn't say. He leaned and watched me closely, probably because he'd never heard the story before.

"I'm not sure I believe it," he said after I had put Petya to bed. "But it's a good story."

"You don't have to believe it."

"Maybe I should. Maybe it would have helped to believe in something. To think someone was watching me. Other than the guards. They were watching me."

"Not quite the same, though."

"No, not quite." He paused. "It was a bit like that, when Vitya first arrived in camp. Did he ever tell you about it?" He hadn't. "They always had the new prisoners squat in the open while I inspected them. I tried to be quick, because they shot the ones that fell down. I saw he had a wound in his side. Looked like a knife. Knowing him, he was probably trying to protect someone on the Kolyma tram. That's what they called the whole process of getting to the gold fields. I didn't know him then, though, so I figured he was just another criminal fighting. I wasn't prepared for him."

"Prepared for him?"

"I know it's hard for you to understand. Sometimes it's hard for me to understand now too. But it never occurred to me they weren't all guilty. They'd been convicted of terrible things. And the way the camps were ... They all acted like animals. It stood to reason they'd always been that way. And it made it easier, knowing I couldn't do anything for them. Every day, I could certify a certain number of men were too sick for work. One for each hospital bed. Not that I could do much for them, especially since the guards kept stealing the medicine for the alcohol and codeine. I just had to hope a little rest would be enough to save them.

"Anyway, I sewed him up and sent him out to the fields with all the others. I didn't have anything to give him for the pain. He thanked me when I finished stitching him. They wouldn't often do that. I didn't know what to say, so I told him not to make any more work for me.

"He came back the next night, bleeding where the stitches had torn. I sewed him up, but I couldn't give him a bed. I knew it would take at least a week for those stitches to heal enough that he could do heavy work. Giving a bed to a relatively healthy man for a week meant others would die. I had a system, you see. It seemed like a good one at the time. But anyway, I knew he'd be back the next night, torn again. I guess that saved us both.

"A delegation arrived the next day to find people to arrest from the staff. I found out the old head of Dalstroi had been purged. That's the office in charge of all the road building and gold mining out there," he said, extending his arm as far as it would go in a direction that might have been east. "I'd known him a little bit, when I was at the central hospital, before they demoted me to that camp. That must have been why I'd been sent out there. But it wasn't enough punishment to satisfy them. They came to my hospital and demanded I confess to conspiring with the Japanese and all sorts of things. And Vitya walked in, bleeding again, and saved me by telling them I was the cruelest son of a bitch he'd ever met. They beat him for speaking to them out of turn, but they let me live. Because the old boss's real crime had been his belief that cruelty was wasteful.

"I took him to my room in the back of the hospital after they left. I wasn't sure he'd survive the kicks to his organs, but at least I could keep him comfortable. I wasn't going to sleep that night anyway.

"I should have sent him back to the gold fields, once he was well enough to stand. That's what the rules dictated. But rules didn't really matter much. No one cared if my system for deciding which prisoners should get a bed made any sense. No one would notice if I chose an underqualified man for my feldsher. He'd probably saved my life, and I needed to save his. An easy job was life there, because you could get by on the rations if you weren't working too hard.

"I wanted to dislike him on principle. He was convicted of terrorism, after all. But it was hopeless. You might as well try to hate a big, floppy dog." I smiled at that. "I tried to keep him at a distance, but that's not easy when you sleep in shifts on the same cot. I gave him basic lessons on caring for the prisoners on the night shift and we cycled, twelve hours on and off. But inevitably, there were a few hours when we both were awake and he wanted to talk."

"What did you talk about?"

"I didn't talk about anything. I had to keep hearing about his wife and child. Once, I thought I could shut him up by asking why he was in Kolyma, but even that didn't do it."

"What did he say?"

"'I hit an informant, and then he told lies about me.' I asked him why. You know what he said?"

"What?"

"'He was beating his wife. And it's what they do.'" He played with his glass. "When he told me about that informant, it made me think. Say maybe one in a thousand prisoners isn't guilty. That's not a bad rate, but how do you know which one?" He looked at me like I might have the answer.

"I don't think you can know, Grisha."

"You can't. And it's harder to send them out, knowing the guards will work some of them to death, if you're not absolutely certain they're guilty. But there was no other option. I only had a few excuse slots to give every day.

"It was around that time that my stomach started bothering me, and that made it harder to sleep. I slept less and less, and I didn't sleep at all the night before the first typhus case showed up." He shuddered.

I saw a few cases of typhus during the war. First there's a fever, then a rash. I don't think that part is painful. Then the disease gets into the brain, and the victim hallucinates before slipping into a coma and dying. Wherever people can't wash and change their clothes, lice find them, and so does the disease. I could only imagine what it could do in a labor camp.

"They overflowed the beds, but the commandant and I agreed to keep them in the hospital," he said. "They'd only get in the way on the work crews. It was like a madhouse, where the screaming never ended long enough to let me sleep, even if I could have. Days and nights got confused, especially since it was summer and the sun never set. I guess it was the lack of sleep that gave me strange ideas."

"Like what?"

"Like all I needed to do was organize them and things would get better. I tried to herd the typhus patients to one corner of the main room, where they couldn't infect anyone else. It was stupid. There were only a few patients in the hospital who didn't show signs of typhus at that point, and they were probably already infected. And they kept crawling around like overgrown rats. I almost got them all together, but one kept crawling out of the corner like his life depended on it. I'd shoo him back, but he'd crawl out again. Then he got up and made straight for me."

"What did you do?"

"I yelled at him to stop, but he didn't. I think he saw some demon instead of me. So I hit him with the only thing at hand—an empty medicine bottle. The shards of glass exploded into my hand and his scalp and he slumped to the floor. I thought I'd killed him. I don't know what I would have done if Vitya hadn't come.

"He checked and told me the patient was alive. I'd just knocked him out. Then he got the others back in their beds and made me sit down while he tweezed the glass out of my hand and wrapped it. I tried to explain typhus corner, but it no longer made sense to me. He patted my back and shushed me like a child, then gave me a spoonful of the sleeping medication. I don't know if he knew I hadn't been sleeping, or if he just wanted to shut me up. And then he settled me in my bed and put a blanket over me to discourage the mosquitoes. After that, we were friends. He kept an eye on me. Stopped me from doing anything else that was stupid. Other than when he let me volunteer for the war."

We sat quietly for a moment. "You should tell him how well you remember that," I said.

"I don't think he wants to hear anything from me. Patients always blame their doctors for not curing them. It's just the way it is."

"You should give him the penicillin before you give it to me," I said. "It might make a difference for him. It doesn't matter for me."

"You don't miss …" He blushed. "Companionship? From men?"

"No." I wasn't going to have that conversation. "And anyway, that's not important. Not when we might save him."

"I think it might take a miracle," Grisha said, then half-smiled. "But if you're right about virgins and angels, then maybe we'll get one." I couldn't tell if he was making fun of me but decided he probably wasn't. "Though I could have used one before too."

"You're alive. Isn't that close to one?"

"Maybe." He started to say something, then shook his head. "I should go. Don't think the angels are going to do the night rounds for me. God knows my feldsher isn't."

I hugged him loosely at the door. "You have to have hope," I said.

He nodded. "It's going to be alright," he said, more to himself than me. "Somehow, it will."

Everything went to hell a week later.

I had seen the articles about doctors killing their Kremlin patients. I didn't believe it. I'd read so many lies that I reflexively refused to believe anything they said. But I didn't think too much about it. There was nobody in Norilsk who was important enough to kill.

Grisha didn't look up at me when I came to pick up Petya. He kept clasping and unclasping his hands, over and over, as if something magical would happen if he finally aligned them correctly.

"Is this the day?" I asked, dreading the answer.

"What? No, no. He had a good day today. Best in a while." He kept fidgeting. "Maybe you should find another arrangement."

"What did he do?" My son looked completely innocent, drawing squiggles on some spare paper, but I knew he could be a handful when he wasn't too sick.

"Nothing. It's just … They came to talk to me today."

He didn't have to say who they were. "What do they think you did?"

"Maybe nothing. They asked me about Dr. Grossman."

"Why? They don't think she's—"

"Seems like they might."

"What did you say?"

"That I don't watch her every second, but I never saw her do anything to the patients."

"Were they satisfied?"

"Not really. They started asking me about myself."

"About your arrest?"

"Yes. But also about my family. My nationality. I told them their guess about nationality was as good as mine since there was no note."

"I assume they weren't amused."

"I wasn't trying to be funny. But no." He sighed. "Maybe I can save myself if I denounce her. But maybe not. She helped get me out of the camp. I might be damned either way."

"I can't tell you what to do," I said, because I couldn't. I had my own rules, but it's a very hard thing to tell someone he can't save his own skin, for righteousness' sake.

"They could come for you too," he said. "Because you see me every day."

"I'm not a doctor."

"They could say you poisoned the bread. If somebody wanted to get credit for finding a new part of the conspiracy."

They could, even though it wouldn't make the slightest bit of sense. "I don't think staying away from you at this point will do much," I said. "Even if I had another safe place for my son. Which I don't."

"You could denounce me. And her. That would save you." It didn't sound like either a suggestion or an accusation, just a statement of fact, like I could buy a thicker coat if I was freezing.

"I won't do that," I said with less conviction than I might have had a few years earlier. If I was arrested, my son would be sent to an orphanage, and I was sure he'd be dead within a month. That was what tended to happen to sick children—they were just ignored until they faded away completely. "I won't."

He didn't look at me. "I would understand if you did."

I tried not to think about it, but the idea would intrude as I watched my son sleep and realized how small and fragile he was. I reminded myself of my rules. I would not denounce an innocent person to save my own skin. But was that how the rule went, or had I just added that last bit to justify that I wasn't really breaking it if all I wanted was to save my son?

Grisha and I didn't speak as we handed Petya off each day. We'd compromised ourselves, perhaps fatally, with all those conversations where we let the truth out. Now he had to hope that I wouldn't denounce him as a precaution, and I had to pray they wouldn't arrest him. Even if they weren't interested in uncovering a conspiracy of killer bakers in league with the doctors, my name would be one of the few he would know to offer if they beat him until he confessed enough co-conspirators. We were yoked together and just had to hope we weren't headed to the slaughterhouse.

Diana

I thought Beria had finally fallen when a man in uniform came to my apartment.

One of his parties had been going on for a while, and he was drunk. The man took him aside and said something that the rest of us weren't to hear. I was torn between joy that I might see him arrested in front of me and fear that they would arrest me too. But then I heard something about Kuntsevo, Stalin's country home. Beria found his pants and left in a hurry.

But I first found out the way everyone did, by wireless. I poured myself a glass of wine. Perhaps I should have felt something. Grief—no. My parents were Trotskyites, and he'd destroyed them. Joy—no, not that, either. The others had washed their hands in blood, helping and encouraging him every step of the way, and one of them would rule. So I didn't toast his memory or his death. I just threw back a glass to prepare for whatever lay ahead.

But then nothing happened. Or rather, the worst things stopped happening.

For the first few days, I thought the killer doctors had simply been pushed out by the more pressing news of the leader's death. But even when the funeral was over, the papers had nothing to say about them, or even about rootless cosmopolitans.

I couldn't get a clear answer on whether Malenkov—the one who took over Stalin's old positions—was an anti-Semite. Khrushchev was, but he seemed to be on the fringes, comparatively speaking. And Beria only attacked people when he would get something out of it.

He later told me he'd let Stalin die by not calling a doctor. I didn't believe it. If there was no doctor, it was because they'd arrested most of the good ones and were too scared to do anything on their own anyway. But I pretended to be scandalized and vaguely aroused by the idea of regicide.

He had the secret police back before Stalin even took his final breath. He had grand plans, and as much as it pains me to admit it, some of them were not evil. His friends sometimes talked about how he'd let the East Germans rule themselves and ensure this country was forever grateful with an amnesty for the slaves in the camps. Obviously, I wanted that for all of the women who'd stood in line with me at the Lubyanka. But I needed him to fall. I could only wait so long for him to get bored and toss me aside.

Notebook of Viktor Aleksandrovich Chekhov

7 March, 1953

My dear Diya,

The world seemed normal when I woke up. By noon, everyone was wailing like they'd lost their mother, wife, and son all at once. I thought maybe there'd been an accident at the refinery or one of the mine shafts, but those happen every month, and life goes on.

I asked the feldsher. He didn't say anything. He looked like a frightened little boy, and I wondered if the Americans had dropped one of those bombs we'd raced to make. What if you and Sasha were under it? What if your skin fell off? I don't even know if that's really what those bombs do, but that's what I thought of.

Then someone got on the hospital loudspeaker with an announcement about the leader's death. And I started to worry about different things. I don't think there's going to be another civil war. But I'm not sure enough to be comfortable.

I don't know what to feel about it, Diya. Our daughter-in-law looked like she'd been crying when I saw her. The doctors looked relieved. But as far as I know, Comrade Stalin never hurt or helped me. And I don't know what his death means for you. Will the big men tear each other apart until somebody's on top? What if Beria wins? What if he loses? What I'd give to be able to telephone you.

But I was saying about when we found out Comrade Stalin died. I signed to Annushka it would be alright, even though I don't know if it will. That he would live on through people like her. Can't blame her for being scared. My students cried over Lenin, and they had lived under the tsar. Kids like her can't remember a time before Comrade Stalin. I'm scared, too, about what will happen next. But you can't say that to a weeping girl.

Your loving husband,
Vitya

Annushka

I did cry on the day Comrade Stalin died, but not for the same reason other people did.

Grisha came over that evening with some bread and a bottle of vodka. I've always hated the stuff, but it seemed right to have a few sips that night.

"Suppose he's not going to answer my letters," he said after draining his glass.

"You wrote to Comrade Stalin?"

"I wrote to anyone who might listen. So many letters, begging for a chance to prove myself. I hadn't really collaborated. Just surrendered when we were surrounded. Surely he could understand?"

"Any normal human being would," I said, which was not the same thing as saying yes.

"I knew each letter was just one among thousands that must be directed to him each day, and that it all depended on what small sample his secretary chose to give him. It was only a sliver of a chance, but any chance was better than nothing."

It wasn't really a chance, just the illusion of one. But it seemed cruel to say it.

"Even with Vitya's extra bread, I was getting sicker. I wasn't starving anymore, but I needed vitamins and minerals that I wasn't getting in a camp diet. I was sentenced to twenty-five years, and I knew I wouldn't last that many months without an easy, indoor job. So I needed to believe Comrade Stalin would save me. I knew he didn't know who I was. But I thought that if he somehow found out about me, he would care. Not that I was anything special. I suppose I thought he cared about everyone. Like—"

"Like God," I finished.

"Yes, I guess so."

I shook my head. "Well, he didn't care about my village." And I finally told him the whole story, how the city people had taken our grain and left us to starve. "And they gave my parents ten years. Ten years, without even the right to send a letter, for stealing a few heads of grain to try to keep their daughter alive. So my only toast is to outliving the bastard." I raised my glass and took a sip, even though I hated the burn of the alcohol.

"Ten years without right of correspondence?"

"Yes."

He took a deep breath but didn't look at me. "Annushka, there is no sentence of ten years without right of correspondence."

"That's what they said …"

"That's what they say when they don't want the relatives to make a scene." He rubbed his eyes, which were starting to get watery from the vodka. "I'm sorry. I shouldn't have said that."

I took a breath. "You're saying they shot them." Him saying it does not mean it happened.

"Yes. But it would have been quick. They picked people who were—efficient—at that sort of thing. I met some of them in the camps after they got purged. I think they would have rather been shot themselves than be sent out there." He shook his head. "That doesn't help, does it?"

It didn't, not in that moment. It would later.

That night, when I went to sleep, I saw my mother and father. Just as they were. Not a day older, not broken by what they had suffered. I ran to them and embraced them, then took their hands to lead them to my home and my son. My father just kissed my hand, and my mother patted my cheek with a sad smile. Then they took each other's hands and walked off, not looking back. I ran after them until I couldn't breathe anymore because I was crying too hard, but I could never catch them. You know how dreams are.

My son felt me sobbing and pushed me with all the might his little arms could muster. "Mama?" he signed, and I could see the worry and confusion written on his tiny face. I never let him see me get upset.

"A bad dream," I signed, though it wasn't really. It was a bittersweet dream that made me face a bad reality. But scary dreams were something he could understand. He gave me his stuffed rabbit and tried to imitate how I'd shush him after a nightmare. I'd been only a few years older than him when I lost my parents and my home. And how much more precarious was his situation, with no father and only a dugout we'd squatted in because no one else wanted it? But I couldn't do anything to change that. I pulled him against my chest, stroked his dark hair, and made my breathing calm down.

The factory was still shut down the next day, to give everyone a chance to wail for Stalin. I didn't go out because I knew I'd want to slap people and scream at them. How could they not understand? Well, they were Russians. They seemed to like being someone's slaves. I think it made them feel secure, to know someone owned them and was responsible for them. I tried not to hate them for it.

Grisha came by at the end of the day, with a broken wooden crate in hand. "Vitya had a hammer, didn't he?" he asked.

"Yes. But what are you doing?"

"I thought we should have a funeral."

"For Comrade Stalin?" I couldn't hide my disgust.

"No."

I chose a spot of tundra where Petya and I had picked wildflowers during the brief Arctic summer. The ground was still hard, so we couldn't drive the makeshift cross very far in. It was too cold to stand outside for a long eulogy, and I'd been too little to really know them as people, so I just said a prayer.

"Thank you," I said as we walked back. I was in the middle, holding my son's mittened hand on one side.

"No need for thanks," he said, and we walked in silence for a bit. "Annushka?"

"Yes?"

"If they arrest me, will you do this for me too? Say a prayer?"

"Yes. But they're not going to arrest you."

"I hope not. It would just make me feel better if you say you will."

"Of course," I said, slipping my other mitten into his. He squeezed it lightly. "I always remember the people who've had to leave."

I had a terrible time keeping that cross upright, along with the others that would join it not so much later. It sank in the mud when the ground thawed, then was locked in at odd angles if I didn't have it just right before the first freeze came. It still gave me something to do for my dead loved ones. I understood why my mother had been so obsessive in weeding Anna's grave. People fade from our memories, no matter how we try to hold onto them. When we tend their memorials, we tell them and ourselves that they still matter, even when we can't hear their voices or picture their faces clearly anymore. It's all we can do.

Diana

It was a sticky summer night in Moscow, and I was sitting at my kitchen table, debating whether to poison the wine.

Were you proud of me, father? I knew he wouldn't be. This wasn't revolution. It was a desperate attempt to get my own freedom, no one else's. Beria hadn't come in a week, but I knew that was just a temporary reprieve. It had happened before.

I had the poison from when the girl had given up trying to remove the mice without violence. I could put it in the wine and let him bleed to death on the inside. The only flaw in the plan would be if he told me to drink some. I wasn't willing to die to kill him. I'd never hated anyone more than I'd loved my own life. I imagined that if my parents could see me, they'd be quite disappointed as I sat there, pouring a glass, swirling it, and then dumping it back into the decanter. I don't know how long I did that, or how long I could have gone on—if there hadn't been a knock at the door.

Two policemen stood on the threshold. They didn't bother with pleasantries.

"What's your name?"

"Diana Sergeyevna Chekhova."

"Is this your apartment?"

"No. Beria ordered me to stay here."

"Ordered you?"

"Yes."

"You didn't want to stay here? Looks like a nice apartment."

"No. I want to be with my husband." A pause. "Would you like to look around?"

I showed them all the evidence of Beria's orgies. "And that was the least of it." One of the policemen looked like he might faint. The other locked eyes with me.

"And what was the worst of it?"

"He said the USSR would never prosper without private property." It was true that he'd said that, though personally, I thought raping little girls was worse. "And called Comrade Stalin all sorts of vile things."

"Are you willing to sign a statement attesting to that?"

"Of course."

I was nervous being taken to the Lubyanka, but I never gave them reason to torture anything out of me. I was like a parrot, repeating any nonsense they wanted. I'd thought the things he'd actually said and done might be enough, but no. They wanted espionage and terrorism and a dozen other things, and I obliged. I needed him dead. Whatever they would do to his wife and son, they'd already decided to do. They hardly needed my evidence to destroy them. Perhaps a woman with more character than me would have insisted on telling the truth. I'd salute her as she went to die in their cellars. But I wouldn't follow her.

Notebook of
Viktor Aleksandrovich Chekhov

---

1 July, 1953

My dear Diya,

It can't be long now. I saw the news in the papers, that they arrested your jailer. Are you already on a train, coming to me? Hope you brought your warmest things. Or maybe we can go back to Moscow. Could we do that? You'll know best.

Waiting for you with no patience,
Vitya

12 July, 1953

My dear Diya,

Something is going on. Annushka told me she doesn't see the prisoners going down in the mine in the mornings. She thinks they might be on strike. Can they do that? Never would have occurred to me not to work when I was ordered to. I feel for them, of course, but I hope they surrender. I don't want bullets flying near our grandson's home. And what if they stop allowing trains into Norilsk until it's put down?

I don't know that's what's happening, of course. The newspapers and the loudspeaker announcers report that everything is fine, the finest it's ever been, no place could be finer. You know how it is.

All of my love,
Vitya

5 Aug., 1953

My dear Diya,

It's all over. They herded the prisoners into an open spot between the watchtowers and said anyone still standing in twenty minutes would meet the machine guns. Annushka heard their loudspeakers. She thought they'd be safe underground, but she wasn't sure, so she gave Petya a bath in the metal tub in case it offered more protection. Don't think it would, but can't blame the girl for trying. She heard the guns, but no bullets came into the dugout. And of course Petya had no idea anything was happening.

Maybe they thought they could do it. Maybe it was just a more dignified death than starving. Annushka doesn't know how many of them died. She thought it would be dangerous to see anything. I'd guess most of them decided to live, though. Who can blame them? We all want to live.

Anyway, everything is settling down ahead of your arrival. You must be almost here.

Love,
Vitya

Annushka

"What fools," Grisha said after the strike was broken and we could visit again. "Did they forget about the machine guns? Now they'll have to work even harder to make up for lost production. They'll die even faster. And no one even noticed. Except you, of course."

"They didn't forget the machine guns," I said. "They decided to taste a little bit of freedom before they died."

"How do you know?"

"Sometimes I'd hear them shouting. And I know how my countrymen think."

"Why, when there's trouble, is it always the Ukrainians?"

"Eventually we get tired of living on our knees."

"You'd rather die?"

I looked over at Petya, who was busy with his truck. "If it weren't for him—"

"What were you going to do? Throw some bread over? They'd shoot you, and you'd die for nothing. No one was coming to help them."

I knew that was true. Norilsk is a camp town. We all knew what happened behind the fence, and I think most of us knew those men were innocent of any meaningful crime. But everyone was waiting for the guards to put down the uprising. Of course, some of the women were married to guards. I understood why they felt that way. I think the rest were just frightened that if those men got a taste of revenge, they wouldn't be satisfied until the whole city was reduced to ashes.

"What would you have done?" I asked.

"If they're nationalists, they would have beat anyone who broke the strike. So I would have rested and eaten as much as I could. I assume the cooks were frightened enough to keep serving bread. And when they brought out the machine guns, I would have given up and gone back to work." He thought a moment. "Maybe not. If I felt sick enough, I might have let them shoot me. It's the only sensible thing to do when you've got a twenty-five-year sentence. But I probably would have wanted to live. Do you despise me for that?"

"What would it matter to you if I did?"

"It doesn't matter to me."

It obviously did. "No, I don't blame you. During the war, I just wanted to keep baking bread and to live another day. I only joined the partisans when it was clear my friend and I were going to die either way."

"So you chose to die on your feet."

"I still wanted to live. So much. I never felt more alive than when I was walking through the forest on my way to scout something out. The smell of the pines, the way the trees filtered the sun ... It all meant so much more when I thought it was the last time. Does that make sense?"

"It sounds nice." Which was not the same thing as saying it made sense. "It wasn't quite like that for me."

"There's not much beauty in a camp."

"No, I mean, during the war. We were pinned down in a forest for a while. But I don't remember anything beautiful.

"I know I can't complain about being there. I could have stayed in the camp, but I didn't. I wanted to do something that mattered. So they put me with the men on the Volkhov front, trying to break the siege around Piter. I'd either stitch them up or amputate. Keep them alive long enough to send them to the rear. And identify who was going to die anyway no matter what I tried to do. There was no time for anything else.

"Maybe that's why I went across the river with the men. I didn't have to volunteer for that. But I did. It was all swamps and trees. No people, no help. And they couldn't get us food across the river consistently, let alone medical supplies. I did my best to rewarm the men who had frostbite, but I couldn't do anything else. After a while, they gave me a dead man's gun and told me to make myself useful. I wasn't much of a shot, but neither were the others, once they started to starve. We ate the dead horses. The one gift that bitter winter gave us was keeping dead flesh frozen." He shook his head. "Maybe there were beautiful things there, even then. But I didn't think to look for them."

"Was that where you were captured?"

He nodded. "We should have evacuated that winter, when we would have had a chance running across the river. But they waited until everything was mud. They couldn't get us anything, so some of the men kept eating the horses after they thawed and started to rot. They always died, because I had no way to stop their insides emptying out. We were so weak when they gave us permission to withdraw in May. I think a few units got across. But not mine.

"The Germans attacked, and the generals ordered those of us who were still there to fight back. I tried. We all tried. But the Germans had fresh reinforcements, and we didn't. They pushed us into a smaller and smaller pocket. Soon, we were surrounded. There were three choices: put a bullet through your own skull, go down shooting, or surrender. I was out of bullets.

"I thought about running at them and ending it quickly, but there were men still alive in the pocket with me. I owed it to them to live. And I … I felt a strange hope. We were going to be captured." He watched me carefully, probably waiting for some sign of disgust. "The Germans are efficient. I thought they might have clean bandages. Of course, helping us wouldn't be their top priority, but maybe there would be enough left over that I could make do? I was good at making the best of inadequate materials. I thought it would be alright. God, I was an idiot."

"I thought the same thing when they came to Kharkiv."

"Did you ... Did you do anything?" Having the thought is treason, but it's difficult to prove what was in someone's head—not that that ever bothered the police. Acting on the thought, that's either a death sentence or a quarter century in the camps.

"No. You?"

"No. Well, I followed their orders. March, stop, march, get in the pen, drop your trousers. They called it a camp, but it was a pen. You wouldn't put animals in there, not after other prisoners ate all the grass."

"Why did they want you to drop your trousers?"

"Looking for Jews. You see, they—"

"I've heard of it."

"They pulled out the Jews and shot them right there." He shook his head. "I'd thought they wanted us to undress for a medical exam. Like the ones I gave. But once they'd checked everyone's ... everyone's body, they just left us in the pen. We tried to curl up in holes someone else had dug in the ground. I don't know how many we lost, between them killing the Jews and shooting anyone who couldn't keep up with the column.

"We were there a few days before they forced us to march to a train station and cram into cattle cars. I don't know how long we rode. There wasn't enough light to tell day from night. Men died there too.

"We finally stopped in a farming region. We were divided up and ordered to work in the fields. Of course we stole everything we could, even though they shot anyone they caught. That was the only way I survived.

"Some of the workers were prisoners of war, like me. Others were women and children—Poles, Ukrainians, Russians, anyone who was in the Germans' way. It was worse for them. The guards and the burgermeisters would beat us if we worked too slowly, or just for the fun of it. But sometimes they'd grab a woman and pass her around or force some girl to live with them. If one of us 'under-men' so much as looked at a German woman, though, the punishment was death. Not that, after eighteen hours in the fields, we had any strength to … Never mind."

"They arrested you for working in the Germans' fields?"

"No, they arrested me for letting myself be captured."

"Why?"

"Well, they didn't take a lot of time to explain it to me, Annushka. It's just the way it was. God, I remember how happy I was to see caps with red stars. It was like coming out of the grave. They fed us and let us watch them machine-gun the guards. So we thought it was going to be alright. But then the police showed up and took over the camp. I remember being called in to talk to their officer. You know what he asked me?"

"What?"

"'Why did you survive?' I just said I was lucky. Which I was. Then he asked me why I'd worked for the fascists instead of dying like a real Russian. I tried to explain that I thought it was better for the men to have a doctor than not. I didn't have any medicine, but I did manage to bandage a few injuries and ran an anti-lice campaign in our camp. We killed any bugs we found, and not one man died of typhus." He was obviously very proud of that, and it's not an insignificant accomplishment. "But they didn't care. They just filled out a form saying I'd been convicted of treason and terrorism and loaded me up with all the others. Who knows, maybe those were the same cattle cars we'd come on." He laughed darkly. "To think, I'd been planning to ask for an assignment in Piter. I felt like I'd done enough and shouldn't have to go back to Siberia."

"You weren't wrong," I said.

"No, but I was stupid. I wrote a letter every Sunday in my first camp, asking them to reconsider my case. I knew I couldn't go back to Piter, not with a sentence for treason and terrorism. But I had this idea I could go to Magadan. Maybe Vitya would help me settle in …" He shook his head. "It wasn't even a bad camp. They let me be a feldsher there. I could have survived twenty-five years of that. But then they put me on a train to Norilsk. Punishment, I guess. For writing too many letters. I don't know why else they'd send a doctor to die in a mine."

"Why do they do anything they do? They probably just picked you at random." That's one of the worse things about this country—you never know what's spite and what's incompetence.

"Maybe. But I was sure I was being punished." I suspected we weren't just talking about the police anymore. "I hated them, the prisoners. Until Vitya. Have you ever seen a camp up close?"

"Only through the fence."

"I'd seen it all so many times. They come in, just ordinary men like anyone else. And in a few months, they turn into animals. Like reverse evolution. The first delousing, they'd try to cover up. After that, they didn't care if everyone saw them naked. They'd go from trying to pick the rotten bits out of the food to eating from the garbage heap. There's not much good in camp garbage. They were worse than animals because they should have known better."

"Hunger does things to people," I said. "I don't think we can judge them for it."

"Well, I can't now." He looked at me, sizing me up again. What would I pardon, what would I hold against him? "I tried to be resigned to it. But my body rebelled. It demanded to live. You understand? The body doesn't know what shame is."

"Were they still alive when you started?"

"What?"

"I was eight the first time I saw someone cutting meat off his dead wife. Breasts and buttocks. She'd already starved, so there wasn't much even there. I didn't really understand what he was doing until a year later. And I couldn't blame him. Not really. Should I?"

He looked uncomfortable, being asked to pass judgment or absolve me. I think in his mind I was some pure angel sent to preside over his fate. "It wasn't your crime."

"No, but it could have been. If I were older and stronger. I'm no different."

He shook his head. "I don't believe that. But, to your original question, no. I didn't eat anyone. I went to the garbage heap. Because they wouldn't give me a job in the hospital or the kitchen, or anything easy. And I wasn't strong enough to earn what I needed to stay alive. If I found something to eat and my head cleared for a few minutes, I'd be disgusted with myself and think I should end it. But it never lasted. I'd wake up the next morning, and the only thing I'd remember was where I'd found a little scrap of rotting meat."

"I'm glad you didn't end it," I said, taking his hand.

"I actually hoped Vitya would kill me when he fell over me in the mine. Not that I knew it was him. Just a bigger, stronger man who was annoyed with me. Because I didn't want to keep starving. But he saved me instead. And I can't do a damn thing to save him."

"No word on the medicine?"

"None. I wouldn't expect it yet. But he's getting sicker, faster. If he gets much worse, there's no point in giving it to him. Not if he can't recover. Not if it's hopeless."

"If they can have hope, we don't have a right not to," I said, gesturing in the direction of the fence. As I said it, I was sure I'd heard it before. But who said it, and when, I don't know. There are so many things I heard before I was wise enough to understand them.

Vitya was getting worse, and not just physically. I'd see him pacing the ward ceaselessly, sometimes accidentally muttering aloud what was weighing on his mind. It was always about Diana and Sasha. It got bad enough that Grisha let me in to try to calm him. That was against the rules, but it didn't really matter. The bacteria hadn't found me to be a receptive host. And the other patients grumbled, but not too much. Even in an infectious disease ward, someone gets special treatment.

"They should be here by now," he said.

"Maybe they were waiting until the strike ended," I said, though I know it's a weak excuse. The rest of the country wasn't allowed to know what was happening.

"It was over a month ago. It's a long trip, but not that long." He got up and started pacing again.

"Please sit, Vitya. You can't waste your energy. You need it to heal."

"But I'm not healing!" he snapped. "Forgive me, child. I'm not angry with you. He's the one who's to blame."

"He's doing his best," I said.

"He wants you to believe that. If Diya were here …" He turned to me. "Can you telephone her? Do you think you could get through to Moscow? Find out when she's coming?"

Anyone who has had the misfortune to use the Soviet phone system knows that wasn't a small thing to ask, but I couldn't say no. I chose a phone at the train station because I thought that would be the most reliable public booth in the city. It was fortunate there weren't many passengers that day who might have needed it because it took me over an hour to get through to her building.

The doorwoman answered. "Who are you and what do you want?"

"Masha Viktorevna Muskvina," I lied. "I'm trying to call my cousin Diana Sergeyevna. She lives in apartment—"

"Not anymore," the doorwoman said, and I could tell she was preparing to hang up the phone.

"Has she gone to meet her husband?" I said before she could be rid of me.

"She left with two policemen. I haven't seen her since." The phone clicked.

I had to lean against the glass of the booth to get my breath. What could they charge her with? It didn't matter—she'd been the mistress, however unwilling, of someone who'd fallen from power. That was reason enough to kill her, if that was what they'd decided to do.

I thought about lying to Vitya. I would have liked to, and God knows I had plenty of practice. If I had thought his death was imminent, I would have done it and been sure it was the kindest thing. But I still believed he might recover, and a lie would be only a temporary solution. He might be satisfied for a week or two, but then he'd inevitably start worrying again, like anyone would. And I felt that it was important that he trust me. He didn't trust many people anymore.

I tried to make it sound less hopeless than it was. He still collapsed when I told him what the doorwoman had said. "She's smart," I said. "If anyone can outwit them, she can." But it wasn't really a matter of brains, and we both knew it was entirely possible no one could outplay them.

"Sasha?" He finally asked.

"I don't know. The doorwoman didn't say anything about him." I wasn't sure which was worse: letting him believe that his innocent son might be in the police's hands or telling him that his son would happily betray Diana, even if it wasn't necessary to save his own life. So I just said I didn't know.

It broke him. Grisha let me keep visiting, but it wasn't clear that he even noticed I was in the room. I'd find his tray sitting on the bed, cold and untouched, while he paced the floors over and over and over. I started slipping the money we'd saved for a bribe to the feldsher and told him to get Vitya anything he wanted. I was thinking that he'd get some kind of food that was more tempting than the hospital cafeteria's slop. I should have been more specific, but I don't know if the feldsher would have obeyed any rules I'd put in place.

He was calmer after that, but not in the way a man is when he's accepted his loss. It was more like he'd left his body. He'd sit on the bed, staring at nothing, only occasionally registering my presence when I shook him. I assumed they'd been giving him more codeine to keep him quiet.

Sometimes, he'd stir. Then he'd make me promise, with words so slurred that I could barely understand them, that I'd get away. That I'd protect my son. That I would wait for Sasha. That I wouldn't let the doctor hurt anyone else. That I'd go so far east that the Germans would never find me and the little girl. He called me Lana when he talked about fleeing the Germans. I didn't know who Lana was or what any of it meant. He'd never told me anything about his life before Diana and Sasha. But I promised it all, because that seemed to let him rest.

And it was too late for the truth. I don't know when he would have been able to hear it, but he couldn't have then, even if I'd been cruel enough to tell him the family he'd loved so much was built on a lie. So I kept lying, promising him that I'd do everything he asked and that it would be alright. I didn't know what else to do.

Diana

I still can't decide if I overestimated my son or underestimated him.

I kept his name back when they asked me for as many of Beria's followers as I could remember. He'd just accepted his help to a position in the police, and I couldn't imagine he was important enough to have done any favors in return. But that was how these men built their power bases—favors in exchange for loyalty. Sometimes it worked, and sometimes their protégés were perfectly content to knife them once their backs were turned.

It was difficult to know who went into each category, though, and the police tended to treat everyone as a true friend of the fallen man unless they proved as unashamed as I was in denouncing that monster.

As soon as I was sure it was safe, I went to warn my son. I didn't know where he lived anymore, so I had to track him down in the dingy little office where he kept tabs on thoroughly uninteresting bureaucrats.

"Mother," he said through clenched teeth when I'd annoyed the receptionist into getting him for me. "What do you want?"

"What a way to talk to your mama," I said.

"Forgive me, I'm just very busy."

"It won't take long." I stood like a statue for maybe ninety uncomfortable seconds, until he decided I truly wasn't going to leave. He let me into his office.

"If this is about Viktor Aleksandrovich—"

"It isn't." I wanted to smack him across the mouth, but I just seethed inside. Viktor Aleksandrovich, like he was some stranger! But that wasn't why I'd come. "You know they arrested Beria."

"Yes, I gave evidence against him as soon as I heard." He paused. "Is there something more, or can I go back to work?"

So all of his going on about the great service Beria was doing for our country had been an act. He was as mercenary as any of them. Relief competed with disgust, and I still can't say which was stronger.

"I'm sorry to have wasted your precious time," I said, turning to go. But I stopped in the doorway to his office. "I'm going to your father."

"You're a fool." He shrugged. "But I can't stop you, can I?"

"What should I tell him? About you?"

"Whatever you want. I'm sure you'll make a fine show of it, whatever it is."

Once again, I wanted to hit him, but I didn't. "You'd know all about performances. Goodbye, Aleksander Viktorovich."

I thought I saw maybe the slightest flash of regret in his eyes, but it was gone before I could be sure I'd seen it. I left his office, thanked the receptionist, and walked away. I wanted to turn, to see if he was watching me go. I knew he wouldn't be. And I'd be damned if I'd give him the satisfaction of seeing me look back.

Annushka

The infectious disease ward was never quiet with all the coughing, but yelling was rare.

They weren't pained screams. They were shouts. I could hear them from the other end of the hallway. It wasn't until I got to the door that I made out what they were, though.

"You imbecilic excuse for a feldsher …" Grisha was nearly purple. I felt sorry for the feldsher, whatever he'd done, so I opened the door a little more noisily than was strictly necessary. Grisha looked over at me and seemed to deflate, then looked back at the feldsher. "This never happens again."

I tried to ask Vitya what had happened, but he couldn't tell me. He'd stopped pacing during my recent visits, which worried me even more. He'd just stare, glassy-eyed, occasionally mumbling something I couldn't understand. I assumed it was the fever, the codeine, or both.

"What did he do?" I asked Grisha after I'd given up on conversation with Vitya. My son had had a bad day, but he was sleeping peacefully in his blanket nest, and I didn't want to disturb him until I had to.

"Imbecilic was the wrong word." He shook his head. "It was actually clever. He's been selling the codeine to higher bidders and giving the patients homebrew. It knocked them out enough that I couldn't tell the difference. Suppose I'm the idiot."

"It never smelled like alcohol in there. I mean, it did, but rubbing alcohol."

"That's what worries me, that his version of samogon wasn't much different." He leaned back. "I should fire him. But there's no one else. Unless you want the job."

"I don't know how to take care of tuberculosis patients."

"Well, apparently, he doesn't either. You wouldn't steal their medicine. I'm joking, I'm joking," he added quickly. "I wouldn't wish this place on you." He looked over at my son. "On anyone."

"Is he …" I didn't have the strength to finish it.

"Not today. No, not today." I didn't ask about tomorrow, because I didn't want to hear that he couldn't guarantee me even that much. "The penicillin must be close."

"I hope so."

"I'll let you know the moment it arrives. Even if it's the middle of the night."

I nodded, but I couldn't say anything more. I just picked up my son, who shifted listlessly as I cocooned him in the blankets. I wanted to believe in the penicillin, but I'm sure my mother had wanted to believe that there would be enough food to save little Anna when they completed that terrible trek to Kharkiv Province.

"Annushka." I turned back. Grisha was standing in his office doorway. He moved toward me shyly, tentatively. We stood facing each other for a moment, and I started to wonder what it was about. Then he pecked my forehead with his lips, so lightly that I wasn't sure they'd actually touched me. "Have faith."

I stood on my toes and pecked him back on the cheek, because it seemed like the appropriate thing to do. The way he blushed made me question that, but I put the thought aside. Men and romance were luxuries I didn't have time for. "I will try."

"Don't go in there," Grisha said when I arrived at the ward the next afternoon. "Petya's asleep in my office. Get him and go."

"Vitya?" I asked.

He nodded. "Most of them are just irritable. He's shaking. He must have been taking more."

So that was where the money I'd left for food had gone. I couldn't be angry with him about it, though. People drink when they don't know how else to survive. "Would it help if I talked to him?"

"I doubt it. I'm not sure he'd know you."

The next day was worse. I could hear him yelling, but I couldn't make any sense of it.

I don't know why I thought I could help. I'd been useless with him even when he wasn't in the agony of withdrawal. But I went onto the ward anyway, thinking I was doing the right thing.

Vitya was pacing again, weeping and cursing incoherently. He looked unsteady on his feet, and Grisha was staying close behind to catch him if he stumbled. Then he looked up and saw me. The sight didn't make him happy.

"Get away, Lana!" he roared, and I wasn't sure if he thought I was a mortal threat to him or that he was saving me from something. "Get away!"

I fumbled my way out the door and pulled it shut behind me. It didn't calm him down. It took the feldsher and three of the healthier patients to hold him until Grisha could give him an injection that stopped his thrashing. Once he was still, they lifted him into the bed, as if it were his coffin. It might as well have been.

"I'm sorry," I said when Grisha locked the door behind him. "I thought—"

"You meant well," he said shortly. "In a few days, he'll remember who you are."

"Lana—"

"I don't know, and it doesn't matter. Nothing makes sense when they're like this. I'll get the boy."

He left me and the feldsher for a moment while he unlocked his office. The feldsher eyed me. "Shame about your … father-in-law? I could make it better, you know. Bogo, he's alright at disease, but he doesn't understand about white fever. Thinks you just dry them out. You see how that's going. Got to ease them out of it. I could get him some booze. Ration it out."

"You want me to pay you to fix the mess you created."

"No. I want you to get the key for the codeine cabinet. Bogo's keeping it all locked up in his office. Pretty soon, some very important people are going to be just as unhappy as him," he said, tilting his head toward the ward where Vitya lay unconscious. "You get me that key, everyone gets what they need."

"Get it yourself."

"Funny, he doesn't listen to me much anymore. But maybe his little whore can persuade him. Or you could steal it from his desk after you blow him. Makes no difference to me."

"You're disgusting."

"Come on, sweetheart. One little favor. One hand washes the other."

I was starting to wonder if he was scared of what these very important people would do if they couldn't get their opium. I wanted Vitya to be better, but I had no faith the feldsher knew what was best for him, let alone that he'd do it. Before I had an answer, Grisha returned with Petya, and I left without giving the feldsher another glance.

That night was much like any other. I coaxed my son to take some bread and milk and gave him a bath to try to make him comfortable. He was so often feverish, and there was nothing I could do about it, other than to wash away the sweat and hold him close as he shivered through the night.

I hadn't fallen asleep yet when someone pounded on the door. We never had visitors. I disentangled myself from my son, who fortunately kept sleeping, and got a knife. I didn't intend to open the door, but

I also knew I didn't have any way of reinforcing it if someone was determined to get through.

The pounding resumed. "Annushka? It's Grisha. Let me in." It was his voice. He practically jumped in when I opened the door. "I've got it."

"The penicillin?" I didn't dare hope. "You're certain?"

"It came at the end of the day. Are you ready?"

I lit the lamp. My son finally stirred. "Does he need to eat with it?" I asked.

"It's a shot. The directions say it should go in the rear." He started to get it ready.

"Don't let him see the needle. He won't be afraid if he doesn't see it." I picked up my son and wrapped him close against my chest while I sang, discreetly lifting the nightshirt to expose his bottom. Grisha quickly gave him the shot. Petya fussed at the pinch, but only for a moment. Soon he was peacefully sleeping again.

"What now?" I asked after I'd laid him back down.

"We wait and let it work. Then hope he can beat back the other." He looked away. "Do you want yours now?"

"Dr. Grossman can't give it to me?"

"I'd rather she didn't know I've stolen four doses of this stuff. I promise, I'll only look as much as it takes to hit the target."

He hit the target, then loaded another syringe and gave it to me. "Just stick the needle straight in here," he pointed to a relatively meaty spot, "and push down." I didn't feel at all comfortable with this, but I did it. "Good, good. I'll give Vitya his once he's calm enough."

"What are you going to tell him?" I asked as he buttoned his pants.

"I'll say it's an experimental treatment. That's not entirely a lie. It might help him, even if that's not what it's for." He picked up the vials. "I'll slap these labels on some saline, and Mrs. Commandant won't know the difference. We did it, Annushka. We really did it."

It was late, but neither of us was tired. The future suddenly carried hope instead of dread. Of course, we couldn't sleep. So, I turned the lamp down and we sat at the table, imagining what we'd all do once Vitya and my son were healthy enough to be around people again.

"You're free too," he said. "You could find love."

"So could you," I answered.

"But it's far more likely for you. You're still young and beautiful."

"I'm not beautiful," I said, because I'm not. I'm healthy, and that might pass for beautiful in a place like Norilsk.

"Trust me on this."

"It doesn't matter anyway. Vitya wouldn't be happy if I told him I was in love with some man. Not when he thinks I should be married to his son."

"You're going to have to tell him the truth eventually, if he's going to live for a while." I knew he was right. You can preserve a dying man's illusions about his son, but not if the man might have another decade to live. I didn't want to discuss that, though, so I stayed silent. He cleared his throat. "I should go. Morning rounds aren't too far off." He set a note on the table. "An excuse slip, in case you don't feel well tomorrow. Or, in a few hours."

I was glad to have it, because I didn't feel well that morning. Nothing significant, just tiredness from staying up all night and an upset stomach. The drug didn't seem to bother my son at all, and he wanted to get up and play for the first time in weeks. It might have been a coincidence, but I wanted to believe it was working.

I went to the hospital in the afternoon, with a vague hope that Grisha might somehow confirm our healing. But a feldsher from one of the other wards stopped me before I got to the stairs.

"Your friend's been arrested," she said.

"What for?" I asked, though I was sure I knew. They'd somehow found out about the missing penicillin. I'd sent him back behind the fence, where he'd surely die.

"Murder."

"Murder? What are you talking about?"

"His feldsher was dead in his office."

"An accident."

"Not with his head like that."

Was it possible he'd caught the feldsher stealing the codeine and gotten angry? No, I knew it wasn't. And even if he had been the type to lose his temper, he'd spent almost the entire night in my dugout.

I don't know how I managed to make supper that night, because my mind was wrestling with itself. I could tell them he couldn't have done it. But they might decide they didn't care and just wanted a tidy resolution. If that was the case, there was nothing to stop them from arresting me. And even if I decided I didn't care about saving myself, there was my son to think of. He might survive an orphanage, with the penicillin working its magic in his veins, but who would he be when they were finished with him?

Letting someone else die when I could save him was not against the rules. I hadn't denounced him, and I hadn't done the thing he was being punished for, so I wasn't responsible. I had asked him to risk everything to save my son, but was there a promise implicit in that? Did he think I was coming to save him? I knew he didn't. I had no doubt he believed he'd been completely abandoned. And I also didn't doubt he hadn't told them anything about me. They might beat him into naming co-conspirators eventually, because they can beat anything out of anyone if you give them long enough. But he wouldn't promise them a religious dissenter turned penicillin speculator to save his own skin.

I watched my son sleep for a while, then I wrote him a letter. I explained that it wasn't that I loved a man more than I loved him. That there are times when we must speak, or we lose what makes us human. That I hoped he would forgive me someday.

There was so much more I wanted to say to him and so little time. I couldn't really tell him about my life, his grandparents, our homeland.

I sat there, trying out one paragraph and another in my head. I didn't want to finish that letter. But I did. "You are the best thing anyone could ever hope to leave in this world. Be good, and try to be happy. With all of my love, Mama."

I felt like I had signed my own death certificate and was suspended, half in this world and half in the next. I picked up my rosary and cried and prayed and cried some more, until Vitya came. I knew he wasn't allowed to leave the hospital, but I didn't ask any questions.

"Promise me you'll take care of Petya," I said. I knew he didn't have long, but every day is precious in forming a child's mind. "You can't let them send him to one of those places."

"Nothing's going to happen to you," he said, taking a seat opposite me.

"I have to tell them the truth."

"What truth?"

"He couldn't have done it. He was here well past midnight."

"He could have done it after." His voice sounded flat, as if he didn't really believe what he was saying. "Maybe he was guilty of other things."

"Aren't we all?"

"Annushka. Don't argue with good fortune, my child." I didn't understand. "I know what he was trying to do. I'm going to protect you until my son comes. It's a shame he has to ..." He trailed off, looking disgusted with himself.

And I told him the truth. About Sasha. About Beria. About everything.

I expected him to push back, to insist that it couldn't be. But he didn't. "I'll talk to them," he said.

"What?"

"It doesn't really matter who tells them he wasn't at the hospital. I'll fix this." He looked at me. "You should sleep. It's going to be alright, child."

I knew I wouldn't sleep, but I laid down next to my son and breathed in the smell of his hair. I didn't believe Vitya could fix it.

I didn't hear him leave, so I must have slept. I would have had so much to say to him if I'd known.

"Hello, Norilsk. I'm sorry to wake you up so early." I jolted awake with a start at the sound of Vitya's voice over the crackling loudspeaker. I didn't understand how that could be, but I ran outside to hear it more clearly. "My name is Viktor Aleksandrovich Chekhov, and I killed the feldsher in the tuberculosis ward last night. I snuck out to get more codeine, and the feldsher was stealing it. I got angry and I killed him. I wish there was more to it than that." He paused. "No one helped me. No one knew. Anyone else you arrest is innocent. You should know that. I let Dr. Bogomolov take the blame because I didn't like him getting close to my daughter-in-law. I wanted her to wait for my son. But my son isn't coming." There was a banging sound behind him—probably someone taking back the communications center. "Goodbye, Norilsk." Then there was a different sound, like something hitting flesh. Then nothing.

I didn't hear what they came up with to explain that disturbance, because I was too busy throwing on clothes and wrapping my son up. The buses weren't running yet, so I walked to their office. I almost turned back once it was time to open the door, but I couldn't let myself do that.

They took me back while my son napped under the receptionist's desk. The room was an office with a desk covered in files and a half-eaten sandwich on a napkin crowning the whole mess. Not made for interrogations. A female officer sat across from me, took out a notepad, and nodded.

"Dr. Bogomolov was with me until well past midnight," I began.

"How far past?" This seemed like a good sign, that she wanted to know if Grisha actually could have done it.

"At least three."

"Doing what?"

"Is that important?"

"You're going to make me guess? Fine. I think you lifted your skirt up for him."

That wasn't wrong, though it wasn't like she'd thought. "I'm not a bad person."

"Who said you were?"

"People might, if they knew."

"So he paid for it."

It was a gamble, but I knew there was every likelihood she wouldn't believe me if she thought I was just trying to save my lover. "With Vitya—my father-in-law—not able to work anymore, things have been very difficult. I've had to pay extra for his care and provide for my son on my own since his father took off. So I need every ruble I can get." She nodded with what might have been sympathy. "So when Dr. Bogomolov said he wanted to … have … me, I thought, *well, better than some stranger off the street. A doctor's probably clean.* You understand?"

"That took all night?"

"He wanted to talk after. To make it seem like—the real thing—I think."

"The real thing?"

"Like love. Not just … that." I locked my eyes with her and let her see the tears forming. They were real, because I was so afraid. "Please don't arrest me. I've only done it this once so I could buy some meat for my son. You saw how little and frail he is. Please, believe me."

She only had one more question. "And what do you make of your father-in-law's statement?"

"I don't know. I've never known him to be a liar. I never thought he could kill anyone, either." And I truly didn't know. Why would he make that up? Why not just tell them he'd seen Dr. Bogomolov leaving and coming back?

They sent me to wait. My son was actually enjoying himself, scribbling with the receptionist's pens. I think I would have liked her under different circumstances. After a while, the female officer told me to go home. I wanted to know what they'd decided, but I didn't dare seem too attached.

I went to tell Dr. Grossman what I'd told them in case they were going to question other witnesses. That's why I was there when he came back all bloody. It was the best we could have hoped for under the circumstances.

"You came," he said, like he was trying to convince himself.

"Of course," I said. He looked confused. "Of course I came."

I helped Dr. Grossman clean him up. He was so slow to respond that I was sure he had a head injury. Then she found the blood still seeping from his right eardrum, once we'd washed away the results of the other wounds.

There was very little I could do for him or my son, so I made meals that were as full of vitamins and protein as was possible, given the limited grocery selection in Norilsk. My son healed slowly. One life-threatening infection is still more than a growing body should have to face. But even though it took months, the pink started to return to his cheeks, and he felt strong enough that I had to watch carefully to make sure he didn't fall off something and accidentally end his life when it was finally beginning.

Grisha's bruises faded over a few weeks. There was nothing I could do for them, other than pack snow compresses to ease the aching. I checked every day to make sure his ear was clean and dry, but it didn't matter. The eardrum pulled itself back together, but as scar tissue. He could understand most of what people said if he looked directly at them and concentrated, but with one bad ear, he couldn't make out lung sounds or the subtler problems with a heartbeat.

Dr. Grossman offered to write him a disability certificate, but he wouldn't take it. He said he wasn't old enough to sit around waiting for death. So she decided you don't really need two good ears for the injury ward—it might even be an advantage not to clearly hear the patients' screams.

Even when he had recovered as much as he was going to, he came by the dugout most days, probably because I was easier to talk to than most people. He and I could communicate a bit with signs, and I was used to enunciating so my son might one day learn to read lips.

"They searched everything, including the dirty laundry," he told me. "I had no idea what it was about, so I just sat on my bed and watched. What reason did they need to arrest me again? The thing that confused me is that they wore ordinary uniforms, not special police ones. I'd expected to be charged with a political crime again at some point." They did tend to rearrest people they'd released when there was a quota to fill.

"I truly had no idea why they were asking me about a murder when we got to their station. Why not arrest me for anti-Soviet agitation or something like that? Then they showed me the photograph. There was the feldsher, with his head bleeding on the rug in my office. They wouldn't bother arranging a scene like that when they could beat me into confessing I'd conspired with Tito to build a bridge to the moon.

"I told them I wasn't there, that I'd stayed out most of the night at a friend's house. But I didn't tell them it was you, to be safe. So they started beating me to get me to confess. One hit me hard enough on the side of the head that I could feel the blood in my ear. After that, it was like they were yelling at me underwater. I must have fainted at some point.

"I came to in a cell. I hadn't signed anything, so I knew they'd be back. It was so cold in that cell. I prayed I'd die there before they pushed me past my endurance. I'd been a fool to mention a friend and put you in danger, and I had no confidence I'd be strong enough not to name you when they began to beat me again. So I prayed for the first time in my life. I don't know if anyone heard me."

"Of course He did," I said, and I nodded to make sure he understood me. And I did believe someone had him in His hands. They were under no obligation to release him just because Vitya had confessed. And fainting during an interrogation can be a small mercy, from what I've heard.

But that didn't change that he'd lost half of his hearing, and Vitya had lost much more. I couldn't believe that was what God had wanted to happen.

I didn't know what to do, so I went to the station to find out where to send a package. I was still sending supplemental food to Polya, who had two years left in her ten-year sentence, but I needed to do this. I would eat less if we were running short at the end of the month.

It didn't matter what I'd decided, though. They told me that he wasn't in a camp, but a mental institution. They don't take letters and packages there.

"Your father-in-law was crazy," the female officer said as she plowed into the pastries I had brought to loosen her tongue. "He claimed Comrade Stalin made him do it. And that—another traitor—was part of the conspiracy." Beria. "Only a deranged mind could say something like that."

"If he was deranged, maybe he only thought he did it," I said, then wished I could take it back, even though I didn't believe he'd done it. If his confession was false, then Grisha was once again the prime suspect.

"Oh, he did it. He knew it was a lamp that broke that feldsher's skull. We didn't tell anyone that." I suddenly felt dizzy and grabbed the edge of her desk. "You alright?"

"I didn't really believe it," I said.

"Well, believe it. You were living with a lunatic."

"I don't know why I didn't see."

She shrugged. "Not a crime, not seeing that someone's crazy. Other things …" She trailed off, since we both knew this conversation would be very different if his offense had had the slightest political motive.

"Yes," I said, because agreement was the only option. But I didn't believe Vitya was insane. Temporarily confused by illness, yes. Broken by loss, certainly. Driven to desperation by the idea that he was about to lose the people he loved most, absolutely.

But he'd spoken clearly enough when he came to see me. He knew what he was doing when he switched on the loudspeaker system. He was taking responsibility for what he'd done, whether he meant to hurt anyone or not.

I wanted to do the same. But I couldn't. The police wouldn't care that I'd lied about Sasha—that wasn't a crime. I couldn't do anything to help Vitya. And Grisha wouldn't even let me confess.

I tried to tell him how my lies had created all this pain. He wouldn't hear me. It was the same thing, over and over: "You didn't know." "It wasn't your fault." "You didn't make him do anything."

At first, I thought he was just trying to comfort me, but gradually I realized that wasn't it. With Vitya gone, I was the only person in Norilsk who'd showed any interest in whether he was warm and fed, let alone happy. The only reasonable thing was to hate me, but he couldn't hate his only friend. Therefore, I must not be guilty of anything, or if I was, I could only have done something small. He would forgive me and wouldn't acknowledge that there was anything to forgive.

I couldn't stand it.

I wanted someone to punish me. I don't mean that I wanted to be destroyed. There are a thousand easy ways to wreck your life in the Soviet Union, if that's what you want. I wanted someone who knew exactly what I'd done to pronounce judgment on me. I'd known since I was a child there was no justice, and it had made me sick. And now there would be no justice for what I'd done either. After all the times I'd wished for God to pour out his wrath on others, I couldn't very well spare myself.

Diana

The blushing policeman told me my horror was dead.

"Did he beg?" I asked.

"So much that they stuffed a towel in his mouth."

I laughed at that. He finally knew what it was like to be gagged.

They kept me busy for a week or two after that, informing on all of his cronies. I didn't mind that in and of itself—those men could hardly claim innocence—but I wished they'd hurry up. I had places to go.

Five days after they finished with me, I was in Norilsk. The train arrived on Sunday morning. The refinery was belching evil-smelling smoke, but the rest of the city was no doubt still asleep, enjoying a few minutes of forgetting where they lived.

It wasn't difficult to find the little dugout. The girl answered the door and looked like she might faint. But she pulled herself together and made me a glass of tea.

"I'll tell you everything, as long as you can keep your face calm," she said. I believe she kept her word. She certainly didn't spare herself. She had that peculiar religious talent for self-flagellation.

It was true that she'd kept her mouth shut, and that it wasn't entirely about preserving my husband's illusions about his son. But that was part of it, good motives mixed with selfish ones, and she hadn't known how the dominos would fall. And anyway, how could I condemn her? I'd just sent men—bad men, granted—to their deaths to save my own skin. I didn't have the heart to hate her, not really. So there was nothing left to do but get on the train to my husband.

The mental institution where they kept him might have been a prison under the tsar, or perhaps a monastery. The walls were stone, weathered just enough to let the moisture seep in from the previous day's rain. The barbed wire fence must have been added in our enlightened times.

A few prisoners—patients in the records—were outside in their identical gray padded coats, walking around with their heads down, staring at the tufts of grass making a valiant effort to rise between the stones. One must have seen my heeled shoes and looked up, because I heard the guard yell and what sounded like a rifle butt hitting a skull. I kept walking.

I had paid the guards to let me in and out, with the understanding the arrangement could continue as long as the money lasted. The one leading me didn't ask me why I was there. I didn't ask him why my husband wasn't even allowed the little daylight in the courtyard.

I did jump when I heard the first scream, but I didn't scream myself. I would never give them that satisfaction.

We walked past rooms where patients convulsed, where they lay absolutely still, and where three or four big men held them down to give injections. They hadn't bothered with anything to cover the walls, and the screams echoed and mixed with each other until it seemed like the stones themselves were crying out in pain. If a man wasn't insane when he entered, he would be after a few days of that.

My husband's ward was quieter. Men paced, sat muttering to themselves, or just stared. Most didn't seem to see me, and I'm grateful for that. What would I have said to them if they'd called out? I would have just kept walking. I wasn't there for them.

My husband's cell—it was a cell, no matter what they said—was about the size of a Parisian broom closet, and therefore perfectly humane by Soviet standards. The window opened onto the corridor and had bars placed closely enough that a grown man would be lucky if he could get his arm as far out as the elbow. The only light in each cell was from a bare bulb flickering on a short cord dangling from the ceiling. The cot lacked blankets or even sheets, despite the chill from the old stone walls.

"Can't have them hanging themselves," the guard said, half-chuckling.

My husband was on the floor, dragging himself from the slot where they put the meals in after pushing a letter through the other way, into the corridor. He looked like a dead man reanimated, the gray of his skin not much different from that of the little hair he had left. The ankles I could see sticking out of the dirty pajamas looked like an incompetent taxidermist had cut away the flesh and simply laid the skin back over the bones. I saw nothing of the dark, handsome soldier I'd married or the bear of a factory worker he'd aged into.

"Is there another Viktor Aleksandrovich Chekhov here?" Of course I knew, but who can help hoping that her pain is really someone else's?

"Only one we have. I can take you back if this specimen isn't to your liking." I wondered if the heels on my shoes were sharp enough to put a man's eye out.

"Let me in."

"I can't guarantee your safety."

"I didn't pay you to guarantee my safety."

He shrugged. "I'll be back in two hours. If you scream, someone might hear you before then."

I nodded. The hinges on the door made a grating sound, as if it had been a while since they'd been used.

My husband looked up at me from the cold, damp floor, but didn't move, except that his face broke into a sad smile. Several teeth were missing, and little red triangles had formed in his gums between those that remained. Scurvy, then. When I was young, I never could have imagined that I'd be so familiar with the many forms of malnutrition.

"It's good to see you again." He didn't sound surprised. "But usually, we're some place more pleasant. The old apartment or the theater. Sometimes we escape and go free."

I spoke four languages, but I couldn't come up with a fitting reply in any of them. I knelt beside him and touched his cheek. "Vitya." That was all I could say. "Vitya, darling."

"It won't be long until I see you again for real." He touched my face lightly, as if he thought I might fade away. "Will you forgive me then?"

"There's nothing to forgive." Maybe that wasn't true, but it didn't matter. "Vitya, please." Please what? I didn't know.

A coughing fit racked him, and he jerked away, bending into himself as he shook. He stayed that way for several minutes, struggling to breathe. When he sat up, bloody sputum surrounded his mouth. And I knew. Nothing I did—bringing him healthy food and warm clothing, even if I managed to find a doctor willing to visit this God-forsaken wasteland—would change the outcome. The infection in his lungs would kill him, probably soon. The fever might never let him out of its haze. If I left and didn't return, he would assume he had been dreaming and continue this horrible not-life as before.

But I would return, I resolved as the guard shut the gate behind me in the evening. I would return, and perhaps I would bring a butcher's knife, or a bomb, or a cake filled with ground glass that would shred a man's insides. None of them would achieve justice, but the cake might come close, if only I could make one large enough to give half this damned country a slice.

I wasn't there when he died. His skin was already cold when the guard led me back. He swore and wondered why Vitya couldn't have kicked off the day before, when he was already making a trip to the crematorium. I couldn't say anything. I pressed a few rubles into his hand to take me along.

He tossed my husband into the back of a truck. I insisted on riding with the cargo. I remember thinking I should have brought scissors to cut a lock of hair. That beast and my son had destroyed everything I had of my husband. Every family photograph. Every little note written for my birthday. Even the shirts I would bury my face in after he was taken because the scent would comfort me. Gone. All the evidence I had ever loved someone, reduced to ash.

I thought it was snowing when we arrived. Cities burn black. Humans burn white.

I gave my husband one last kiss before they loaded him in. I watched as they shut the door, and even then, I didn't take my eyes off. The guard touched me lightly on the shoulder.

"You want a ride somewhere?" I shook my head. "It's not like he knows you're here."

That was when I screamed. At him, yes. But not just. And then I was sobbing instead of screaming. I was on my knees and I couldn't see through my tears. The truck rumbled off and the world was mostly silent. I stayed there, kneeling on the ground, as little flecks of ash caught on my coat. I took off my scarf and laid it on the ground to catch them. And I folded them up and held the scarf to my chest like a newborn child.

I thought about going to stay with the girl in Norilsk, but there was nothing for me there. And besides, it wouldn't have been kind, reminding her of her mistakes every day. So I went back to Moscow. I found work in a store, serving a new generation of rich Party wives. I hated every moment.

When the shop closed for the night, I walked or found a place to sit. And I plotted. Vengeance is so much sweeter than grief. I turned plans over and over in my head. I didn't know how to build a bomb, and all the old revolutionaries who did had long since been executed. The big men had food tasters, and how would I get close enough to poison them anyway? The same problem for a knife. So it had to be a gun. You can find anything on the black market, if you meet the right people. I said I needed the gun to protect myself from a jealous ex-lover. The man who sold it said he didn't much care.

And I waited. And waited. I would take trips to the country, get away from the picnickers and practice. I wasn't bad.

I would have done it, if I had gotten a chance sooner. But then I happened on my son and the talking mannequin he'd married. It was in the park by the river. They were pushing a pram. I thought about pretending I had never seen them and running into the Lubyanka and shooting everyone in sight just to get it done with. But I had the absurd desire to find out if the child had gotten my husband's dark eyes. So I decided to get my revenge by making my son's life hell instead. I think I thoroughly succeeded in that respect.

My granddaughter did get those beautiful brown eyes. I spoiled her, so she loved me, but I got the better end of it. When I looked at her, I could pretend something was left of my husband other than the ashes in that little scarf and my fading memories. I told her stories about her grandfather, mostly so I wouldn't lose more of him than I already had. The sound of his voice had gone silent, and the edges of the picture of him in my mind were starting to fade away like an old photo in an album. So I told her all the silly things he ever said to me, and how he would have loved to pull her on her sled. And when she asked how he died, I told her the Party killed him. For no reason at all.

I also told her that we were Jews, and that the men on top had betrayed us. It was cruel. I made her a stranger in her own country. But I'd rather that than let her grow up into a soulless machine like her parents. I don't know if she'll remember any of it when I'm gone—which will be soon, if the hard ball of flesh I feel in my breast is what I think it is. All those monsters who run the country will outlive me.

When I found that, I decided I needed to do something more than make my son's life hell. I'd never gone back to check on Vitya's old notebooks that I'd stashed away. It seemed too risky. But a woman well on her way to death doesn't worry so much about risk anymore. And I was determined the truth wouldn't die with me.

I wanted to show them to my granddaughter, to make it all real for her. But she's so young. Too young for the full truth of everything people can suffer. Will she forget her grandfather and me because I coddled her? No. No. She will remember. A person who believes she has a soul can never become one of them. And she will tell her daughter, who will tell hers, for a thousand generations if we must. And someday, we will tear them down and grind them into the dust.

Letter, written approximately January 1954

Dear ~~Grisha~~ Grigori Nikolaievich,

I guess I've forfeited the right to speak with any familiarity. I hope you haven't torn this letter up yet, though I don't blame you if you have.

I want you to know that I wasn't lying when I said I was glad to find you again, and even happier when you got out. It probably doesn't seem like it now. Though I was as surprised as you that she had made the suggestion that got it done. No, probably not as surprised, because there were things I didn't know. I just sensed a strong mutual unease.

Then I walked in that one day and saw the two of you. She said you were just talking, but she fumbled when I asked about what. I saw nothing wrong, other than the guilty look on your faces. But I thought it was best to ask you not to come anymore. I really thought my son was coming. You could be a brother to her if you wanted, but she belonged to him.

And then you said I was sick and had to be kept away from them, even though I didn't think so. I was tired from working long hours. I coughed from the dust in the mine. I woke up sweating from nightmares. I lost weight because I was setting aside food for the boy. It all made sense, you see? I didn't want to believe you'd lie to me, but I knew you were lying when you said I'd get out some day. People went in there, and they only left when they died.

I didn't want to believe the worst of you, but I had to protect her. No matter what that meant. I'd see you two talking, and how she looked more sleepless and worried with every day. She wouldn't tell me what was happening. I understand why now. But I thought you were putting pressure on her. I was worried she'd give in before Diana and Sasha came.

And then I learned my wife was gone, and probably my son had been arrested with her. Why did I live if I would never see my wife again? I wouldn't have lived. There would be no reason for me to draw breath. I didn't care about getting better anymore. I saw no reason to force myself to eat, to endure those terrible injections, to move from my bed. I couldn't sleep, but I wanted nothing more than to close my eyes and never wake up. I thought about using my bed sheets to end it all.

The feldsher started bringing me samogon with the money the girl had left so I could buy better food. I felt guilty, having him spend her money on alcohol, but I couldn't stop. It was the next best thing to death, being so drunk that nothing mattered, that I was almost unaware that I was still alive. I understand why you smashed his bottle, though. You didn't understand.

It wasn't long after that that the nightmares started. I say nightmares, but I thought I was awake. I hadn't been able to sleep for days, because I was shaking and sweating and my heart wouldn't stop racing. And then the dead started to visit. My mother, Lana, Masha, Diana, Konstantin Fyodorovich, all the people I had hurt or not been able to help. The men I'd left to bleed out in the swamp. The children in that little village whose name I never knew. The women raped to death on that ship. The boy who'd been shot after we stole his gold. The prisoners I'd beaten because the thieves ordered it and because I'd wanted to live. And so many more. God, they filled the whole ward and spilled out into the halls. "You failed us. And now you'll fail her. You'll let that monster tear her apart like a piece of bread. You have to stop him."

And then I wasn't in the ward anymore. The little house was dark and quiet. I had to break down the door with the red paint. The stench was thick. Like a battlefield crammed into a one-room house. I lit the lamp anyway. They were on the ground. The little one was holding the big one. At first I thought they had rotted away. They had, some. The gasses had already burst out. But they had some skin, stretched over the bones. I knelt beside them. I couldn't bear to touch them. I had to touch them. I pushed the hair out of the little one's face. A rat was chewing on the nose. I crushed its skull with my boot, and I kept stomping. And when I couldn't anymore, I dropped to the floor and cradled the dead child. And I heard a child's voice, saying, "Why didn't you save me?" And I woke up sobbing.

The feldsher had forgotten to lock the ward when he left. He would do that sometimes. Before, I would be good and stay. Not that night. I broke into your office. I didn't want to hurt you. Please believe that. But I had to get her away from you. I had failed so many people in my life. I couldn't fail again. I had to stop you. And then I felt someone, in the dark, grabbing at me. And I defended myself. I took a lamp and smashed a skull. And then I ran back to my bed.

I woke up with blood on my hands and my shirt. I must have coughed on it. I felt shaky, like I'd just had a terrible fever break, but when didn't I? I washed myself, and then I tried to think. I'd dreamed of going to the little house in Norilsk and finding them dead. The big one and the *little one. And I'd run my hands through the little one's long curls—that wasn't right. The little boy had straight hair, and his mother kept it cut short. Not them. And then I dreamt I had killed you to protect them, because they weren't dead yet, even though I saw them dead. I laid back and closed my eyes and tried to remember the last time that I was awake and thinking clearly.*

And then someone screamed. They found him in your office. The feldsher. You know that. And I wondered. Had I done it? It was all a dream. But I wasn't sure. And I said nothing when they dragged you away.

I got away under cover of night. They hadn't found anyone else to keep an eye on us after dark. I had to get to her. Maybe they had already interrogated her, if they knew you'd been seeing her. Would she know what to say? I had to find her.

She didn't seem surprised to see me. She was there, at the table, preparing to risk her life to save you. I tried to tell her she didn't have to, that maybe this was for the best, as horrible as it was. Then she told me the truth. I promised I would make it right. I told her to lie down and rest. And I whispered my goodbye.

There was no one in the communications office at that time of night. Maybe there was supposed to be, but there wasn't. The door was even unlocked. I fiddled with the controls until I found the right ones. It was vital that everyone hear.

And then I hesitated. I guess I felt like a man falling from a building, who'd like to keep falling forever. Anything is better than smashing into the ground. I breathed as deeply as I could, just to feel the air in my lungs. And then I coughed up blood. So I switched the microphone on and confessed what I'd done, and that I'd done it alone. I had just enough time before they broke in and flattened my head with a nightstick.

Once I came to, they started interrogating me with their boots. I told them I'd just gotten angry, that I'd done it to make you suffer. They wouldn't believe it. So I told them Lavrenty Beria had made me do it. And Stalin had been involved somehow. I laughed because it felt good to say it. And once I started laughing, I couldn't stop, except when their boots knocked the air out of my lungs. And then they sent me to this place.

Now I'm here, writing it all down. There's so much more I could say to you, but most days I'm too weak to write. The people I loved come to me now, and they aren't angry. They're just waiting. I won't keep them long.

What good does it do to tell you I'm sorry? There's nothing I can do for you or anyone else, and nothing I can say can fix the damage. You're a good man, to hear me out. I'm not fooling myself that you've forgiven me. Just know that I don't begrudge you any happiness you and the girl manage to claw out of this rotten world. I hope the two of you will heal and feed people, and maybe, maybe know some peace. And if my soul still exists somewhere, it will smile.

Annushka

Diana Sergeyevna sent me the letter folded into the textbook where she'd written her testimony, with instructions to give it to whoever this Grigori Nikolaievich was, if I knew him.

I invited him over for dessert and silently handed it to him while we waited for our tea to cool enough that we could drink it. Then I went and played with my son, so he wouldn't have to feel me watching his face. My eyes did keep drifting back to him, though.

He folded it up and set it aside. "It's much as I expected. He read his fears into every word and every glance. That sometimes happens from the fever and the stress of facing your impending death. And the samogon the feldsher smuggled in couldn't have helped." He sighed. "I should have fired that feldsher so many times. I shouldn't have left him in charge."

"You couldn't watch Vitya and the others every hour," I said. "Everyone needs to sleep."

"But if I had just been there that night …" he trailed off. "Would it have made a difference?"

"I don't know," I answered honestly. "But if I'd told him the truth from the beginning—"

"He wouldn't have believed it." There was a good chance that was true. "I wanted so much for him to care about me."

"He did," I said, gesturing toward the letter.

"Not enough." He shook his head. "Then again, you can never compete with family. Or so I've heard."

"You're family to us," I said.

"What kind? Am I your brother? Your husband?"

That took me by surprise. He'd never been bold enough to ask. "I can't be anyone's wife. I can't even imagine, not after him."

He took a moment to answer. "It's up to you. But it's a shame if he took that away from you too."

We didn't talk about it again, not for a long time. We talked about everything but that. I thought about it, though. Did I want to know what it might be like to be touched by a man who cared about me? At first, I was positive I didn't want to take the risk, but the more I thought about it, the more I wondered what it might be like. Other women seemed to consider it worthwhile. And the thought crossed my mind that, even though he thought no woman could ever want him, someone else eventually would. And I would have to let my friend become someone I saw occasionally and had polite, hurried conversations with because I had no right to claim anything more.

It was Christmas again when I finally decided to take the risk. I had made the layered cake, and Petya insisted we should bring Grisha some. I hadn't come to the hospital in months—he always came to see me—so I needed something, and he'd never turned down cake before. I bundled up my son and trudged out into what seemed likely to be the warmest part of the twenty-four-hour night.

Grisha was in his office, bent over paperwork. A new rug mostly covered the blood stain on the floor. I knocked, then knocked harder, then opened the door and slammed it again. That got his attention.

"What's the matter?" he asked, checking Petya's forehead with his hand.

"We have cake!" my son signed with the big gestures he used when he was excited.

"Ah, cake," Grisha signed. "But I don't have three forks!"

"I think it froze solid while we walked anyway," I signed. "So you'll either have to wait for it to thaw and eat it all yourself or come see us tonight."

"Come see you?" He forgot to sign, which made my son stamp his foot.

"It's a special occasion," I said, though I substituted Christmas in the signs. I had my back to the door, and there were no windows in the office to spy on my hands.

"I don't have anything for Petya," he said. "I don't have anything for you either, except maybe some soap."

"I didn't ask for anything."

He glanced over at the desk. "There's nothing here that can't wait until tomorrow. If you'd like me to walk back with you." He blushed. "To help keep him from getting lost in the snow."

"I think I would like that," I said. And he smiled until the apples in his cheeks, which most people don't know exist, came through.

We didn't get married until about two years later, when they started tearing out the dugouts and we needed to apply for an apartment in the new buildings they were slapping up around town. We'd made our commitment before God, sealed with secrets we could never tell anyone else. Their papers meant nothing to me.

Some months after we made it official, when we were lying in bed as Petya mumbled in his sleep, Grisha took my hand in the dark and pressed the signs into my palm. "Do you think God planned this for us?"

I wasn't sure how to answer. The people I'd outlived deserved happiness at least as much as I did. And it hardly seemed inevitable. If I had told Vitya the truth, would he have kept me around long enough to save his friend with some bread and a well-timed hint? And if I was meant to lie and save Grisha, did that mean our happiness meant more than Vitya's and Diana's? I've chased that thought around my head without ever quite knowing if I was justified. So I didn't answer. I wrapped my hand around his, kissed his fingers, and hoped it's enough.

Summer 1957

This is the last thing I'll write in this apartment in Norilsk.

We're going west, to Omsk. Most schools for the deaf are in cities where you need permission for residence, which someone convicted of treason and terrorism won't get. Grisha offered to stay behind while I went with my son, but neither Petya nor I wanted that. So, we'll still be in Siberia, but without the months-long nights. It's the best we can realistically hope for.

Petya is looking forward to school, mostly because he doesn't understand what it will be. They'll insist he learn to speak, all the while drilling into his head that he can't say anything that's true. But perhaps that will help keep us safe. There will be a clear dividing wall in his mind, between what's spoken out in the world and what's signed at home.

I must finish this and get rid of it before he starts to learn to read, though. He can never know that his mother wrote an illicit book, let alone compiled others' seditious words. So it will all go as crumpled packing paper, cushioning a nice set of tea glasses I'm sending to a certain friend who was released in a different part of Siberia. And she will get it to someone else, who knows someone who knows someone with a job at a printing press who can dash off a few copies overnight. I don't doubt each of them will make their own little changes to cover our tracks. If I somehow got my hands on a copy—which I won't risk—would I know my own words?

Sometimes I try to imagine some future where everything is different. Where people aren't forced to lie to save themselves and their sons. I can't, though. What would I say to such people? What use would they have for me? Surely, they wouldn't understand any of it, from keeping this from my son, all the way back to crushing baby birds because I was starving. Everyone around me now would understand, if I could tell them. They might arrest me for some of it, but they would know why I did it all. These residents of some blessed future surely would find plenty to fault in me, though.

Sometimes I think it would be a beautiful thing, to be blamed.

Acknowledgments

A special thank you to my sister Heather Hart, who was the first person who heard about this book and read several versions. Your feedback, while sometimes not exactly what I wanted to hear, made it better.

Thank you to my good friends Steph Eldredge and Celia Llopis-Jepsen for their help editing the earlier drafts, and to Andy Marso and Alex Miller for reading and reviewing the nearly finished product. Thank you to my former teacher and longtime friend Annie Stahl, for encouraging me to write all those years ago.

Thank you to the team at Mission Point Press, and especially Misha Neidorfler. Your belief in the book and your professional dedication improved it every step of the way.

Most of all, thank you to my husband, Justin, for never letting me give up on this book (and for not getting scared off when he saw how many books about the Stalin era I had in my apartment). Your support, especially through these long days of early parenthood, means everything.

About the Author

Meg (Hart) Wingerter started writing this book right out of college, because pens, notebooks, and library books were about all she could afford for entertainment on intern wages. It took nearly eight years, five jobs, four states, one pandemic, and enough research to create a freshman-level course on early Soviet history, but at the end, she had a novel.

Wingerter lives in the Denver area with her husband, Justin, and daughter, Claire. She covers health for *The Denver Post*, and has been published in *The Oklahoman*, *The Topeka Capital-Journal*, *The Muskegon Chronicle*, and *The (Lancaster) Sunday News*. She has been recognized for her journalistic writing, and beat Mitch Albom for top columnist in Michigan in 2012. Despite what the trolls may tell you, this is her first work of fiction.

www.ingramcontent.com/pod-product-compliance
Lightning Source LLC
LaVergne TN
LVHW092011090526
838202LV00002B/104